Stanley James

D1713448

Stanley James

Clyde Henry

To order additional copies of this book, contact:
Xlibris Corporation
1-888-795-4274
www.Xlibris.com
Orders@Xlibris.com
50696

Dedication

— To my most loving wife Janet, without whom this book would not be possible,

— To my father George, mother Beata, sister Georgette, and bother Lyle,

— To my daughters Katara, Athena, and Aletheia, son-in-law Matthew Zachmann,

— To my grandchildren Kaden, Isaac, and Eian,

— To my many friends who helped proof the manuscript, and the many incredible people at TRIAD Architects, especially Rena Harper, whose corrections on the first draft were invaluable,

— To the wonderful community of support at the Ohio Writers' Guild, and most importantly . . .

— To you, who have taken your time to learn the story of Stanley James.

A Warning

In an old Russian fairytale, a young man rides through an idyllic forest on a horse named Thunder. Suddenly the trees are silent, the winds halt, and the patterns of dappled light stand still. He looks and sees a golden feather on the path. He understands, as do we, that this is the call to adventure. If he picks up the golden feather, his life will be irreversibly changed. The horse named Thunder speaks, "Do not pick up the feather, just let it be."

For Jake, the feather was a speck no larger than a comma on a brown envelope. For Mindy, it was a smudge of paint. For me, it was a word nearly said in a careless conversation. And for Stanley James, it was the fear on a young boy's face. Those of us who picked up the feather were changed forever; but what about those of us who followed the horse's advice? What happens to the heroes who don't answer the call?

Oh, one more thing, my friends. I will warn you now. This is no ordinary tale. While it appears innocent enough, set in the pleasant landscapes of rural Minnesota, populated by bright boys and girls living in a carefree time, it disguises itself like a pretty golden thing. It is waiting for you—waiting for you to turn its pages and pull you in—until you, too, are irreversibly altered.

I have warned you. There is still time to heed the advice, to close the cover and walk away before these pages become the stuff that magic feathers are made of.

The New Age

Optimism Rises as the Modern Age Dawns

The war was behind us and hope sprouted in America; it was the unanimous belief that the children born in this new age would live in a world filled with endless potential. Optimism hung in the air like the heavy scent of . . . I should write something like "the scent of sweet gardenias on a summer's night," but I have never smelled such a scent, although I did once smell a gardenia at the Franklin County Conservatory in Columbus, Ohio. No, the optimism was different from that. It was more like the smell I experienced one summer evening when I was ten. Three of us had been swimming at Lake Darling-Carlos Bridge, and we were riding home on our big-framed bikes. My dad bought my bike from a customer at the gas station when his son had moved on—to cars and girls. It was rusty and dented, but we planned to fix it up. "Fix-it-up" is always the plan of poor people who buy damaged things, but the plan is seldom implemented. The things just continue to disintegrate faster than they can be fixed up, and the energy expended becomes disproportionate to the value gained. So, as I was riding the bike—still in its decaying condition—we passed the fresh-cut summer lawns of the vacation homes that lined the shores of the locally prestigious Lake Carlos. The smell was a sensory delight known only to young boys who rode down these gravel roads to swim or to loiter in hiding places where the rich could be watched from afar. It was a blend of smells that perfectly merged the aroma of freshly-cut fescue grass, pine needles, and the human scents of sweet bourbon evaporating into the evening sky, and soft perfumes that rolled from the skin of middle-aged women like a mist announcing their presence. The odor was spiced with the peppery smell of dog shit that had been inadvertently run over by the efficient new gas-powered mowers.

The complex smells of that evening were more like the scent of optimism that existed in those days, a rich composite of scents that stimulated and inspired the sprit. The emerging national myth instructed us that we were all part of a classless society on the verge of a new modern world. The future was for everyone. We would enjoy the wondrous inventions and have adventures like those seen by over 40 million people at the Brussels World's Fair, which was written up in *Life* and *Look* magazines for those not fortunate enough to have personally attended.

In Alexandria, Minnesota, where I grew up, even a family like mine, living on the edge of poverty, believed that we, too, were middle class, as all Americans were. But just as in George Orwell's *Animal Farm*—where all the animals were equal but the pigs were more equal—in Alexandria, and in most of America, some of the middle class were more middle class than others. The optimism of the 1950's had also infused the Catholic Church. They began the largest parochial school building campaign in history. Millions of children fathered by returning Catholic soldiers would fill the seats of the newly fabricated plastic desks. The process of injection molding permitted the efficient production of strong durable melmac seats and backs in a deep mauve color. At the time, however, we were not so sophisticated as to call it mauve, so we merely called it "dark pink." Like the efficient production of these plastic products, so too, the new schools would mold the new Catholic citizens. We would be of a single form and our values would be as consistent as the plastic colorant was from one batch to the next.

Nuns by the thousands were flocking to the convents and these women of God were ready to staff these new institutions. Yes, nuns by the tens of thousands were marrying Christ. Christ was eternal, and fortunately so, because the millions of young men who otherwise would have courted these girls had vanished in the war. The young girls entering the doors, however, did not think to themselves, "Well, all the men are dead, so I might as well become a nun." The competition for the few men that were left was so robust and intense that it was over before they had decided to compete. The "bad" girls had gotten all the men. They, the future nuns, were of a higher sort. Their man was above the drinking, the back seats of old cars, the cigarettes, and the swing music that tempted others. Their man would not smell of the barn like their fathers and brothers, or knock them around after a binge of drinking and gambling down at Charlie's Corner Bar or the Knights of Columbus Hall. Their man was the son of Mary. Only her son, with his soft effeminate eyes and glowing skin, was worthy of them. He would be their companion in a clean, safe community of fellow wives. They did not enter the convent because they had lost; they entered it because they had chosen not to compete.

The new Catholics would be different from the generations before the war; they would not speak German, Irish, or Italian, or drink too much beer and fall away from Mother Church and into the sins of the flesh. Education, yes, education—not the suffering prayers of mothers and old women—was the new efficient method of creating the perfect Church.

The bishops boasted, "Give us the children and they will be indelibly formed." An even higher authority than God or Mother Mary backed the church fathers' boasts. Scientists—the new prophets—had determined this truth, and had developed the new theology and set the parameters for success. The bishops perceived the new church as being founded on the new Catholic Intellectualism, not the embarrassing miracles of Fatima, and Lourdes, not on figurines that smiled at sick children and cured them, but on Jesuit priests with doctorates in Psychology, Philosophy, and Physics. The intellectuals believed that their churches would soon be vacuumed clean of painted plaster statues, fountains of holy water, and all other superstitions. But no one had taken the time to tell this to the millions of steadfast parishioners, or the simple parish priests that attended them. They went on crossing themselves, and sprinkling sick children's beds with the blessed water, and placing braided holy palms under their pillows.

The new Catholic leadership still believed that there was evil in the world, but now the evil was not so much to be found in the supernatural devils that once prowled the earth—or even in the Protestants. One still had to be careful not to be deceived by Protestants, but now they were only in error. The men who had fought and died alongside Catholics in the Great War were no longer in an evil alliance with Satan, but only misled. While they were not the devil incarnate, they were still to be avoided, particularly when it came to marriage. This abhorrence of mixed marriages was also shared by a majority of Protestants, who did not want their children under the spell of a Papist.

Eva and Bill

My Aunt Eva did not heed this advice. She fell in love with Bill—a soldier with a grin so large that it was nearly comical. It looked like it had been cut from a larger photograph and pasted onto his head, stretching nearly to his ears. The rest of him was quite typical. He was a man of normal height, green eyes, and blond hair, just beginning to ripen into deep tones of wheat. She met him when he was on leave, and as in so many stories of those times, they wrote letters. By the time he was assigned to the reserves, they were deeply in love. She dreamt of her wedding, and he dreamt of a life where he would never have to leave her side.

Aunt Eva was beautiful with a capital "B." She had long dark hair, a rarity for a German American, and large blue eyes that were as out of scale as Bill's smile. The church, while not encouraging these marriages, did permit them, provided that proper protocol was followed and that the Protestant partner agreed that the children would be raised Catholic.

Eva and Bill's wedding was not in the church, nor were they accompanied by parents, relatives, or friends. There was no Mass for them, no reception in the church basement, no ride through town with boots and cans tied to their car. That would have demonstrated approval. Tolerance was permitted, but approval was not; that would have been too much.

Yet, she looked forward to June 24, 1950. It was to be their day all the same. The bride, the groom, the bridesmaid, and the best man arrived at the priest's house at 7:00 PM. He would be finished with supper by then. They stood on the porch, knocked, and waited. After five minutes, the priest opened the door. Without a greeting, without even a nod of recognition, he read from the text the minimum words required to unite the couple. Then without congratulation or comment, the door was immediately closed. The groom looked at his disgraced wife. He felt an emotion unfamiliar to him—anger, an omni-directed anger. This anger was not so much at the priest, who he knew was only playing his role in the scene. He felt anger at himself. He could have converted, as many intended spouses did. Then his wife would have walked down the aisle triumphant, with a husband and a convert. "How wonderful," all the women would have said. He would have—converted, that is. He had no particular faith in institutions, nor did he really want any. He didn't convert because of his mother. She cried with more intensity than when his father died when she learned that the girl he was seeing was a Catholic.

It was at the wedding of his younger brother. His brother, Herman, was marrying a good Protestant girl from the same county but the next town over. Bill brought Eva to the wedding. The young couple, as all young people are, was blinded by the blaze in their hearts. They believed that his family would see Eva as he saw her. They, too, would fall in love with her and they would accept her. It was the first hurdle—next would be her family, a higher hurdle. While Eva tried to join in the ceremony, even at the cost of her soul, his relatives noticed that she did not respond automatically, did not seem to even know the last sentence of the Lord's Prayer, and started to cross herself several times, before stopping and pretending to brush her hair aside.

Eva did not get the required permission from her priest to attend the Protestant wedding; she was afraid that permission would not be granted and the hope for the day would be lost. If she attended after asking and being denied permission, she thought that she would be excommunicated. But if she attended without asking, she would only be committing a mortal sin. A mortal sin causes one to go directly to hell upon death unless confessed and forgiven by the priest; such are the keys to the Kingdom of God held by the Church. She reckoned that she would not die before making it to confession on Wednesday. If she were really repentant, she calculated that she would only have to suffer a short time in purgatory. A brief period of suffering later for the potential outcome of the day was well worth the risk, and those in love are always willing to take a risk.

Repentant she would be, not because of her sin, but because of the turn of events that day. She said three rosaries in the hope of enlisting Mother Mary in her scheme; but Mother Mary, it turned out, was planning a different fate for her. In Catholicism, only two forms of the female deity are revealed—the Virgin Maiden, pure and filled with promise, and the Mother, maternal and loving. But in the wiser, older traditions, she is also revealed in her third form—the Hag, old and wise. In this form, she sometimes moves fate in strange and twisted ways; she conjures twists of plot that ultimately reveal brilliant truth and redemption. It is from the womb of the Virgin, Mother and Hag that the world's redeemers are born. On this day, the Secret Hag Mary took the beseechment call, and mixed a drop of bitter remedy into the jumble of life.

Hearing the suspicions being circulated about Eva at the wedding, Bill's mother said to the guests that questioned her, "Eva might not be Presbyterian, but there has been a Methodist or two in the family before, and they made perfectly good Presbyterians." Eva's religion, after all, was the fault of her family and not herself. This was only a stopgap measure. The dike would not hold long, so his mother confronted William, as she preferred to call him, directly.

"Eva is Protestant, isn't she?"

This phrasing would permit a simple nod, and avoid entirely the question of which kind of Protestant. Oh, God, she might be Lutheran; or there was some kind of Baptist church that had moved into the western part of the county. What kind? That could be dealt with later.

"No," came the nearly whispered response.

"Oh, Lord, she's not Catholic is she?" his mother immediately said, stripped of the ability to craft a more careful query.

"Yes, she is, but she is wonderful." Bill said without moving his lips.

She covered her mouth, and collapsed. The scene was a familiar one a half-decade earlier, when mothers received telegrams announcing the deaths of their sons. They were at first brave when they went to the door, but soon felt their legs collapse under them. The officers delivering the news or the telegram carrier knew this, and were ready to catch the falling mothers, who generally escaped with only slight bruises.

This message was different. The death notice messages always included locations with strange names that had earlier been marked with pins on the maps that hung in kitchens. The message soon would be followed with a small gold-starred flag to hang in the window. This would replace the blue-starred one. This meant that a son had been sacrificed to the glorious god of nation. Pride would replace him in her heart, and wherever she went solemn whispers would announce her as the mother of a crucified son.

For Bill's mother today's news was far worse. Shame would replace him. Whispers and silence would announce her as the woman whose son married a Catholic. Her father had been a local leader of the Ku Klux Klan in the 1940's in Iowa. Minnesota, Iowa, and Wisconsin didn't have many Negroes or Jews, so the hatred had been heaped on the Catholics. Minnesota had never been an overtly violent place, except for lynching Indians, which they had accomplished here in greater numbers than in any other area in the country. But even as the Klan song "The Bright Fiery Cross" said, "Catholics, Negroes and Jews all had their place in America, too." It was just that their place was not to be married to our children, nor to be the parents of our grandchildren. This was not the South. But it had been the North that had fueled the Klan in greatest numbers, financed it, and legitimized it in the decades before the war. By 1950, it had been discarded and was no longer part of the landscape, but still, Catholics had no business mixing. She had hoped Bill would soon join the Fraternal Order of Masons, and be a member of the local Blue Lodge, as his father had been. The lodge was a good way to get ahead, as her husband had done. But with a Catholic wife, how could this be? She would never be permitted to join the Daughters of the Eastern Star. Her tears were mixed with fear, grief, and pain. Bill's brothers, sisters, aunts, uncles, and friends gathered. Eva stood terrified as glances jetted from her to Bill's mother. Bill held his mother in a reverse pose of the Pieta. Here, the son held the mother. Mothers know that men—that is, men that have been raised strong—if asked to choose between lover and mother, will choose the lover and will suffer the loss of the mother silently. They will numb their hearts and harden their souls, and in the end, will not be able to love either. Bill's mother, having raised such a son, was wise enough to know not to ask him to choose. Instead she formulated a compromise—a compromise that could bridge uneasy gaps in families and in society. She begged in a pleading voice, which not even Satan could have denied, "Son, tell me you won't convert."

One word would save this day and cast the fate of future days. "No, ma, never." A pain hit Eva's chest—the kind of pain that gets you when you swallow a bubble of air—not sharp, but dull, dry, and hard. She knew he had to say it. She would never broach the subject. A subject that, while it had been nearly constantly on her mind, she had never spoken of, never asked him. Now she would never think of it again. As Eva stood there, she was unaware that Bill's religion harbored as deep a hatred against her faith as hers did against his. The founders of his church demanded that every convert confess a belief that her beloved Pope was the Antichrist, and while the American church had softened its beliefs on the demonic qualities of the man, they still demanded that their sons and daughters not marry with infidels, Papists, or other idolaters, so that they would not be unequally yoked. And she, my beautiful, naive Aunt Eva, was a Papist in their eyes, with damnable heresies. Yet on that day, in a barely-spoken compromise, Bill's mother surrendered him to a satanically sealed woman, while saving him from following her into idolatry and hell.

Bill's mother recovered. She was a little embarrassed. Everyone was polite to Eva and treated her graciously. There was no beer to ease the tension—only very, very polite conversation, which illuminated her embarrassment. While she would never be one of them, they did not hate her. How could they? Her only crime was to fall in love with one of them. She was rather a fascinating curiosity—stunning, but suspected of being dirty.

That night in the back seat of the 1939 Ford, there was something different. The excitement changed; the thrill of sin and the hope for salvation instantaneously had become a routine event. Yes, she loved him; maybe she loved him even more. But now it was the kind of love people have after long years of marriage—a love grounded in reality, not in dreams.

On their wedding day, no family was there. Her church demanded it be a Catholic ceremony, a ceremony devoid of honor on the stoop of the priest's house in Freeport, Minnesota, just a few yards away from the beautiful German gothic church that had been built before the First World War. The church that Eva had attended from her birth, where she had imagined her wedding over a thousand times, where she had received her first communion, and where she had attended weddings and funerals too numerous to count.

Sally May, Eva's friend from work—a Catholic, though not very good Catholic, a woman with a reputation and a weakness for both soldiers and drink—was her bridesmaid. None of her six sisters were willing to step onto the porch. A Catholic man, Ralph Horner—who had served with Bill James in the army and lived only six miles away in Melrose—was his best man. Bill didn't know Ralph very well, but a Catholic was required, so Ralph agreed. Jim Hill, Bill's friend from birth, did not come. He spent the day haying on a farm in Douglas County over near Kensington rather than step onto the doorstep of a priest's house. There were no other attendees.

Eva's bridesmaid had ordered a small decorated cake from the Sauk Center Bakery. After the ceremony she opened the white box that she had so carefully held in her lap on the ride to the church, and there it was. This was a nice surprise. Eva cried. It was a hint of what a wedding should be. Seeing it snapped the numbness from her soul.

"Let's take it to mom's. We'll celebrate, please come over." She had told her mom that they would be stopping over after. All four drove over, three in one car, and the best man who had met them at the church drove separately. The best man—feeling very uncomfortable—announced in advance that he would not be able to stay long.

The bride and groom were giddy and excited; the painful ordeal was over, and now they would celebrate and get on with life. Eva held the cake in her hands and Bill knocked, the attendants stood behind. The door opened. Eva's father and mother stood there, my grandparents. Grandma looked afraid and defeated. Grandpa just looked mean. Grandpa took the cake, pushed his way through the small group and tossed it into the street, which was only a short distance because the house stood nearly on the sidewalk. He then turned around and without a word walked back inside, motioning Grandma with a glance to follow him. Grandma's eyes spoke clearly to Eva. They said, "I tried. Oh God, how I tried," as she too walked inside and the door fell closed behind them.

The bridesmaid spoke in short, nearly inaudible, obscene phrases, and the best man quickly said goodbye and exited their lives. They dropped the bridesmaid off at her apartment, and she bade them farewell with something like, "Don't let those idiots hurt you."

Eva replied, "I won't, and thank you so much. I'm so sorry, so sorry."

The bride and groom then drove to their two-room apartment over the dry cleaners on the outskirts of Alexandria. Bill had started working at the dry cleaners a month earlier. The owner was older, and even spoke of the possibility that Bill might have an opportunity to buy it someday. That night, as they lay together in a metal-framed bed, listening to the dripping bathroom faucet, Bill broke out in one of his famous grins that had a propensity to bubble into laughter.

"Eva," he said, "I don't give a damn; I'm the luckiest man on earth. They can't make us feel bad. They can't hurt us. I love you and nothing will ever change that."

Life, yes, life rushed back into Eva and washed every sad and shameful thought out of her soul. How could she not be happy, seeing his disproportionate smile? She laughed and they opened the bottle of gin that he had picked up the day before at the Alexandria Municipal Liquor Store on North Broadway. They mixed it with a bottle of Squirt and before long they were jumping on the bed laughing, hugging, and melting into each other.

As they spun about, so did the fate of the world. Late that night it became June 25, 1950, on the Korean peninsula, and thousands of men, men bent on uniting their land, swept over an artificial line and descended on Seoul. By Monday, Bill knew he would soon be called back into service. By July he was called, and by August he was gone. Eva took over his job at the dry cleaners; they didn't want to lose the opportunity that the owner had spoken of ever so briefly.

Stanley James and I Enter the World

Six months later, I was born on December 20th. My cousin Stanley, Stanley James, was born to Eva and Bill James the next day. I was born on the last day of autumn, and he was born on the first day of winter. The nurse told Eva it was a good sign; the days would be getting longer. He brought the light. In ancient times, he would have had special honors bestowed on him as the first child of the new year; but unfortunately, we now use the Gregorian calendar so those honors went to the first baby born on January 1, 1951. He had missed it by 11 days, or 368 years, depending on how one views the error in the celestial calculation.

Our mothers were in St. Mary's Hospital together, in the new part of the hospital that opened just six months earlier. They were in the hospital for seven days at a total cost of just $72.48, including the $2.00-a-day nursery fee. My dad got word of my arrival from the doctor in the father's waiting room, and Bill got a telegram from the Red Cross. It was good that we were born at the same time. Our moms shared the joy together. So much of their lives had been, and would be, hard. These were golden days, as the snow fell outside, and their babies were carefully tucked in beside them.

We were baptized in two different ceremonies—he first with three other babies, then I a week later with one other—all in the newly built St. Mary's Catholic Church. My mom and dad were his godparents, and mine were Aunt Hope and her husband John. We were all part of this modern world into which babies were exploding, like popcorn. It was a blessing that Bill was in Korea. That way there was less to explain, and his mother wasn't able to plead for the child's soul before he was lost to a Catholic baptism. Perhaps she did plead with him by mail and we just never knew. Perhaps Bill simply didn't answer the letters. Or maybe they just got lost—a lot got lost during that war. Maybe they went to the wrong Seoul.

Before I Remember

As a gardener is responsible for the products of his garden, so the family is responsible for the character and conduct of its children.

Unknown

The House of My Grandparents

Eva was the ninth of twelve children; my mom, Faith, was her sister and the fifth child. Hope and Charity, the other two of the three virtues followed her, but Charity died when she was just seven weeks old. When Faith and Hope were introduced, people habitually said without thinking, "Where is Charity?" Then, when given the explanation, they felt awful. Faith and Hope always tried to think up some kind way of telling people, or preventing the question, but never could solve the problem.

When Eva was born she was handed to my mom, who was then nine years old. She was told that Eva was her baby to take care of. The time for dolls was over. Faith changed Eva's diapers, fed, cleaned, and dressed her. Eva took over the doll that had been Faith's, and life's rhythms continued. The home in Freeport where they were raised was one of dark secrets, and icy coldness. Grandpa demanded absolute obedience, and would flaunt his authority at every opportunity. At every meal he was served first, then the boys that had been confirmed in the church—and thus were men—were served. Grandma and the rest of the children all sat perfectly quietly at the table and watched them eat. If a single sound was made, or someone wiggled in her seat, the offending child would be sent from the table. Grandpa ate excruciatingly slowly so as to savor every moment of authority. When he and the other "men" had their fill, then the rest ate. The older boys soon learned the game, and enjoyed asking for seconds and thirds of the choicest parts of the meal.

20

Faith Escapes into the World

My mother was the most educated of my parents. She managed to graduate from the eighth grade, while my dad only passed the sixth grade before the responsibilities of wage earning took precedence. After mom graduated, she went to work for a well-off local family, the Nelsons. For thirty-five cents a week she kept house and cared for eight children. Young girls were plentiful in the town, so the promised wage was never paid. If she left another girl would take her place. The Nelson woman thought, girls like that should be happy just getting room and board—the room being one shared with the three youngest children, and the food being the family's leftovers. These leftovers were often hastily eaten from the children's plates while she carried them to the sink—before the father demanded scraps for the hogs, or if it was meat, for the dog.

Then—the miracle of miracles happened. She landed a summer job with a rich Jewish family from Saint Louis Park, the wealthy district of Minneapolis. They, the Jews, had just arrived at their summer home on Lake Osakis and had asked at the corner store if anyone knew of an honest hardworking girl who was available. Indeed, Mr. Freeman did. He arranged for Faith to be at their house that very day at 4:00 PM. Had they not hired Faith, she would have been without employment. The Nelsons fired her at once. They suspected something was afoot when she asked for part of the day off.

But she was hired. This was the jackpot. Jewish women took good care of their maids, paid them every week, never deprived them of Thursdays off, and even let them run off to Mass for an hour on Sundays, after breakfast and before lunch. Faith proved to be such a good worker that when the summer ended, they took Faith back to the city with them. She had escaped.

Dad was from Freeport also, but was twelve years older than mom. He left Freeport when she was only six, so he had not known her there. He was earning good pay, working in a war production factory in Saint Paul. On Thursdays after work the guys would go downtown, because that was a good time to meet maids. Maids made good girlfriends. They were alone in the city and didn't have annoying families to question their behavior—only their employers, whose main interest was that they got back on time and were not too tired to work the next day. Of course, the maids always pretended to be young women of leisure. Their exposure to fashion and taste would have fooled the most discerning aesthete—but it was Thursday, and so they were maids. Faith was particularly classy. She had the style and the walk of a high-class lady. She had even learned to imitate the speech of the well-to-do. As she would lay out her lady's clothing she would carefully study the cut, material, and the sewing, determining why it fit so stunningly, what shoes to wear with which dress, and how fashions changed throughout the year. She could have deceived anyone, even those of the upper crust—but not on Thursdays.

One day Faith heard her madam talking with her daughter-in-law. The daughter-in-law had a reputation among the maids of the neighborhood. She was complaining about how hard it was to keep good girls. The solution conceived by the women was to give Faith to the daughter-in-law. At the daughter-in law's home, Faith was only permitted to eat potatoes—all the potatoes she wanted insisted the woman. But her promised wages were paid erratically. It was a shock to discover that all Jews were not alike, that some were not as generous as others. She was trying to figure out how to get another position. The woman surely would not give her a reference if she left, and she could hardly ask the woman's mother-in-law for one. Who knows what stories had already been told. My dad solved the situation by suggesting that they marry.

The Plan

He had a plan. When the war was over, he planned to open a gas station in Alexandria with the money he had been saving. They could include a small café in the plan that she could run. Alexandria was a town with a lot of good fishing lakes. Even now, with gas rationing, summer tourists were flocking there. Surely after the war even more resorts would open. There they would build a life.

But for now, he suggested that she get hired on at the factory where he was working. They were hiring women. He knew the guy from the other division where she would have to work. The rules would not permit her to work with him. But with two factory jobs they could save even more money to implement the plan. She liked the plan, but was uneasy about the factory work. A few years earlier she would have jumped at the chance; but now she had begun to see herself as a lady. Not a real lady, one afraid of hard work, but as a lady with restrictions on what she did. And there was another concern, too. The women who worked in the factories became hard and manlike in their looks, and their language became coarse. She feared this. She had so carefully learned other lessons; she did not want them to be so quickly forgotten.

She would first try one other possibility. The next Thursday, she wasn't able to leave until after breakfast and a number of requests beginning, "Oh, Faith could you just get me this and that before you leave?" But at last she was free. Wearing not her best dress, but an appropriate Thursday dress—a black dress with a white collar accented with white cloth covered buttons, white belt, and black shoes with the new silk stockings that dad had gotten her, topped off with a black hat and white gloves—she entered the front door of the downtown Dayton's Department Store. The help flocked to her. She quietly asked where the employment office was. When she arrived at the proper door, the woman assumed that she was there to complain about an attendant, and was stunned that she was seeking employment. With her looks and poise, she was hired for the hat department, to begin in four weeks when the fall hats came in. Even during the war women wanted to be fashionable, and hats were still made—sometimes from recycled items, and sometimes from the discards of factories turning out war goods. Their production returned to being a cottage industry where women worked at night producing them for a little extra cash. The hat department was one of the most prestigious areas of the store; however, the pay was lousy and commission-dependent.

She decided that they would be married on Saturday, August 1, 1943. Her new job would start the next Monday. She would need to quit her current employment as soon as she got her pay. The pay would be late, but she couldn't wait too long. When it was three days late she asked about it, saying that her mother was very ill and that the family needed the money. The lie would surely only be a venial sin, because it was told to get what was rightfully hers. She did worry, however, that she might be punished by an actual illness descending on her mother. So that night she prayed not only for forgiveness, but also said a rosary for her mother's health. Timing was difficult. She knew that she would give notice the day after she was paid, and that she would be asked to leave immediately without references.

She couldn't stay with her fiancé—that was unheard of; and she did not want to return home—that was too frightening. Her oldest aunt, Aunt Helen, agreed to take her in, and help her plan their wedding during the interlude.

The trick worked, her boss paid her three-fourths of her wages. She gave notice the next day, and was asked to leave. The remainder of her pay wasn't mentioned and Faith decided that there was no need to mention it. She would only hear a litany of reasons why she should not be paid, "suspicion of drinking coffee, eating something other than potatoes, eating too many potatoes, not cleaning the toilet well enough." Why even ask? Such women never paid, and always had sufficient justifications to satisfy themselves. She was already packed and had said her good-byes to the rest of the staff. She arrived at Aunt Helen's, and even though it was 10:30 in the morning, Aunt Helen brought out the bottle of dandelion wine that her husband Hank had made the summer before. They toasted her freedom and the future from tiny crystal glasses that had been handed down in her family for two generations.

The Marriage Begins

The wedding was back in Freeport. Both being Catholic, they married in the Church—a simple wedding, with friends, family, and a lunch in the church basement. Faith began work at Dayton's Department Store. Saving was difficult, as she was required to always dress appropriately. While she carefully shopped the basement the same day items were moved down, it was still costly. Rich women often lacked entertainment in the afternoons, so they would amuse themselves trying on hats for hours. Faith hurried about serving them, even though they had no intention of actually buying one. They might come back when the hat had been moved to the sales room, but full-price sales were few, and the work required long hours of standing and an always pleasant demeanor.

Then, after Christmas, she was promoted to head the Bridal Veil department. Commissions were much higher there, and the possibility that the women who came in would actually buy something was also higher. She began on January 3rd, but the big rush and the big money wouldn't be until May and June. But lookers, only a few of whom had already met a young man, were coming in already to look or to dream. She would try to convince them to put the veil in lay-a-way so that it would still be available. She would say, "You never know with the war, there may not be any later." Then one Monday, Valentine's Day to be precise, a day that should be good for veils, Faith was called into the director's office and asked directly.

"Faith are you with child?"

She had tried not to show, but it was obvious now. She was into her fifth month. She had to quit. They could not have a pregnant woman working in a classy store like Dayton's, not even in the maternity department. One month later she miscarried a baby girl. After two weeks of recovery she began work in the factory assembling seat covers for bombers.

When the war was over, they did build the gas station and attached a café, but they didn't have money left for a house, so they moved in under the café. They only intended to live in the basement until they could afford to build a house across the alley. But as the years rolled by, the dream faded. The basement under the cafe became a comfortable place, or at least their place.

A few years passed, and in 1950 she was pregnant again. This time, it was me. Being the owner of their own business was great for them. No one could tell mom she had to quit. The kitchen of the café had stairs that went down to the living quarters in the basement, so she could slip down the steps and check on things—like a napping baby—while checking on an order. They even had another woman working there, Millie. Millie worked during lunch, but could also fill in when mom had to go somewhere.

Stanley James and I were born in the year that marked the mid-point of the century, 1950. The year that Smokey the Bear began fighting forest fires. The year that Charles Schulz, an unknown Minnesota cartoonist from St. Paul, syndicated "Peanuts." The year that the Soviet Union announced that they had the atomic bomb. As I have said, it was a time of unprecedented progress.

The Mercy of Saint Maurice

Faith and Eva stood outside on an exceptionally hot Sunday night in July 1953. They had spent the day together at the Lake Brophy picnic area with the kids—the kids being Stanley and me. Eva had been working nearly twelve hours a day at the dry cleaners.

Her hands were discolored, and her voice was becoming hard from her new smoking habit and the chemical-laden air she breathed in the shop.

Dad stayed home to work at the gas station. Sundays were good days for gas sales, and that summer the tourists were coming in ever-increasing numbers. On Sunday they were in a hurry to get home, so there was no need to keep the café open. On Sunday the big money maker was ice—ice for the coolers filled with fresh caught fish. They would pay for frozen water. We made it all week—then on Sunday we cashed in. Yeah, they complained plenty about the price, but they paid fifteen cents for a block, rather than have their fish go bad.

The full moon rose and Eva thought, "I wonder if Bill will see the moon tonight? I wonder if that war will ever end? I wonder what the hell God was doing, letting thousands die again?"

The last account she read said over thirty-three thousand GIs had died. Would she soon be one of the women who got the damnable telegram? She wondered, but did not say. The children were present, so she only said, "My what a wonderful moon tonight." Then she prayed a silent prayer to Saint Maurice, the patron saint of soldiers and of female cramps, something else she was feeling at the moment. Why Saint Maurice reigns over these diverse areas of creation is much too long a discourse to repeat here, so let me only say that in Catholicism many convenient pairings occur in the jurisdiction of saints. Only God and the Pope can explain it.

Her prayers were nearly instantly answered the next day. The war ended and troops began to be withdrawn. Not all, but most of the men were coming home. Bill, she learned in early August, would be among them. By then her cramps were also gone; the timing was great for his return. Saint Maurice truly did understand the needs of tender women, virile soldiers and young lovers.

After he returned, they both worked in the dry cleaners. The owner worked only a few hours each day. Then after only two months, he offered to sell the building and business, land contract, with payments over the next 28 years. The owner retired and moved to northern Florida near Gainesville, just a half-mile from the Swanee River. When the tenant that rented the other two rooms upstairs moved out the following spring, Bill and Eva expanded their living quarters to include the entire upstairs and remodeled the second floor into, what was to them, a grand apartment.

These were glorious years. Bill had never done carpentry and Eva had never painted, but together, along with Stanley, they were a family learning from the Popular Mechanic's Encyclopedia of Home Repair. They believed that all things were possible, and they were right. They worked on the apartment at night and during the day in the dry cleaners. Little Stanley played behind the counter and greeted the costumers as they came in. They had fixed up the business too, painted a new sign. "Fast Clean" they called it. They said they could clean anything in 24 hours—and they did, even if they had to work all night.

They knew that when Stanley started school it would be easier. They hoped that by the time he was in the first grade they would have one of the new houses being built to the west of them. They would then rent the apartment that they had worked so hard on, and their good fortune would flow like the rays from the sun. Then they would have time for fishing on the weekends, for picnics, for trips to the cities to visit the Como Park Zoo and ride on the swan paddleboats.

Mom and dad, Eva and Bill, and hundreds of others made a good choice when they located in Alexandria. Alexandria grew rapidly after the war; it would soon approach a population of over 6,000. Alexandria became the largest town between Fargo, North Dakota, and St. Cloud, Minnesota. So large was Alexandria that parents from Garfield and Nelsonville warned their teenage sons and daughters of the corruption that might be found in the city, only seven miles away. They warned their children to stay away from those big town kids, as surely they would want to lure them into a life of alcohol, drugs and sex.

School Days Begin
1956-1957

At each stage of development the child needs different resources from the family. During the first year, a variety of experience and the availability of the parents for attachment are primary. During the second and third years, stimulation of language development is critical. During the years prior to school entrance, information that persuades children they are loved becomes critical, and during the school years it is important for children to believe that they can succeed at the tasks they want to master.

Jerome Kgan

A New School for a New Age

In 1956, the town opened its second elementary school. While the nation's south struggled with racial integration after the Brown versus Board of Education of Topeka decision, the residents of Alexandria were able to live their lives without racism or bigotry. Obviously, we were all white.

On the west side of our thriving community, new ranch homes were being built on new streets with alphabetized tree names: Ash, Birch, Cedar, Douglas, Elm, continuing all the way to Maple. Many of the new homes had attached garages, and price tags of eight, nine and even one for twelve thousand dollars. The new professionals who had attended college on the GI bill and then started their families were occupying these homes. These neighborhoods were not divided between Catholics and Protestants, but by the new determinants of community segregation: money, education, and profession.

The new school was Lincoln Elementary. The old school was Washington. It was decided, I guess by the Board of Education, that all the children on the west side of Broadway would attend the new school, and that all the children on the east side would attend the older school. We lived on the west side of town, the northwest. I visited the new school with my mother, who had dressed herself as if it were Sunday. It was still summer, so she wore a white hat, gloves, and shoes, and a light blue dress. She looked like the ladies in the magazines that she paged through until the corners were all tattered and that I was not allowed to touch with my dirty hands. The other mothers were dressed nearly identically to her. They, too, must have read the same magazines. That is how the world must work, I reckoned. You read the directions in those magazines, the ones with the shiny covers, and then carefully followed the directions and you would be all right, just like everyone else.

I was not dressed so similarly to the other boys. They all had new black shoes, and pants with thin black belts and silver buckles. I had an old pair of brown shoes that we got from a customer as payment at the gas station. They had bought the shoes for their son, but he outgrew them faster than expected, so they traded them to dad for two gallons of gas. I wasn't wearing the black or blue pants; I wore tan shorts with an elastic waistband. They had white socks and shirts; I had blue socks, my favorite shirt and a clip-on bowtie. Mom made the shorts and shirt. The shirt had red and green stripes, and the bow tie was yellow and brown. I guess the other kids must have gotten a kid's magazine that mom and I didn't know about.

Lincoln School was modern, with large windows beneath each of which was an orange panel on which the shape of a duck, rabbit, cat or dog was embossed in a cream color. It had shiny aluminum doors and window framing. The halls had animal shapes in the vinyl floor tile—just like the window panels—and the rooms . . . . Oh, the rooms had endless shelves with toys. Yes, toys—wood blocks, puzzles, trucks—and they had small chairs and tables all shiny and new. And kids everywhere! These would be my friends. And best of all, my cousin Stanley James would be there.

The dry cleaner was on the west side of Broadway—way at the south end. Wow, we would be able to play together every day with all these toys. Our moms were going to try to get us both in the morning kindergarten. There was nothing dirty or shabby in this school. This school was like the pictures of the expensive homes in the other magazine that my mom read. Then, just as we were leaving, I saw the playground—two slides, monkey bars, an orange merry-go-round, swings with black plastic seats and teeter-totters in a row. School was better than the heaven that the priest had talked about last Easter. Heaven didn't have any of this good stuff. School was the best!

Then, about a week before the first day of school, it was determined (I guess again by the School Board) that because of bus routes, and in order to more evenly divide the students between the two schools, the kids who lived north of Lake Winona should attend Washington School. That way there would be room for expansion at the new school. Coincidentally, Lake Winona separated the town like the railroad tracks of industrial cities. To the south were the new homes; and to the north were light industries and poor homes. The gas station-cafe where we lived was on Highway 52 across from the Land-O-Lakes milk powderizing plant, which was next to the sewage treatment plant. Both dumped their refuse into the north end of the lake, as did the local electrical power plant. On the gravel road behind our building, simply referred to as the alley, were eight very small homes, two old farmhouses, and seven children: Danny Carlson, a boy older than the rest of us who wore glasses already and was an altar boy at the church; Sharon Stosonberg, a Lutheran girl a year older than us who played the piano as did her mother; her younger brother who was only a toddler; her new baby sister; and my friend Tim Harris and his big brother, Brad. Brad had an eye that didn't quite work right. He wasn't blind; it just moved strangely. Brad was the same age as Sharon. Tim was my age. The Harris boys were very tan, even in winter, and they had dark curly hair and brown eyes. The bothers didn't belong to any church. Their dad was in the army, so we never saw him. They would sometimes go to see him; but he never came to Alexandria. So, we only knew their mom. She was very pretty, with the typical blond hair of the majority of the Scandinavian population of the town; but she didn't talk to anyone very much and no one ever came to see her.

The fairground was to the west of the alley, and around it was a smattering of other homes with no real plan or arrangement to them—but none of them had kids, only old people. Yes, bussing would be better, they said. The five of us school-age kids all walked to a single location about a block from our homes to be picked up by the bus, then it made two more stops—each time gathering two more kids. In all, nine of us were picked up, and then curiously the bus drove past the children waiting in front of their homes on Cedar, Douglas and Elm Street—children that would be taken to the new Lincoln School.

Washington School, while old and scruffy, was enlivened with a mob of rowdy kids. The playground was stocked with a myriad of playthings, and life continued. Kindergarten was a wondrous time—even without Stanley James. He remained at Lincoln, but was the only child to attend who did not live in a ranch home on a perfect tree-named street.

But even the people in those houses were not feeling as secure as they once did. It had been a year of alarming developments on every front. The Russians now had the H-Bomb, too. Rock-n-roll had not gone away, and Elvis Presley was unchecked in his destruction of the morals of youth. And when the Soviet Union drove their tanks into Hungary that November, we were all stunned. While everyone in Minnesota was a Democrat, we were glad that Adlai Stevenson lost the election. Ike was a military man, and these were dangerous times. For us—the children—evil had two names: they were Satan and Nikita Khrushchev. We knew both sat lurking in the wings waiting to destroy us. But of the two, we knew that Nikita was more to be feared. Because when the voice on the radio talked about him, the men listened; when the priest talked about Satan, they slept.

First grade began at Washington in the prescribed order, with reading: "Look! Look, Look. Look. See Sally." At the end of the year my report card was mixed, with wonderful reviews for reading comprehension, and glowing reports of my creativity in art and craft activities, but disappointing remarks in speech, and a clear indication that I did not grasp phonics at all.

I would not be returning to Washington in the fall of 1958. St. Mary's completed construction of a new parochial elementary school that would open with grades 2 to 5. First and sixth grades would be added the next year. While the Benedictine nuns from St. Cloud operated the hospital, a teaching order of Franciscan sisters from Little Falls was to open a small convent and operate the school. Five nuns would come initially, one for each grade and one to keep house. The fifth grade teacher, Sister Rose, would double as principal for the first year.

Stanley James and I would be together at the new Catholic school. The only nun we had ever known before was our Aunt, Sister Anne.

She was a wonderful and cheerful person. We did not know that—like other creations of God—nuns came in many varieties. We were excited about everything the new school would bring, but mostly we wondered what would be on the playground.

Summer and the Return of Warmth

As one can imagine, winters are hard in Minnesota. Nearly every winter, someone or other died—either freezing to death walking from a stalled car, or passing out somewhere and getting covered with snow. The coming of spring and the melting away of four to six feet of snow is a dramatic change for us, and we are always ready to make the most of this season's all too brief delights.

During the summers, we were set free to wander about as we pleased. Even in this area of town, safety—or the lack of danger—was taken for granted. One morning I made a beeline to Tim's house, and we decided to walk down to the lake to see if there really would be tadpoles there, like we saw in the last issue of our Weekly Reader.

Tim's brother Brad called to us on our way, "Hey guys, you have to see this."

Danny had found a nest of four black birds. He was killing each of them in a different way. Brad missed the first one. Danny put lighter fluid all over it and then lit it on fire. That was really cool, Brad told us, but all any of us saw were the charred remains. Danny put more lighter fluid on it, and lit it again for us, but now that it was no longer animated, it no longer made an agonized sound. It only produced a rich odor of burnt protein and feathers. Intoxicatingly disgusting—but more like seeing a good car wreck after the bodies are removed, instead of the momentous crash of objects. It lacked the power-thrill that it had earlier supplied the observer.

The second and third killings Brad witnessed himself, and eagerly gave us his firsthand testimony. The second was drowned in the lake.

"Danny was real smart. He didn't just toss it in, like way far out—that wouldn't have taken very long and he wouldn't have been able to see it close up. He held it gently by the feet and pulled it under for only a few seconds, then let it come back up, then held it for a few seconds more under the water. Each time he made the time under the water just a little bit longer until it kind of started to die. Not really all at once—kind of slow, you know. Then, he decided to keep it under for a long time before it was completely dead, so that he could feel it die in his hand. The next one he decided to hang. He got a string, tied it around its neck, and then hung it from a low tree branch. That one might still have some life left in it."

They were still checking it from time to time, but thought it was all gone.

"What are you going to do with the last one?" Tim asked Danny, wondering if there could still be any other ways to kill something.

"Smash it with a rock, I bet. That's what my grandpa did with the kittens they didn't want." Brad chimed in with both enthusiasm and authority.

"No, you'll see. This one I . . . I've been saving for the best." Danny announced with pride.

We all paraded off in the order of our births. Danny led the way carrying the sacrifice, followed by Brad, who was waving a branch in an attempt to keep the mosquitoes away. Then came Tim, who was clanking an old tin can with a small gray-green rock, and myself. I was given a task of carrying a big stick that I lazily dragged behind me.

There also seemed to be two adult birds that leaped from branch to branch as we walked—following us. They chirped, although it almost sounded like screaming, or the sound bad brakes make when you're trying to stop fast. I wondered if they could be the mom and dad birds. No, that would be nonsense; birds don't care about their young. They aren't even animals—and if cats don't care when their kittens are smashed, birds couldn't possibly care. And after all, these were blackbirds, not robins. Robins are good birds. But blackbirds, well they are just birds no one cares about. Anyway, animals neither thought nor felt pain like we did, they were just instinctual, or something like that.

Our procession took us to a huge ant pile on the edge of a small grouping of trees on the property that Mr. Lane owned. These were the kind of big ants that are both black and red. They bite, so you had to be careful. Mr. Lane was an old man who didn't like kids. Sometimes we called him Mr. Meany. We couldn't understand why he didn't like us. If he saw us playing on his land, he would say. "I think you kids had better get along before you get in trouble."

But he had some of the best stuff on his property. Cool stuff like the big ant pile. We came here from time to time with big sticks or even a shovel to mess up the pile. Then we would watch the ants run around like crazy. One time when we had a shovel, Danny had found a bunch of ant larvae; those are the ones that look like white worms but turn into ants. Danny tossed a flat rock into the destroyed pile, and then pulled some of the larvae from the sides onto the rock. He waited for the other ants to come to try to carry them back. When they got there, he would smash the little worms. It made the other ants more frantic as they tried to carry the bundles of emerging life back to safety, only to have them smashed—one by one. Our attack on the ant pile would sometimes be accompanied with matches being tossed at random and, when available, firecrackers.

We sometimes pretended that the ants were Koreans or Japs and that we were bombing them. We had all heard funny stories about how the gooks would run around, even tear off their clothes when they were on fire. After the villages were bombed, we—that is, our guys—would then get to walk in and shoot everyone that was left. It wasn't a sin, though; it was war. It is not a sin to kill animals or people in war, only to kill people like us, you know.

Danny took the big stick that had been in my care. He pushed it real deep into the ant pile stirring up a frenzy of activity by digging a pit. The pit was totally covered with crawling ants and larvae. He didn't stop to smash any of the larvae, but when the pit was of a suitable size, he dropped the last bird into it, and then stood by with folded arms to watch the action. The action was disappointingly slow. The ants crawled on the bird, and it peeped, but there wasn't any blood. Danny thought the ants would eat the flesh from the bird in a few minutes. That's what would happen in a movie. But they just seemed to crawl around it, more interested in gathering up the larvae than in consuming the little critter.

I took the opportunity to ask Danny why he was doing this to the birds.

"Well," he said, "I'm going to be a priest, a missionary priest. My mom is already saving so I can go to St. John's. When you're a missionary priest, you see a lot of suffering, so you have to be prepared. You wouldn't believe some of the stuff those pagans do. They worship strange gods, you know. Gods who like to see a lot of torture and stuff like that. If I'm a priest, I have to be strong, so I don't throw-up when stuff like that happens. How would that be, a priest barfing in front of everyone? No one would convert after seeing a barfing priest, would they?"

"No, I guess not. I guess you gotta do it for God," I agreed.

"Yeah," Danny continued, "it's just like being a soldier. They get to see a lot of stuff, too. I heard my dad tell my uncle that one time they burned the wiener off of a guy with a blowtorch, because he wouldn't tell them where the other bad guys were hiding or something. He said they had so much fun doing it, they did it to a couple of other gooks that they knew didn't know anything, and do you know what they did? I mean, what the gooks did?"

"No, what?" I asked.

"They lied, they said that there were men hiding in a hut somewhere. But it was a lie, and that's a sin, but those gooks are pagans and they don't know no better. That's why I'm going to be a missionary and tell them not to lie. Not to lie to the Americans who are there to help them. After they burned off their wieners, they shot them real good for lying, first in the balls, then they put the gun in their mouths and blew off the tops of their heads. Because they lied, you know. You know, lying in war could get people killed; they were just lucky that no one was hurt."

On the way home we did see remarkably small tadpoles swimming in dark schools near the shore.

Second Grade 1958-59

Hail Mary, full of grace. The Lord is with thee.
Blessed art thou among women, and blessed is the fruit of thy
womb, Jesus.
Holy Mary, Mother of God, pray for us sinners, now and at the
hour of our death.
Amen.

St. Mary's opens its doors

In those days, parochial school children were not allowed to ride the public school busses, so mom took me and picked up Stanley James for the first day. Eva had taken a part time job at the laundry of the Douglas County Hospital. She worked there in the mornings and then helped at the dry cleaners in the afternoon. Bill opened the dry cleaners at six in the morning, and worked until closing at about 6:00 PM. But often they needed to work late into the evening to get everything done. About her part-time job, Eva would laugh and say she can't get away from doing the wash; it was her job growing up, too. The part-time job was only for a while, until they had enough money to make a down payment on a real house—a house for Stanley and, they hoped, more children.

Mom took us to school for the first day. We listened to the Everly Brothers singing "Birddog." But as we approached the school, she became nervous, as if we were doing something disrespectful—not quite a definable sin, like chewing gum in church. So, she quickly switched from the Minneapolis Rock & Roll station KDWB to the local KXRA where a male voice with a Chicago inflection was enthusiastically informing us of the success of our country's nuclear testing. All that summer it was a popular topic in the news. Soldiers were watching the tests close-up, wearing dark eye protection, everywhere from Nevada to the Atoll Islands.

News of the tests on Bikini Atoll caught our attention and Stanley James whispered in my ear, "I wonder if the blast blew off the Bikinis?"

I tried not to laugh because I didn't want mom to ask, "What are you boys giggling about? This testing is serious. The Russians have even bigger bombs, and with the pipeline storage tanks in town, we could be a target."

We were all taken to the gymnasium, where we were efficiently labeled with nametags that also served to identify our grade and our teacher. We were filed according to grade in neatly aligned rows of chairs. Our moms and the one dad who came stood in the back. It was all giggles, a few tears, and lots of wiggles.

Monsignor Ward walked up to a microphone that had been set up on top of a portable platform. The platform looked like a folding table, only lower, and with a different kind of surface. When he walked, the sound of his footsteps echoed from under the stage. The sound was both strong and authoritative but with a rhythm that told us that he was also gentle and happy. Like Santa might sound as he walked across rooftops on cold winter nights.

He began, "In the Name of the Father, and the Son, and the Holy Spirit, bring your blessings to this fine school and to the children that you have given into our care. May they grow to love you more each day, and may they know your grace and mercy. And, too, bless the nuns from the Little Falls Convent of Saint Francis that have been sent to us, and the cooks and staff who will guide and care for these little ones through the years." Then he spoke directly to us and told us how fortunate we were to be the first class to have such a beautiful school and so many people to care for us and to shape our lives.

The Franciscan sisters stood dutifully by, occasionally quieting one or another of the children. Then he began calling out the names of the children starting with our grade. When we heard our names we were to stand and line-up and follow our teacher back to the room.

He began, "Anderson, Clare; Anderson, Douglas; Baker, Robert; Bundy, Susan;" and continued until he reached "James, Stanley;" when no child stood. I poked Stanley but he was looking straight ahead at Monsignor Ward and paid no attention to me.

"James, Stanley," was called again. People begin to look around. "Is there a James, Stanley here?" he asked.

Then Stanley James stood and announced himself in a loud defiant voice. "I am Stanley James, not James Stanley."

Susan grabbed Clare's arm, expecting that Monsignor would immediately discharge a lightning bolt from his hand and obliterate the child on the spot.

But Monsignor simply laughed and said, "Alright, Mr. Stanley James, welcome to St. Mary's."

Everyone smiled in polite agreement with Monsignor's handling of this defiance. Everyone that is, but Sister Mary Ann. Sister Mary Ann was our teacher. While she said nothing, she did not understand why Monsignor dismissed such insolence so lightly. She was a woman that believed in justice. She was a woman more comfortable with the God of the Old Testament, the God who believed in and perfected justice. Punishment, she believed, could only be dealt out to those that deserved it. But like the God of the Old Testament, she believed that an opportunity to do so should never be missed.

She would not have long to wait in order to mete out justice. After reaching the room, the first lesson of the day, described in educational literature, as the "Lets make it fun and break in easy lesson," was to draw a picture of a house.

"Does it have to be my house?" asked Stanley James. "I don't really have a house."

I was glad that he asked, because I didn't really have a house either. I didn't want to draw the gas station with an arrow to our house under it.

"In here we raise our hand and wait to be called on before we speak. Is that understood? Class, say, 'yes,'" was our new teacher's calm, but firm reply.

All of the students said, "Yes," except Stanley, who instead raised his hand.

"Stanley, why didn't you say 'yes'?" Sister inquired, still calm, but now colder.

"Because I hadn't been called on, and you said never to speak until we are called." Stanley proudly informed her, not with insolence, but rather with pride that he had listened so very intently to every word, and was the only one who had followed her instructions to the letter.

"Not unless I tell you to say 'yes'."

"Well, then," said Stanley James in a voice like an attorney who had just caught a witness giving inconsistent testimony, "I guess you made a mistake. You should have said that to begin with."

"You are not to correct adults."

This time, Stanley was not challenging a man, confident in his authority and therefore not compelled to use it. He was confronting a woman, unpracticed in her authority and eager to exercise it. "You are going to find out what happens to boys who sass adults, something you should have learned a long time ago."

"OK," said Stanley James as bright as day. "That's why I came to school, to learn things."

She couldn't take what she saw as impertinence a moment longer. Crack! A slap was fired across his face faster than a car sliding into a guardrail along Highway 52 at the sharp turn just west of the fairgrounds. A look of surprise replaced Stanley James's open confident appearance of a few minutes earlier. All the kids put their eyes down to their papers except me. I wanted to see what Stanley James would do. He raised his hand.

"Yes, Stanley." She asked, suspicious of what he was going to say.

"What did you do that for? I didn't do anything," he said, confused.

She rushed to him, took him by his earlobe, twisted it, and dragged him from the room. I think I heard or felt his head smash against the newly painted block wall. When she returned, she was alone.

"Are there any other questions?" she asked in a proud tone, like someone who had just defeated a worthy opponent.

We were all afraid, but I still needed to know, must we draw our own house or not.

I raised my hand and said, "Can it be any house, or does it have to be our house?"

"Stand up when you ask a question." I stood and repeated the question with trembling lips, hunched shoulders and shivering fingers.

"You may draw any house you wish," at last, I was told.

I began to draw a wonderful big house with a large blue-gabled roof, four Doric columns, windows with colored glass squares in the top third, a chimney, and front steps, bushes and trees. It was like the houses in mom's magazines. She would show them to me and tell me about each of them—what style they were, and what kind of people lived in them. The people who lived in the magazine houses were always rich people. Sometimes they were also famous or powerful. But always they were rich. The other kids were surprised. We were silent, but I could see how one-by-one the kids would stop and look at my picture in amazement.

Sister Mary Ann said, "Stop for a moment, I have something to add."

While she was talking, Dave whispered very quietly from behind, "Let me see yours." I lifted it and held it off to the side for him to see. When I looked back at Sister Mary Ann, she was walking over.

She took the picture from my hands and said calmly, "Some students have not learned to listen. Art class is not for students who don't listen. Take your chair to the front of the room and sit facing the wall."

After art, Stanley James returned to the room with a bump on his forehead. Our eyes met and our telepathic conversations confirmed that these nuns were not the same as our aunt, Sister Anne.

Lunch was great, but first we had to go to eleven o'clock Mass. This we learned we would have to do everyday. The cooks made sloppy Joes, with green beans and applesauce. Then if that wasn't the best, they buttered slices of fresh bread and put them on large red trays, and we could eat all the bread we wanted. After lunch, we went outside to play for twenty minutes. Lunch and recess were the two best times of the day for any boy.

The next day, we settled into our routine; we would walk to school, and I would meet Stanley James at the corner where Johnson's Dairy was. Stanley, Dave, whose mom and dad owned the dairy store, and I would walk together. The public school bus would pass us most days in the next block and the kids on the bus would yell, "Cat Lickers," or "Mary Worshipers," out the windows as they drove past us and passed our school, to be let off at Washington. I could recognize some of the boys from my kindergarten and first grade class, but I didn't think they knew who I was any longer. I had become the "other."

The next day the first thing on the agenda was another getting acquainted activity. We were each asked to say our favorite food when called on. First was Mary McDaniel, a pretty red-haired girl all the boys had a crush on, but we didn't use such a word. We only said, "She's not all that bad." Translation "Wooooww." She stood up along side her desk and said in a clear sentence, which by the second day we understood the routine to be, "My favorite food is cherry pie."

"Very good, Mary" said Sister Mary Ann.

Mary was visibly proud and relieved. Her father was an attorney in Alexandria and her mother sang in the choir and served on a lot of the town committees. She was, in second grade, already on her way to following in their preordained footsteps.

Next was Dave Johnson. He stood, but didn't quite have the formal structure down. "I like watermelons, because we can spit the seeds and not get in trouble."

Sister Mary Ann looked a little annoyed and simply said that it was very low-class to spit seeds and that he should learn to remove them with a fork. He was about to defend his actions when he remembered Stanley's encounter the day before for correcting Sister Many Ann. So, he simply said, "Yes, Sister." He was learning the role of authority and the role of the controlled. It doesn't matter whether they are right or not, it only matters that they are in control.

Next was my turn. I didn't like to talk in front of people, they sometimes didn't understand me and didn't listen, but if I didn't talk I would be disobeying, so I said, "I like ham-a-burgers."

"What did you say?" She sounded almost like a cat might sound that had found a mouse. That is, if cats could talk, which they can't.

"I like ham-a-burgers."

She smiled in an almost snicker that signaled to the other kids that it was appropriate to laugh.

"Come up front and stand here beside my desk," she said coldly. "Now say what you like again."

"Ham-a-burger."

She and the class were now openly laughing.

"Say it again," she calmly demanded.

I knew I must not be saying it right, but I didn't know how to say it, and I had to say it. I was crying as she made me say it again and again, each time signaling the class to laugh. It became even funnier because each time I couldn't stop myself from adding additional h's.

"H-hh-hhham-a-b-bbur-bbburger, h-h-h-h-hh-hhham-a-a-a-b-b-bbur-bbbur-g-g-ger."

I looked at all the faces of the kids and the face of Sister Many Ann, and only Stanley James's face was not laughing. His forehead was furrowed and his expression was one of bewilderment. A look not unlike that of weird Tony, the 50-year old man who rode a bike around town finding pop bottles to turn in for the three-cent deposit, and who still lived with his mom and dad. We had been told to stay away from him, because he wasn't all there. He, too, wore the same frown of confusion, didn't get the jokes people were making. and didn't know he was the joke. As I looked at Stanley James, I was disappointed, because I knew he wouldn't be able to explain to me why everyone was laughing. He didn't know, either.

There would be other words during the year—"Chim-a-knee," "Rut-a-beg-gas," and many more. Each time a new word was found, a new episode of the same old sitcom would occur. I would be paraded to the front of the class and would be asked to repeat the word to the laughter of the class and Sister Many Ann, until I cried and could no longer move my lips to form any word.

By the end of the year, I stuttered so badly that I would hardly speak to anyone except Stanley James. Being silent was not really so bad. It changed my relationship with the world from active participant to an observer. One who observed every detail from a kind of white invisible cocoon that pain could not penetrate. But now this cocoon was only thinly spun and still soft and plastic.

For music, we were combined with the third grade and had their teacher, Sister Gene. We all loved her. She was lively like an elf, only bigger. She was not beautiful to look at, short and dumpy, and her face was deeply pitted with holes and lines. One of the girls said that she must have had a lot of pimples when she was a teenager and that's why she became a nun. I only knew that she was the liveliest person I had ever known. She would sing with us, and sometimes jump up from the piano and start to clap her hands and dance. She would get us all jumping up and making noise. Occasionally, one of the other nuns would come to the door and knock. After she completed her doorway conversation she would turn around and say with an expression like a child caught in the cookie jar, "We need to be a little bit more quiet." But some days she would take us outside to sing as loud as we could.

Killing Danny

Fall is a very short season in Minnesota and the daylight hours fade quickly, so after school I would race over to Tim's house. He and his brother Brad were still going to Washington, as did Sharon, because they were not Catholic. I, of course, knew that they were going to hell and that kids like Sharon would want to influence me into becoming an evil Lutheran. But Tim didn't have any religion, so I figured I was safe with him.

Danny was becoming a problem for Tim and Brad. Danny was too old for St. Mary's. He was a seventh grader, so he continued in public school and road the bus with Brad, Tim and Sharon. When they got off the bus, Sharon's mom was always standing on the porch and would watch Sharon walk or run home; but Tim and Brad lived all the way down the alley and Danny lived even further down.

As Tim and Brad would walk, Danny would walk behind them and push them, and say "Get out of my way, you little farts," and other things like that. They would try to move off the road, but Danny would just move to the side right behind them and tell them to keep walking. Then he would push them again. One time when he had pushed them down, he put his foot right on Brad's private parts and said, "If you don't walk faster, I'm going to smash your balls like grapes, both of them." Tim told me all about it when Brad wasn't there. His brother was scared and didn't want to say anything. After Brad got home he would change his clothes and run over to Sharon's house, and they would sit on the porch. She was teaching him how to play the piano. Sharon's mother gave lessons, but Brad's mom didn't have money for that kind of stuff. So Sharon would teach him for free. He liked being inside, safe inside, away from the possibility that Danny would hurt him.

Tim and I went over to talk with Sharon and Brad but saw that he was crying. "I don't know what to do; Danny wants to kill me. He said that next summer he's going to take all my clothes off and push me down Mr. Lane's sewage tank, the one with the big cement cover that stinks, the one that the men were pumping out last Thursday. He's going to do it, when it's full again. I'll drown in Mr. Lane's poop." Sharon was very calm and simply announced that we would have to kill Danny first. It would have to be done today. Having decided what needed to be done, without any discussion, the next topic was simply to decide the most effective way to do it. Poison—that would probably be best, because he was so much bigger than us. Brad seemed to have recovered his composure at the possibility that his problem would soon be over.

I was very pleased to announce that I could contribute to the enterprise. "We have Stanley Gluc at home. My mom said it is deadly poison. Deadly, that's the best kind of poison. She said that even one drop would kill you, so I'm never to even touch the bottle. I'll run home and get it." I returned in record time, out of breath with the bottle safely concealed under my shirt.

"But how are we going to get him to eat glue?" Tim asked with notable concern.

"Some of the kids in my class eat paste, but I don't think he would eat it. Besides, he would see the skull and crossbones on the jar," I pointed out.

"It really has a skull and crossbones. That really is good poison," said Tim.

"I know!" said Sharon. Her keen mind had devised a solution in seconds that would have taken a military strategist years to conceive. "We will buy a gumball, then we will cut it in half and glue it back together."

Sharon had a penny that she was willing to contribute, and Tim and I ran to the cafe and popped the penny into the gumball machine by the door. Brad pulled his jack knife from his pocket and the plan proceeded. As we waited for it to dry, we discussed how we would deliver the gumball. We couldn't just give it to him. If someone saw us, we would have to go to jail. At last, it was decided that we would put it on the outside of his windowsill. He would look out and say, "Look someone left me a gumball on my windowsill," he would open the window and bite into it eagerly, and his mother would soon find him dead.

I was selected to deliver the gumball for two reasons: first, I was the youngest, and if we got caught I would have to go to jail for the shortest amount of time; and second, everyone knew Catholics had confession and if I didn't die before my first confession, I could confess the murder and not have to go to hell.

The glue was returned. So little had been used that no one would be the wiser. But can you imagine the horror that Brad, Tim and Sharon shared when Danny appeared at the bus stop the next day and said, "What the hell are you looking at?" Obviously the plan didn't work.

We never figured out how our carefully conceived bid for freedom failed, but we never tried again. The next week, Brad and Tim's dad was transferred to Texas, and they were moving. Brad was glad. He packed his stuff the day the news came. But Tim and I were sad. I thought I would see him the Friday that they moved, but by the time

I ran home from school, he was gone—just a pile of trash sat out in front of a house without curtains, a sure sign that life had left the womb of the structure. I saw a broken brown shoestring in the trash pile. I knew it was Tim's. He broke it the day before, and his mom said that she had a new one under the bathroom sink. I picked it up, took it home, and carefully placed it in my box alongside the other mementos of my young life's passages.

We Decide to Be Atheists

The next weekend, new renters moved into Tim's and Brad's house. I saw a trailer pull up to the door and ran to see if a new friend might replace Tim. To my disappointment, it was only a girl moving in—a girl a year older than Sharon, so she was two years older than me. Her dad was a truck driver, and he had parked his truck in our alley, much to the annoyance of the other neighbors. I liked it. It was big, powerful, and smelled of diesel fuel—pungent, and if you smelled it long enough, it made you a little dizzy, kind of like bees flying around behind your eyes.

The new kid, Janie Parker, was a very confident and worldly girl. The kind that ends up committing suicide in her teens, because when you have it all figured out, there isn't much of a reason to hang around. But now she was ten, and her world knowledge was still fresh. By the time I had gotten to Janie's house, Janie had already found her way to Sharon's house. Oh well, I might as well meet her. They were on the porch. I walked up, and Sharon was warning her about Danny. She saw me, introduced me, assuring Janie that even though I was Catholic, like Danny, I was a good kid, and had tried to help them kill him. She could trust me.

I stayed and listened to Janie's stories. She had been around to places that I had heard of, but had never known anyone who had been there. She had already lived in twelve different places, and the longest that she had ever lived anywhere was two years. She had even lived in California for almost a year; she had seen palm trees and both oceans. Her mom had been married three times, and this dad was the second one she remembered. The first dad, her real dad, she had never seen. He had to go, before she was born. She liked her second dad the best and, it was a big secret, but her mom was still married to him. Her new dad and mom were just pretending to be married. They were "shacking up," as her grandma called it. Her mom said that it was common law marriage, but not to tell anyone, because if they found out, the landlord might throw them out. Janie said she didn't care if he did. She didn't like the house. It wasn't as nice as the one in South Dakota anyway.

Sharon asked her what church she went to.

"Oh, I'm an atheist," she said.

Sharon was much more informed about the different kinds of churches in town. For me there were just Lutherans, Presbyterians—that's what Stanley's dad was—and all the others.

"I don't think we have any of those in Alexandria," Sharon replied. "If Atheist is kind of like Lutheran, maybe you could come to my church."

"No, that means I don't believe in God and neither does my mom. We just believe in love."

"How can you not believe in God?" I asked.

"Well, no thinking person does," she replied. "Can God do anything?" she then asked.

"Well, sure He can."

"Does He know everything?"

"He sure does."

"If He can do everything, can He be surprised?"

"I guess so."

"If He knows everything, how can He be surprised? You can't be surprised by something you already know. That would be dumb. And if He can't be surprised, then He can't do something that even you can do. So, He can't be real. Do you think He can change the future?"

"Yes, I think so." This I was certain of, because we were constantly praying for various outcomes.

"Well, if He knows what's going to happen, then how can He change it? If He does, then He didn't know what was going to happen." Janie was firing one shot after another and my head started to spin. After a few more rounds—some concerning big rocks, and something about if everything needs to be made, who made God?—she was making a lot of sense. So Sharon and I decided to be Atheists, too.

Sharon went inside and told her mom of her new conversion. She soon reappeared with a reversal of conviction. "Mom said that the Bible says that Atheists go to hell, so I don't want to be one."

"How do you know the Bible is for real?" Janie quickly retorted.

"Well, King James said it was really true, and he was a King, so it must be. Besides that, so did Jesus." Sharon was even faster than Janie on the comebacks.

Janie wasn't sure, and it appeared that her carefully rehearsed arguments were melting away. I didn't know at the time that Catholics didn't believe in the King James Version of the Bible, but I did learn later that the Pope had also agreed with Jesus that Atheists go to hell, and that was even better than King James. So, that was the end of my brief flirtation with Atheism, but not an end to the questions that Janie had raised.

As for Janie, after this one incident, I never saw her again. Her new dad and mom got into one heck of a fight the following Saturday night, the police came, and the next day her new dad was gone. The neighbors were glad that the truck was gone, too. By Monday, the car was packed, and Janie and her mom were gone. The landlord came over and cleaned out the rest of the house. He took some stuff home and piled up the rest for the trash man. Sharon and I made reports of what the pile contained to our moms, and were given instructions as to what items we should drag home. But if anyone should ask, our moms had not told us to do it.

Sharon got the best stuff; there wasn't much boy stuff until I found a magazine just for boys. It wasn't *Boy's Life*, that one we got at the school library. It was *Playboy*. It didn't have any games in it to play, but it did have pictures of women with no clothes on. You could see their boobs and everything. I knew I should hide it and did so right away. I put it under a pile of old books that were under the steps that lead up to the kitchen of the cafe, and decided to tell only Stanley James.

Stanley, Aunt Eva, and Uncle Bill came over for Thanksgiving that year. As soon as it was safe, we headed for the stairs where my treasure was hidden. We loved looking at the pictures. We slipped into the furnace room, where the boiler that heated the café and station sat like a giant steel tank. We hid behind it, in a warm spot on an old rug that mom had washed and left in there to dry and then seemed to have forgotten. We didn't know why we liked looking at them, but we did. We heard Aunt Eva calling, so we hid the magazine again—this time under the rug—and then started talking about other things, the first thing that came to mind.

I thought I would try out Janie's argument on Stanley, and then see if he decided to be an Atheist. If he did, then I would tell him about the Bible, so that he wouldn't really go to hell. I started by asking him if God could ever be surprised.

He thought for a while and then said, "Well, I guess He could, if He wanted to be."

"Well," I replied in the same rehearsed way that Janie had, "if He knows everything, how could He be surprised?"

"Well I don't know, but sometimes I dream and I am surprised by my dreams. Sometimes it's a funny surprise, but sometimes it is a scary surprise. But I know that the dream is just in my head and that I am making it up. If I'm not making it up, who is? So, how can I be surprised by what I dream; but I am? Does that mean that I don't really exist, or that my dreams don't exist?"

"Gosh, I guess not." I didn't even have to tell him about the Bible. He had figured out something else, and I kept thinking about it and wished that Janie were still here so I could get her with that one. That would stump her.

Then he said, "Maybe that's what God is like. Maybe we are all safe in His dreams, and when He wakes up, then we will be a part of His waking thoughts too. Maybe that's what happens when we die."

Aunt Eva said, "What are you boys doing in there? Come out, it's time for dessert."

The Christmas Play

November came, and it was time for the first Christmas play at Saint Mary's. We would learn the songs in music class, but Mrs. Perkins, a volunteer with a "strong musical background," was in charge of the production. Mrs. Perkins, before she got married, worked at St. Benedict's College, and had been an assistant director on two theatrical productions. Both received good reviews in the *St. Cloud Times*, Stearns County's largest newspaper. She had also helped with last year's senior class play at Jefferson High.

The older students would be assigned the roles of Mary, Joseph, the shepherds, etc., and the younger classes would sing two songs each that accompanied the drama. On the first day of rehearsal, Mrs. Perkins began by saying how important it was that we all sing very loud. No one would hear us if we were like mice. The gymnasium was a very large room and needed a lot of sound to fill it. Then she arranged us with the tall boys in back, the better-looking students in the center, and the others on the ends. Stanley James was the tallest boy in class, so he was in the back row; I was short and placed on the end. I knew that I would not be able to sing loud; I was afraid that I would say the words wrong. I hoped that Mrs. Perkins would not notice. Mrs. Perkins had brought her friend, Mrs. Nelson, to play the piano. Once she had us all arranged, she said, "Now remember, sing out."

We started "Joy to the World." Halfway through, she stopped us and pointed to Stanley James, and said, "You, the tall boy in the back."

Yes, she had recognized Stanley James; he was singing the loudest of everyone. His voice had filled the gym. I was very proud of him and in my heart wished that I could have sung so well.

He pointed to himself and said, "Me?" visibly proud at the honor of being recognized. We had been told in music class that Mrs. Perkins might select a few children to sing some parts by themselves. That's called a solo. I knew that Stanley was being picked, and from the smile on his face, he knew it too.

"Yes, you," she said. "Just move your lips, and don't make any sounds." One of the older boys who was practicing his role as the third shepherd laughed, but when Mrs. Perkins turned to look at him, he was instantly devout. Stanley James moved his lips silently, but with a little tremble, and looked confused. He had done what was asked, why was he told now not to make a sound? Our understanding of authority was becoming increasingly consistent. The play proceeded and the right children were heard, or barely heard, which might have been the plan all along, since Mrs. Nelson's excellent piano playing pretty much covered the less-than-perfect children's voices.

After the play, flowers—six roses and babies breath—were given to Mrs. Perkins and Mrs. Nelson. They were told how very wonderful they were, and what a gift they had been to the children. Mrs. Perkins was very gracious and simply said that she wanted to do it for the students. For them, having such an opportunity would strengthen their self-esteem and self-assurance. In her own life, the theater had meant so much, and she only hoped to pass on a little of her experience. Then, she also thanked Mrs. Nelson, for not only playing the piano, but also for helping her during the many hours of sorting through all the Christmas music and helping her decide which pieces should be played. Christmas came and went. On January 3rd Alaska became a state, just two days after Fidel Castro took over Cuba. A lot of the grown-ups were surprised to learn that Cuba wasn't a colony anymore, and several discussions ensued as to whether we should permit this change to happen. As we walked to school after break, we discussed if we would have a new flag with forty-nine stars, or if they would continue to use the old ones until Hawaii joined the union in August. If they did keep the old ones, would we still have to say the pledge of allegiance to the old flag?

"That wouldn't be right," said Dave. "It's not our flag anymore."

"But new flags cost a lot of money," Stanley James said with some authority, though why he would know the cost of flags was uncertain.

Maybe the nuns could sew a new star on the old flag and then another next summer. Well, they had not done either, and we still had to say the pledge to the old 48-starred flag. The next five months rolled on, and then at last the year came to an end; it had only been a time of temporal suffering, not eternal damnation. No more Sister Mary Ann. Next year Sister Gene was teaching third grade. She was fun. Next year I would be in the room down the hall close to the playground. With Sister Gene, school would be great all the time.

Third Grade 1959-1960

i am an advocate for the segregation of the mentally retarded in high schools, for i feel that the current system of inclusion and integration does nothing but hinder everyone's education . . . mentally retarded or not. it only seems logical to have the children who are mentally retarded in another room where teachers can focus solely on the problems of the student, and to be able to educate them in the best way they see fit . . . .

DanBrownFan
Posted: 11-29-2001, 08:12 PM
The Teachers' Forum
http://www.theteacherscorner.net

The Great Divide

At the beginning of August, a letter arrived from St. Mary's. It was a newsletter concerning new developments at the school. Grades 1st and 6th were being added in the fall, but we knew that already. The 6th graders would be primarily last year's 5th graders—with the addition of two new students that had moved to Alexandria. Both the 1st grade and the 2nd grade would, however, be new kids. Also, it was determined that in order to assist children who needed extra help, a special room would be set up. In this room, there would be 3rd, 4th, 5th and 6th graders. The room would be called the Ungraded Room, as the students may or may not move from one grade to another in any given year. Students completing work in the Ungraded Room would move on to public schools when it was believed that they were capable of handling the work in 7th grade. Sister Mary Ann agreed to be the teacher of this special needs classroom, and took a six-week course at St. Benedict's College to prepare her for this challenge. The second page in the letter contained the names of the students who would be in the Ungraded Room. Yes, I was there, and so was

Stanley James, along with 16 other students selected for this special room. When we heard that we would again have Sister Mary Ann, our hearts plummeted. I felt like the child found in a burlap bag with rocks. She was dropped from the bridge into the deepest waters of Lake Osakis early in the summer. It was a horrific crime, but at that moment I wished in my soul that I had been that child.

Also in the special 3rd Grade was Dave, whose father ran the dairy. His mother was very fat, and was often laughed at behind her back by the other women. Sometimes even the nuns expressed disbelief at her size.

Joining us in the third grade was George Ann Tailor. George Ann always had the corners of her collar or the end of her dress ties in her mouth, twisting them and talking nervously—often to herself—in words that were not comprehensible. No, actually she was not talking to herself. It sounded more like she was talking to some thing—or some being—that no one could imagine. If you asked her who she was talking to, she would gaze at you for a moment like she didn't understand why you had asked such an obvious question. Then she would begin talking all the same. She was able to read, and filled out the worksheets and tests perfectly, and as neat as a monk. Then she would push the papers on the floor and continue to make sounds. During music class in the second grade, Sister Gene tried to talk with her; sometimes she held George Ann on her lap and sang to her, but George Ann would just suck her thumb and hide her head like a puppy. All the nuns knew that this approach had not worked. It only encouraged this baby behavior. Sister Mary Ann was more resourceful in dealing with this silly immaturity.

Jimmy was also in our class. Jimmy was the whitest boy I had ever seen up to that time. Two years later, a family with two albino children joined the church. They were whiter—but for now, Jimmy was the winner. His skin was white, and his hair was light blond—the color and texture of corn silk just when it sprouts from the top of the cob, before it turns green and then yellows into dark brown. His eyes, unlike the albino children, were a pale blue, almost washed away—the way old blue jeans look after too many washings in hot water. His body, too, looked like it had become limp and softened from an equal number of cycles in the machine. He was thin, but not the thinness of children who don't have enough to eat. Their thinness was different; their thinness defined the shape of a child's frame and long muscles. Jimmy's thinness was more like an under-stuffed doll, a very white Raggedy Andy doll, with arms and legs that appeared to be unable to stand. He had no muscles, and his bones seemed to be made of a soft cartilage. He was not feminine in any way. There was not enough of him to be feminine; there was none of the energy or giggling excitement of girls. No, just the kind of desperation that kittens have when their mother is killed and they begin to starve.

He didn't seem to notice himself. He was always lost in some dream world—a world that was despised by Sister Mary Ann. To her, a daydreaming child was the equivalent of an adult alcoholic, and probably would become one. Daydreaming was a practice that caused work not to be done, and whose course could not be controlled. It was a weakness that was pervasive in the Ungraded Room and from which we were unrelentingly jarred. But for us it was a private escape that we all used to slip away for seconds, minutes or hours into worlds where there was no school, where all the girls were naked, where magical things happened, and where we were the heroes. In our daydreams, we were the smart kids that rode white horses to triumphant rescues. Our dream worlds were our real worlds. As I dreamt, I wondered if the other children were in the same world or a different world. Surprisingly, we never discussed our daydreams. Whether privacy or shame kept us from talking about them, we never did.

Jimmy's mother was a strong woman; she walked almost like a man, and spoke looking down—not with any shame, but with downward glances. Sister Mary Ann devotedly gave her detailed reports on Jimmy. She seemed to be the only mother that Sister Mary Ann enjoyed talking with. They seemed to whisper for a long time as equals or as co-believers in the same world view, one that the earth's other inhabitants were unable to grasp. I even saw them laugh on a few occasions. Not a hearty laugh like the boys made when someone farted; but a smug, upper class laugh—the way an amateur actress playing a French woman laughed. They always smiled when they parted.

Jimmy's father was also thin, but not in the same way. He was one of those men whose head appeared too large for his body, and could well have been the model for the first bobble-head doll. Yet, he was a very refined, handsome man. He smiled a lot, and spoke very quietly, more quietly than his wife. They operated the local gift store. The store sold Hallmark cards and small knick-knacks. They were expensive for Alexandria. Getting something from the Langley's Gift Shop was like a New Yorker getting something from Tiffany's. Because they sold such expensive things, we all thought that he was very rich, so we found it hard to understand why he was in the Ungraded Room with the rest of us.

Jimmy's visits to our other world, the world of unspoken dreams, were too frequent and he traveled far too deeply into the unknowable fathoms. I watched him with his head down on his desk or cocked to one side, and some times he would jerk and move parts of his body much like a dog does when he is asleep, with small erratic motions. Yet Jimmy's eyes were wide open, staring into space. Even when they moved, he was not aware of the room, or us, or even his own being. Then, instantly, he would come back. Some days he would pop in and out four or five times in ten minutes, even during a class. One time when he was called on to read out loud, he stood, and then after every three or four words he slipped into a daydream, moving his jaw and twitching his eye. Sister Mary Ann had to shake him awake. She knew they had a television, and suspected that was the problem, but his mom insisted that he was limited to only thirty minutes each night.

In the Special 4th grade was Melinda Wilson, the girl who had a scarred hand with small nubs for fingers. People said that she was born with a webbed hand, and that the doctors cut her fingers apart. The arm that supported the hand was small, and hung casually at her side. Her head always seemed tilted to that side as she walked, sat, or stared into the sky.

Dale was fat. His fatness made him seem mean, and a lot dumber than he was. His soul was hard—not brittle with softness inside like a shell of a turtle, but hard like a very firm mattress. He was in our 4th grade. When the kids made fun of him, he tried to smash them against the brick wall of the school. Sometimes he waited for days; then when he saw them he would maneuver them into the corner, and keep ramming his fat body into them. The look on his face never gave us a clue to his feelings. He looked the same when he was being teased, beaten, or pounding some asshole kid. He always looked the same.

The other student was Robert Circle, and he was really cool. He had lived in the Twin Cities, in an apartment, and knew all the cool words. He thought we were all real square, but he was always willing to mentor us in Coolville and beatnik stuff. He only had a mom. His dad was real cool, but he didn't live with them anymore. He went to New York, to do poetry and explore life. His mom came home to live with her parents and worked at the Woolworth Store.

The 6th graders were all boys, and they hardly spoke to us. They had their own club. Then there was Jeff, Timmy, Billy and all the rest—all with their defects and strange behavior. It was as if all the children that would not fit perfectly between the pages of a beautiful book had been swept up and neatly deposited in the room at the top of the rear stairs, now known as the Ungraded Room.

First Day in the Ungraded Room

This year did not start with a "fun" lesson. Those were for little kids. We needed to get right to work. We had a lot to cover, and if you fell behind there would be a gaping hole in your education for the rest of your life. This worried me. I knew that some day, perhaps if I ran for President, a reporter would ask, "What is the capital of Vermont?" and I wouldn't know. I would have to say, "Sir, I wasn't paying attention that day," or lie and say, "Oh, I was absent that day, and yes, it was an excused absence, so it's all right that I don't know." But what if they checked and found out that I wasn't absent, that I was there, sitting in the second row and not paying attention. The next day it would be smeared all over the newspaper: "Presidential Candidate Lies. He was there the day they covered the capital of Vermont, but he failed to pay attention." Of course, as a third grader I was very naive, and didn't realize that it is the nature of politicians to lie and that a bigger headline would be: "Unfit for the Presidency—Candidate Caught Telling the Truth."

Beginning the first day, and each day thereafter, we were assigned three worksheets to complete. We loved these sheets—with their scent of light blue mimeographed printing fluid. We held the pages close to our noses and deeply breathed in the clean pleasing smell. It made our minds spin a little, like a child-dose of crack, letting our souls waft off for a moment. I think that Sister Mary Ann was pleased at how eagerly we welcomed our homework.

But soon for the slower kids and me, it was like when adults received bills that can't be paid. If we failed to complete the work, then the page number was recorded in a small book. The book was about two inches wide and six inches long. Sister Mary Ann made it from scrap paper, and punched holes in the top into which she fastened two silver rings. Each page had the date, and then the names of students who had not completed their assignments. Whenever we were not in a required class, the oldest paper due was taped to the wall, and we stood in front of it throughout the day until it was completed. We could not ask for help until it was done, and done correctly. We could not make mistakes; we were not permitted the forgiveness of an eraser. This was truly the rule of the God of the Old Testament. No forgiveness, no assistance, and a certainty that the commandment could not be obeyed. We were trapped in a cosmos that demanded infallibility and action. By not acting, by simply standing in front of that sheet hour after hour, we committed no error. By acting, by placing a mark into one of the boxes, there was a certainty that at some point we would fail, and then the wrath of God—in the person of Sister Mary Ann—would powerfully descend upon us.

At first, we only stood there during regular class time, but soon there was no recess for those who could not complete their work. Then there was no going to Sister Gene's for music, no art, no science, only standing with the page taped to the wall until it was done. It was like being locked out of paradise, locked out of all the events that made life bearable. But the expulsion did not happen quickly like Adam and Eve's expulsion from their garden. Each new denial was planned and savored. Like a cat playing with a wounded mouse, or Danny drowning a bird. Each new deprivation was skillfully chosen for the precise moment, so as not to extinguish all of a boy's hope too soon.

The first time we were not allowed to go to Sister Gene's for music, I was standing at the wall, stealing peeks at the clock all morning. The pain in my knees was agonizing, so I was shifting from one foot to the other, looking down with my head, but then twisting my eye up to catch the corner of the clock in my sight. Clock-watching was forbidden, and if we were caught staring at the clock, we would be placed directly under the clock at one-and-a-half arm's length, and then pushed forward until our fingers touched the wall. In this position, we were told to stare up at the clock. If we wanted to watch the clock, we could watch it all morning. The pain that developed in our fingers, arms, and necks was excruciating. We fought tears—another sin—and breathed slowly, feeling each breath, trying to push the pain out each time we breathed out. We then were asked repeatedly, "Are you enjoying watching the clock?"

To which we would answer, "No Sister, watching the clock is a waste of time."

"Then why do you do it?"

"Because, I'm lazy." We tried each time to be very sincere in our reply, because we were never sure what the criterion was that would gain our release.

Sister Mary Ann did not see me sneaking peeks at the clock, and at last, the last tick came. I turned around and started to get in line when she said, so very calmly and inquisitively, "Where do you think you're going?"

"To Sister Gene's room for music," I replied.

"Where?"

Quickly rethinking my phrasing for fear that I might not have formed a complete sentence, or might have addressed Sister Mary Ann incorrectly or with the wrong inflection, I stood straight up, hands at my side, and said, "Sister Mary Ann, I am going to Sister Gene's room for music class."

"There is no music for boys who don't do their homework. Anyone with work to do will be staying here."

Stanley said, in an eight-year-old voice that demanded justice, and without even raising his hand, "That's not fair, Sister." The last word sounded of desperate disappointment.

The reply was not long in coming. Her hand reached out and securely grabbed his hair, hair that was as thick as the fleece of the 4-H sheep at the county fair, and rammed his head into the side of the desk on the right side of the row, and then into the edge of the desk on the left. The desks took flight, hitting Melinda. She screamed, but caught herself mid-sound, so as not to exacerbate the incident, and quickly said without raising her hand, "I'm all right. I'm all right. Really I am."

But it was too late.

"Look, you almost hurt Melinda. See what you did?" Then, without letting go of his head, she dragged him over to a desk and pushed him down, placed a dictionary in front of him, and said, "Now you have work to do, too. Copy all the 'S' words."

Who's on First

In the 1950's, come October, the most important topic on the minds of eight-year-old boys was who would win the World Series of baseball. Even though none of us had ever seen a major league game, we, too, were in the thick of it. Douglas said, hands down, the White Sox had it. But Bill said he thought it would be the Dodgers. His cousin lived in Los Angeles and sent him a postcard with the whole team on it.

Then I added, "I . . . I . . . think the White Sox, they're the best."

"What would you know about it?" Joey Turner, a kid from the real third grade, said in a condescending voice, deflating our excitement. Joey's father was an attorney in town. He was kind of big, just like his dad. Not fat like Dale, just a little big, like the men down at the VFW. His mom always wore a mink coat. She either had two of them and a mink stole, or she had a long one that the bottom zipped off, providing her with both a jacket and a stole. The women often talked about this possibility; but oddly, no one appeared interested in simply asking her. I couldn't understand why they were so reluctant to find out the answer to a question that so enthralled them. In any event, Joey's mom always had every hair in place, as did he. He always wore the perfect blue or white shirt and black or blue pants. One of his shirts had his initials embroidered on the pocket in the same color as his shirt. He said it was chic, and then informed us that chic meant real cool. "Real cool."

"I . . . I . . . know a lot," I said in reply to his inquiry as to what I knew.

"Crap, you don't know anything, you're a retard."

"Wh . . . Wha . . . . What's a retard?" I asked, having never heard the word; but from the sound of it, it didn't seem chic.

"You're in the dumb, dumb, retard room. You're all retards there."

The sound hit me like walking into a glass wall. I knew that there was something that grouped us, something transparent, a common denominator; but I didn't know what, or that it had a name. Now hearing it, it not only rang true, but it defined us. I knew instantly that it would be what defined me for the rest of my life. It was as if a coat, larger than the one Joey's mom wore, but made of rock, had been wrapped sufficiently tightly around me to both paralyze and hurt me. I couldn't talk, I tried to say something, but not even the stutter came out. I looked around. Robert already knew we were retards. Stanley James knew it, too. Some of the other kids were off playing, or were so unaware of language that the six letters had no effect.

Stanley James didn't hesitate. "Do you know what retards do?" he asked Joey.

"You retards dribble on yourselves and eat snot," Joey replied.

Well, that was true, some of the kids in the Ungraded Room did generally have saliva dripping from the corners of their mouths. And Jeff, George Ann, and Timmy all liked to eat snot, mostly their own.

But Stanley James said, "When we're not eating snot, do you know what we do?"

"No, what do retards do?"

"We rip the heads off dickheads, Dickhead."

Stanley began to step forward, but Joey's friends grabbed his arms. Some others grabbed the arms of Robert, the only other boy in the Ungraded Room with the manhood to fight. With Stanley and Robert's arms locked by two boys each, firmly behind them, Joey began hitting Stanley in the guts. Joey pounded like he was hitting the punching bag that his dad bought him and hung in his garage, his garage on the nice street with a tree name.

I had seen him the summer before when I walked by on my way to Stanley James's place. The garage door was open and he was out there by himself, talking to himself and just hitting the red bag, over and over. I just watched, and then he saw me and asked, "What the hell are you looking at?" I ran away, but now I couldn't run, and I couldn't speak. I just stood there. Robert tried to break away; he would have fought, he would have hit them, and his mom would have been called, but he didn't care. I guess that's what being brave is—not caring what the consequences are.

They didn't even bother holding me. I was too weak of soul to fight, too afraid that my mom would be called, too terrified of what Sister Mary Ann would do to me. We never for a moment thought that Joey and his friend would get in trouble for hitting Stanley James, or any of the rest of us. No, that wouldn't happen—couldn't happen; the kids in the regular class were like, well, like grown ups with rights. We were, well, I guess we were retards. I was a retarded coward who stuttered; and now at least I knew who I was.

The rest of the year was lost in day dreams until that May, May 5th to be exact when we heard that the Russians were claiming that they had on May 1 shot down a U-2 spy plane. Our government said it wasn't true, so of course it wasn't. "Just a bunch of damn communists making stuff up." the men said. Monsignor Ward said that even though it wasn't true, we should remember the pilot in our prayers because it must be a really bad time for him. Two days later the CIA pilot, Francis Gary was paraded before the cameras. The Paris Summit which we had once hoped would end the cold war collapsed when Khrushchev walked out and threatening retaliation against our U-2 bases. The grown-ups thought we would soon be at war. No one questioned our president's repeated lies, everyone knew it was all right to lie to the communists, and that they were just wrong, to have shot down our spy plane over their county. But for us, summer was just around the corner, so everything was going to be all right.

A Priest for all Tourists

The beginning of summer brought the tourists to Alexandria—the crowds of farmers from Iowa and factory workers from Minneapolis who stayed at the many resorts that "weren't modern." That meant they didn't have indoor bathrooms, but they were on the lake, and came equipped with a fishing boat tied to a dock. For an additional 50 cents a day an outboard motor could be included. These were on lakes like Lakota, Mary, Louise and nearly a hundred others that the glaciers from the last Ice Age left.

The wealthy summer people came from Chicago and the Twin Cities' suburbs. They came to large summer homes on the large deep lakes—like Carlos, Le Homme Dieu, and Darling—or stayed at the Darling Dude Ranch or Blake's By The Lakes with their own golf courses and gates that prevented those not similarly blessed from entering the grounds.

But at the Catholic Church, rich and poor flocked in every Sunday morning. More Masses were added. The fishermen came to the 6:00 am service to get it out of the way; the late partiers came at 11:30; and between these there was a Mass every half-hour. One was ending as the next was beginning, just like the movies of those days.

People came as late as they could and still fulfill their obligations (which was just before the offertory) and left as soon as they could (right after communion started); but come they did. It was a mortal sin to miss Mass. Every spring parishes across the country preached, "Vacation is no excuse, and with the number of fatal car crashes that the newspapers report daily, you had better be prepared."

Fortunately, the arrival of the tourists in Alexandria coincided nicely with the arrival of a crop of newly ordained priests from St. John's Seminary just 50 miles down the road near St. Cloud. Generally, there was a nice overlap between the arrival of the new priests and the departure of the priests from two years ago, who would be assigned to their own smaller parishes in the fall. The smaller parishes were located in small farming communities where church activities tended to be minimal during the summer, but began to heat up in the fall with catechism classes and preparation for Christmas.

This year's new priest was Father Reed. He was unusual in appearance for Minnesota. He had black hair and black eyes. Only two other men in the parish had these features, and all three were important men in the lives of the parish boys. There was Mr. Pearson, who helped out at St. Mary's School with playground duty and hung around after school to watch the playground. He was Susan's dad, and we all thought he was cool at times and harsh at other times. His hair had the slightest touches of gray, just beginning to speckle in among the deep black color. Then there was Officer Beecher. He was the young police officer that started with the force in Alexandria a year earlier. He was not tall like Father Reed or Mr. Pearson, and he was slightly shorter than the average guy in church, but not by much. He was very good looking, like a model that might be photographed for suits in the J. C. Penney's catalog, and like a lot of shorter men he had developed his muscles so that he had a masculine appearance and looked taller than he was. His hair was curly and cut short and his skin was always tan—not the dark red tan of a farmer or the deep brown tan of the rich teenage boys that came to the lakes in the summer and laid on their docks in the afternoons—his tan was the golden bronze tan of the leading men in summer movies.

As for Father Reed, he was the antithesis of tan. He was white. His black hair and beard stubble made his skin look even whiter; the contrast between the parts of his face where his black beard would grow, and where it didn't grow, was extreme. The bottom of his face always looked like other men's faces after two or three days of vacation without shaving; but if you looked closer, you knew that he had just finished shaving. To try to minimize the difference, he would shave twice a day, once in the morning, and then again at 4:30 if there were any services or events that night. He was tall and had a body like a basketball player, but lacked the grace and confidence of one. He was shy, but the ladies all thought that he was very handsome, and they would have drooled when they saw him if it were not a sin. He must have sensed this sexual tension because while he tried to be very calm and speak with a very priestly voice, the whiteness of his skin could not hide his blush.

Unlike Monsignor Ward, who typically wore black pants, a simple black shirt with a white collar, and a small triangle of papal burgundy for his priestly uniform, Father Reed preferred to wear more formal priestly attire—a long black cassock with small buttons all up the front terminating at the top in a white collar, tied at the waist with a wide sash with fringe at the bottom. While this attire should have been less revealing, the tailored shoulders and uniform-like cut clearly showed that Father Reed lacked the flab of many of the previous priests that had served at St. Mary's.

He was different from Monsignor Ward in a lot of other ways. Both men came from Stearns County, where most of the priests that served our parish came from. Monsignor Ward, it was said, came from one of the old wealthy families there. His grandfather owned one of the granite quarries near Cold Springs, and had supplied the granite for the St. Cloud penitentiary. It was the third longest wall in the world—only surpassed by the Great Wall of China and Hadrian's Wall in England. It was 20 feet high and so thick that two guards could easily pass as they walked on top of it, and it was solid granite. The wall was built to last for a thousand years, and the financial foundation that it provided for the politically connected Ward family would also last as long. Monsignor—whose real name was Isidor, though we weren't supposed to know that—was the Ward family's oldest son. When he decided to enter the priesthood, his father was relieved that he had produced a spare son, named Thomas, to take over the family business. His dad figured that he now had bases covered, heaven and earth. And though he would have preferred that the first son take over the business and the second become the priest, he understood that God, too, wanted the best, and was content with God's choice.

The family, however, always insured that Monsignor Ward was comfortable, got the assignment that he wanted, and was promoted in the church. As for Monsignor, while he didn't depend on such things, he never refused them. He took particular delight in one fringe benefit of being from a family with means. Each fall, the Sunday after the new cars came out, his brother arrived after the 11:30 Mass with a new, top-of-the-line Cadillac for him. Monsignor always acted surprised and just stood there looking pleased. His hands were clasped together in a comfortable gesture in front of him, and he would ask if it was really for him. He walked all around the car examining it, but never touching it, just keeping his hands together and beaming the biggest smile of the year. Some of the men, men who themselves might be considering such a purchase, also gathered, looking at the new style—which in those days changed considerably every year. His brother opened the door and sitting on the seat would be the biggest bottle of Chivas Regal Scotch available in this county. No one in Alexandria knew what Chivas Regal Scotch was—it was not available in the local municipal liquor store—but they knew it must be very expensive. Monsignor's brother would stay until after dinner, then he would drive Monsignor's old car, a one-year-old Cadillac, back to St. Cloud. It was said that Monsignor didn't actually own the cars—his brother kept them in his name, and paid the insurance on them, and so forth. The parish liked the arrangement because it meant that they only had to maintain one car—an old Chevy station wagon that would be assigned to Father Reed.

Coming from such a family, Monsignor had the ease that comes from the assurance of success. He was always well-liked, had done well in school, and felt relaxed being with other men of management. When the bishop came for his two visits each year, the men would go golfing and dress—not in priestly attire—but in casual golf clothing. As they drove through this tourist community, they didn't look much different from the men who ran Champion Gas or Kellogg's. Even as a boy I envied that ease; it was so different from other men who were in a desperate contest for means, status, or the pettiest of powers.

Stanley James, Dave, and I lay on the cool grass in late August after a blistering day of 101-degree heat without air-conditioning. "Did you hear about that Olympics over in Rome?" Stanley asked, and then continued before I responded. "People from all over the world, even commies, are going there to play games," he told us, as if it was the latest news.

"Yeah, I heard."

I knew all about it. It had been happening forever—not always in Rome, but somewhere, every four years. They had people from Africa and those other funny countries, but they didn't play baseball or other American games. They just ran, jumped, and stuff. I guess it would be too hard to tell them all the rules in those foreign languages. Running was all right.

"Stanley, if you were in Rome, you would beat them all," I said. Stanley James was the fastest boy in Alexandria, or even in Minnesota, or in the whole world. He could run like it was no one's business.

"Maybe I will go one day. Maybe in 1968, when I'm all grown up, I will go. And if I do win, I'll sell the medal, I hear that the medal is pure gold. Then with the money, we will buy a car, and we'll all drive to Texas and become cowboys."

"We can't drive," I said.

"In 1968 we will, we will be able to do whatever we want." Stanley assured us.

Fourth Grade 1960-61

"The world is very different now. For man holds in his mortal hands the power to abolish all forms of human poverty and all forms of human life. And yet the same revolutionary beliefs for which our forebears fought are still at issue around the globe—the belief that the rights of man come not from the generosity of the state, but from the hand of God."

John F. Kennedy
Inaugural Address
Friday, January 20, 1961

The World is Starting to Turn Upside Down

Teenagers were doing Chubby Checker's Twist; of course, we snickered at them. We said it was silly, but sometimes, when no one was looking, we did it, too. Then we laughed and pushed each other over. We couldn't imagine doing it in front of a girl.

This year we made the usual commitment to try harder, to not get our names in "the book," and to have art, music, and gym—or so were the plans. We were still in the retard room; and yes, Sister Mary Ann would still be our teacher.

Talk of a Catholic running for President was on the radio and all over town. He was a Democrat, but still everyone thought at first that Nixon, the current Vice President, would be the next President. Eisenhower was OK, and Nixon would know how to deal with those Russians. But I think all the nuns wanted Kennedy to win. They didn't say anything; however, we took home a lot of papers about what an important duty voting was—and we never did that before. After the TV debates, everyone was fired up. They thought we had a winner.

The school news that parents and kids were talking about was that the school would begin a program of volunteer tutors for students with reading and other difficulties. They would work mostly with students who had the potential and the willingness to achieve, but who just needed a little extra help. This was touted as a very innovative concept at the time. Eight volunteers had been trained. Two would be assigned to each of the 4th through 6th grade rooms, and the retard room would get two of its own. One of ours was Mrs. Beasley. Mrs. Beasley was a certified teacher with a college degree. Two of the sisters, Sister Rose and Sister Vincent, also had college degrees. The others had completed two-year teaching programs. Mrs. Beasley loved teaching, but of course had to stop when she married and started a family. Her son was at St. Mary's in the regular 4th grade. She started the program and trained the other teachers. Because she was not being paid, the other wives did not frown upon her teaching activities. It wasn't as if she was a working wife or something like that. The other volunteers in the program weren't really teachers, just six other moms and Officer Beecher.

Everyone thought it was great to have a man volunteer, especially since Monsignor Ward and the nuns all knew that some of the boys did not have a good male role model at home. Oh, all of the dads were in the home, except Robert's and Billy's, but some did not attend church regularly, some drank, some were known to eye women in an inappropriate manner, and most were distant from their boys. Most, if not all, did not meet the expectations that Catholic men should aspire to. Having Officer Beecher there would be great.

Billy's dad died in the Korean War; he really hoped to have Officer Beecher, and immediately said he couldn't read a word, which was a lie. He could read really good. Robert always told us he didn't need a dad. But the look of blank distance on his face after hearing about Officer Beecher betrayed him. Even a boy of nine could see his plight. More than anything, he secretly ached for a dad, but only his real dad. His loyalty to his dad obligated him to hate any man who might be more caring, more dutiful. In order for his dad to be the best dad—and the best dad is what every boy wants—all other men must be reduced to a level beneath his own.

The problem of where to find space for the new program was overcome by clearing out a small storage room under the south stairway. Another space was located in a small office that was part of a locker room. Although the school was built as an elementary school, there was a locker/shower room downstairs. It was designed with two doors—one door led directly into the downstairs boy's bathroom and the other opened into the gymnasium. A small combination office/storage room was included in the design so that the men of the parish could use the facility for church league basketball. Even though the office was intended for use by a volunteer coach, it had become a storage room for junk that should have gone directly into the trash. The acoustics in both of these spaces were far less than desirable for teaching, but since each tutor would only be working with one child at a time, everyone agreed that they would be fine locations for starters.

Altar Cloths Burned

On the third day of school, the kids waiting at the front door were talking in whispers when we walked up.

"Did you hear what happened?" Clare whispered in the loudest, most excited tone possible while still being a whisper.

"No," replied Stanley James, also whispering but not knowing why.

"Someone tried to burn the church down. The altar cloths were lit on fire, but the fire stopped when it reached the corners, it couldn't get to the flat part," Clare explained, sounding almost like a news reporter.

"Do they know who?" asked Stanley.

"No, but we think it must be the Protestant boys, the boys who call us 'Cat-Lickers,'" Doug proclaimed.

"Or my dad said it could even be grown up men. They burn nigger churches in the South, and maybe they want to burn ours, too. The Protestants are always planning to kill us, you know," Joey pronounced with absolute certainty.

"That's not true," Stanley James said in a tone nearly on the edge of anger, but calculated not to be inflammatory. "My dad is a Protestant, and he ain't planning to kill anyone."

"Maybe it was your dad, maybe you told him how to do it," Robert said, joining the growing consensus.

"I didn't! You're lying!" Stanley James's body was now tightening. His feet were automatically moving into position for a fight—his left foot pointing directly at Robert, and his right foot perpendicularly placed about two feet back. This is the posture boys take when fighting. The position prevents them from falling down backwards as they attempt to dodge a blow, and if the blow makes contact, it permits them to spring back with their compressed hands becoming deadly artillery.

"Why are you getting so mad then?" Robert sensed the danger, and knew instinctively that while Stanley was slightly smaller than he was, his anger was greater and would give him the advantage. Robert wanted to avoid the conflict; they both did. Like the poles of a magnet, the boys were either pulling tightly together or being dangerously repelled.

"I'm not," Stanley replied, but his stance did not change.

"Are, too," came the near automatic retort from Robert.

Then Dale, the fat kid, delivered the first push to Stanley from behind. Stanley—not expecting such a move—fell forward into Robert.

"What the hell are you doing?" Robert said to Dale as he forcefully pushed Stanley to the side. "I can fight my own battles. I don't need help from you or anyone—no one—do you hear?" Now his voice was louder, shaking, wanting to cry, but already trained not to reach that breaking point.

Just then, Mr. Pearson walked over. "Boys, what is going on?"

"We think that Stanley's dad lit the church on fire," Doug announced, like a boy who had just solved a mystery.

"Why do you think that?" Mr. Pearson spoke in a composed voice that had just the slightest nuance of disguised skepticism in it.

Joey, who made the original accusation, explained, "He's a Protestant, ain't he? And not even like a Lutheran—he is a real bad one, the kind that gets divorced."

Why a fire in the church and the practice of divorce should have any connection can only be known in the immature minds of boys and men of learning.

"That's why you think he did it?" Mr. Pearson asked, now looking a little like Fred MacMurray, with one eyebrow raised.

"Yeah, and Stanley could have told him how to do it, too," Joey continued.

Mr. Pearson got a very serious look on his face, the kind of look men got when talking to us about communism or the Committee on Un-American Activities and stuff like that. Then he said very sternly, "What you boys are doing is very dangerous. You are making up rumors. If you spread those rumors, people might believe them, and very bad things could happen. You have no proof that Mr. James did anything. It has happened that boys or girls have thought something is true just because they think so, things that later turned out not to be true. But do you know what happened before they found out it was just a rumor?"

"No," Joey replied for all of us, in a single word. With Mr. Pearson, we didn't have to reply in complete sentences.

"Before anyone found out, people were killed because of it. So, saying something that you haven't proven is very wrong. Don't say it again," he concluded.

"You . . . you . . . you mean it's a sin?" I asked, overcoming my stutter for this important concern. The always-present concern at Catholic schools is the anxiety over the state of everyone's soul.

"I think so," he replied.

"We never learned about that one, I'm going to ask Father Reed," said Robert.

I was going to ask if it was a mortal sin or just a venial one, but thought I had better not. If it were only a venial sin, Dale and Robert would be sure to continue to say it. I hoped that they considered it a mortal sin.

"You do that, but in the meantime, stop spreading gossip," Mr. Pearson concluded and walked away.

Joey then said sneeringly to Robert, "You better confess what you did."

"You said it too," Robert replied.

"Did not!"

And the endless arguments of boys continued.

The next day, the hot summer came to an end. Cool fall breezes replaced the stagnant air. Then it turned harshly cold. The Olympics in Rome that were a constant background story all summer came to an end on September 11th. We had heard all about Americans, Africans running without shoes, Italians who set records, and wrestling in the Basilica Maxentius. We couldn't imagine wrestling in a Basilica and not getting into trouble. Even slugging someone in a parish church was a mortal sin. Yet the Pope let them wrestle in the Basilica? Rome had to be a lot more fun than Alexandria. By their end, we knew all about the Games, and we were racing, jumping, and horsing around more than normal   each believing that one day we, too, would be a winner and carry home the gold.

Clyde Henry

Learning about Pagans

World history was my favorite subject that year. We learned about strange and exotic worlds of the past, from Egypt to England, all in a continuous parade of progress—progress that culminated in the America of our time, where we no longer lived in ignorance like those people of the past. But not everyone was as lucky as we were, at least not yet. We learned about places that were still backwards and primitive, where people even today practiced paganism. Where they made wooden images and then dressed them, prayed to them, chanted to them, and gave them food. How stupid these pagans were, we thought. How could they believe that some statue they made could have any power, or be alive, or enjoy the food they brought? Sister Mary Ann explained to us that while even simple reason would show people how silly such beliefs are, it was Satan working in these cultures that persuaded them to believe in the power of these idols. We must pray every day to Mother Mary and to the patron saint of missionaries, Therese of Lisieux—known as The Little Flower of Jesus—to help them. She then took out a holy card with Saint Therese's picture on it, and pinned it to the bulletin board surrounded by a ring of gold foil stars that she had pasted on a blue background. Next to it, she placed a picture of Our Lady of Guadalupe. Our Lady of Guadalupe is really Mary—the Mexican Mary, not the American one. She used Our Lady of Guadalupe because Mexico was a foreign country where they talked different. Robert asked if there were pagans there, and Sister Mary Ann said, not exactly. Although they were Catholics, they were not very educated. So, we needed to send missionaries there, too, to teach them English. That way they could learn if they were following all of the teachings of the Church correctly.

These two saints, Therese of Lisieux and Our Lady of Guadalupe, were going to be our two special saints this year, to help us understand the need for missionaries to lead natives from their misunderstanding to the right ways. Under each image, Sister put a small paper plate. For every Rosary that we recited to one of them, we would be permitted to place a silver foil star on the plate as an offering.

"If we give each of the saints a full plate by the end of the year, just think how hard they will work to help our missionaries in the field. Because for saints, our prayers are like food, and we must make an offering everyday so that people around the world will stop making sacrifices to all those pagan gods."

Stanley James raised his hand.

"Yes," Sister Mary Ann said, giving him permission to speak.

"I think you are wrong. How can Therese of Lisieux be the patron saint of missionaries, when Monsignor Ward told us that Francis Xavier is? He is a Monsignor, so he should know." Stanley James was pulling rank. He knew that a monsignor trumps a priest, and a priest trumps a nun any day. How would she get out of this one?

"They both are. Either can be prayed to for missionary help." Obviously, Stanley had not studied his history of the saints thoroughly. She then continued, "You shall never again question me that way. Stanley, you will write one hundred times, before you again sit in your chair, 'Saint Therese of Lisieux, also known as Therese of the Child Jesus, The Little Flower, and The Little Flower of Jesus, who was canonized on May 17, 1925, by Pope Pius XI, is the patron saint of missionaries, African missions, air crews, aircraft pilots, Australia, aviators, Belgian Air Force, bodily ills, the diocese of Cheyenne, Wyoming, diocese of Fairbanks, Alaska, diocese of Fresno, California, diocese of Juneau, Alaska, diocese of Pueblo, Colorado, florists, flower growers, foreign missions, France, illness, loss of parents, parish missions, restoration of religious freedom in Russia, Russia, Spanish Air force and tuberculosis.' And if you ever again address me as you did, you will do the same for Saint Francis Xavier and ten other saints. Is that understood?"

"Yes, Sister Mary Ann," Stanley James said in a respectful voice.

But there was something—something not detectable from his voice but perhaps radiating from his soul—that said he would not accept her authority, that he would not yield. She knew she could conquer his body and demand physical obedience, but his spirit remained strong. She feared his spirit, the spirit of a boy, because she could not stop the questions. Questions that she knew would keep bubbling up from his soul's inquisitive depths. Questions that would one day defeat her. One day he would question everything, even the God whose rules she lived by, and he would try, no, maybe even succeed. Succeed at what?

As this vision turned her stomach, it was mixed with another indefinable emotion, a strange attraction to him that repulsed her and excited her at the same time. Her face dissolved into a face of loathing, loathing for his power and loathing for her attraction to his strength. He said nothing more. He only stood there trying to remember what she had told him to write, wondering if he should reach into his desk for paper, or if he would be allowed to hold a book under his paper while he wrote.

Her body moved suddenly, as if he had somehow insulted her. She grabbed him by his right ear and twisted it while his head tilted to that same side in an attempt to avoid the pain. She dragged him behind her gray Steelcase desk and in a motion that was part pull, part throw, and part directional gesture, she placed him in the kneehole of the unit.

"Stay out of my sight. You boys make me sick."

It was a familiar place—the hole, as we called it—for many of the boys in the Ungraded Room. For some reason, one of us found ourselves in the kneehole for part of every month. Once one of us ended up there, it became the punishment of choice for several days. Then, like the clearing of the skies after a round of rainstorms, her attraction for the "boy-in-the-hole" punishment ceased, and the room returned to a level of terror that was only grueling, but not irrational. Stanley knew what was coming next. In about ten minutes, Sister Mary Ann had another expression on her face—an expression that was mostly blank, except the outside corners of her eyes would tighten. They pulled her eyelids until they began to close just a tiny bit. Then she sat in her coastered chair, grabbed onto the edge of the desk with both hands, and forcibly rolled her chair and herself into the kneehole of the desk, smashing the occupant against the sheet metal that covered the front. Slowly at first; then, as if the first sound signaled the charge, the pace got harder and faster. She smiled in a near laugh and looked at the class, who were expected to mimic her sneer, but not to laugh very loud. Most of the girls responded at once. But some of the boys who had been in the hole had a harder time pasting the proper expression on their faces. Most, in the end, however, managed a brief bow to her wishes with a forced grin. That is, all but Stanley James, who just stared with his frown.

We Celebrate Our Lady of the Holy Rosary

The school was built so that when one entered the building, the lower classrooms were down a half level. These rooms were set into the ground about three and a half feet. Their windows provided a view of the grass in warm months, and were partly covered with snow in the winter. There were two staircases that connected the floors, one at each end of the central hall. The south stairs were the main stairs. These double stairs had a large entry foyer with a ceiling that rose the full height of the entry to the top of the second floor. There a statue of the Blessed Virgin looked down on the children entering the school. The main restrooms were located at the top of these stairs, with a smaller set located on the lower level directly below.

The second stairs was located on the north end of the building. The Ungraded Room, our room, was the first door to the right at the top of these stairs. When we looked out our window, we could see the parsonage across the street and a little to the north, just across the street from the church. That was the house where the priests lived. The parsonage was originally built as a house for a single family. They weren't even a Catholic family, so I suppose the priests had to do some kind of special blessing before moving in. It was acquired in the forties, and they had lived there without difficulty ever since. The large porch was enclosed with lots of windows, and an offset door was added. The enclosed porch space was used for two offices—the larger one was for the pastor, now Monsignor Ward, and the smaller was for the assistant priest, now Father Reed.

It was interesting watching the comings and goings from the parsonage. Young couples planning to marry made appointments and came nicely dressed, nervous, and smiling. Women in their thirties came wearing sunglasses and black scarves, even on hot days. Old women came, and so did the occasional bum, looking for a handout. Families came sometimes, and from our vantage point we were the first to see the new kids that would appear in a few days on the playground. The parsonage was a busy place and the priests were constantly coming and going themselves. We saw them leaving for the hospital with the holy sacrament; or trying to end a conversation with an old woman so that they could dash—nearly running—to the church, where congregants and the altar boys were already waiting with candles lit for Mass. Or answering the phone call that announced that the latest victim of an accident was a Catholic, and that last rites were needed.

It was Friday, October 7, the day that is called Our Lady of the Holy Rosary. On this day, all the classes met in the gymnasium for a special recitation of the rosary. A Boy Scout, as part of his Eagle Scout project, worked with Officer Beecher to prepare the program. In addition, he planned a rosary-related project for each of the grades to complete during the week. Our classroom project was to make large rosaries from cut strips of paper that we pasted together forming a paper chain rosary. There was one blue strip after every ten white ones, until it was five decades long. Then we connected it with another blue strip to the three white links, flanked by two blue strips, standing for Faith, Hope and Charity and then to the cross, which was made from yellow paper.

Only five students in our class actually made one. Six of us were being punished, and stood along the wall in front of some piece of incomplete work, either homework or repetitive sentences of "I shall not do something or other again." Three kids weren't able to cut well enough with their scissors and so ruined their sheets. Two kids just cut their paper into tiny pieces—they didn't have any idea what they were supposed to be doing. And then there was George Ann, who ate most of her paste within the first few minutes after Sister Mary Ann passed it out. She had to sit with the paste jar on her head and watch the rest of the class during the project. She was constantly reminded that she knew what would happen if the paste jar fell, although it was never actually revealed.

The completed rosaries, along with the other decorations from the other classes, filled the halls on our way down to the ceremony. The event started with Officer Beecher wearing his blue police uniform, complete with all the shining bars and polished leather boots and belt, carrying the flag of the United States. Along side him, Danny Johnson, the Eagle Scout candidate, carried in the Papal Flag. The two flags were placed on a small platform flanking a kneeler that was placed in the center, directly in front of a table on which a garden-sized plastic statue of Mary the Mother of God was placed. We all said the Pledge of Allegiance. Then the Eagle Scout candidate read a short speech about the importance of dedicating ourselves to Mary, the Protector of America, and that if enough Americans said the rosary everyday, surely she would protect us all from Communism. Officer Beecher then stood at attention facing us; we knelt on the gym floor, while Danny knelt on the upholstered kneeler with his back to us, facing the Mother of God and led us in reciting the five Sorrowful Mysteries of the rosary. Each mystery requires ten Hail Mary's and a group of five is one time around the rosary. We were glad that we didn't have to do all twenty mysteries—that is four times around and is hell on your knees. It is generally only required if you've done a really, really, really bad sin.

Returning to our classroom, the girls walked in a double line, followed by the boys, and then by Sister Mary Ann. It was a good arrangement. We never knew who she was looking at, and the girls were always better behaved and less likely to talk, or walk silly, or any of the other things boys were apt to do. The stairs were not enclosed. Coming from the lower level after five steps, you reached the landing where the outside door was, and then made a U-turn to continue up the remaining nine steps. As we turned, there, taped to the railing above the lower stairs, in the fullest possible view, was an eight and a half by eleven inch drawing of a man with his pants pulled down, showing his wiener, and balls, and everything. The picture was drawn in black color crayon—all but the mouth, which was red crayon—and his wiener was really, really big. The man was drawn really good. Every finger and even the buttons of his opened shirt were drawn. There was something else drawn too, but it was hard to make out. It looked like it could be another person, but really small and drawn really dumb—like a first grader would draw it. At first, everyone pretended not to see it. Then George Ann just started squealing, kind of halfway between a laugh and a scream. She pointed and kept making the sound as she stepped from side-to-side putting one foot on top of the other. Everyone else just stopped; we were afraid to say or do anything.

Sister Mary Ann said very calmly, "Children go directly to the room and take your seats."

While we were sitting down, she went to her desk, got out a large manila envelope, and walked out into the hall. She soon returned with the captured drawing safely contained. She then sent Dave to the office with a note. Dave returned, followed by Sister Rose a short time later. The two nuns walked out into the hall with the envelope; then returned. This time the envelope was sealed.

Sister Rose addressed the class, "Does anyone know anything about the picture that was hung on the railing?"

We all just sat there; then George Ann said, "I know. I know it was a dirty picture, a real dirty picture," her voice taking on the same squealing sound as when she was standing on the stairs.

"I mean does anyone know who drew it, or how it got hung in our school?"

This was a relief; for a moment I thought we were going to have to explain to Sister Rose what the shapes that were hanging from between the man's legs were. We all just sat there, trying not to look guilty—which we weren't—but having been guilty so often, it was difficult to look natural when asked an indicting question.

We assumed that because of the quality of the drawing, and the fact that we had been with Sister Mary Ann all day, it would be difficult for any of us to be guilty. Anyone could have put the drawing there anytime that morning. The doors of the school were never locked. Even an adult could have done it, although it looked more like a kid drawing than a grown-up's. Sister Mary Ann tried to think who had left the room—only Jimmy taking the lunch count down to the office, but that was in the other direction, and the drawing was too good for him. Then there was Robert, whom she had taken out in the hall after observing him taking a suspicious glance over George Ann's shoulder. But she hadn't left him out there alone; just a couple of well-deserved slaps across the face had handled that matter. She hadn't left the room all morning, so no one would have been able to slip out the door, and if they had, someone would have told. She made sure of this by always giving out a holy picture to the first student to tattletale after she returned. These were like paper baseball cards—but with saints on them, from old paintings—and the back contained a prayer. Most of the prayers told you how many indulgences or days off of purgatory you got for saying them. We always compared them, because sometimes the shorter prayers with easier words were worth more than the hard ones.

The next day, it was as if nothing had happened. Sometimes when Sister Mary Ann's desk drawer was open, we could see the edge of the manila envelope, and knew that the matter had not gone away. It was simply waiting in abeyance; waiting like an evil serpent to slither forth at some moment when we would least expect.

A Catholic Boy's Erector Sets and Midnight Mass

Christmas came. We opened our gifts on Christmas Eve. I got the usual socks, underwear, pants, and also an Erector set. This was a very cool thing. It was like getting a hundred toys in one. You could make whatever you wanted. However, my set was the small one, and you could only make a few things. But next year I could ask for more parts; and if I kept asking for more every year, year after year, in about ten years I would have the biggest set any kid ever had. After we opened the gifts, mom took me to church for my first midnight Mass, or at least the first that I remember. If there were others before that, I had slept through them.

Tommy Thompson, Jr.

A new boy came to our school right after Christmas break. Tommy was neither tall nor short; he had green eyes, and the standard light reddish-brown hair. His hair was short, straight, and the front was combed up in kind of a butch. Not a flattop, because only the front stood up; the rest simply lay like fur over his normal sized head. What wasn't normal about him were his dimples, and the smile that advertised his friendliness. He was in the regular fourth grade room, but said "hi" to us retards, and didn't seem to even know that we were undesirables. We hoped he didn't care.

His dad was really cool too. He came to work at Willard Brothers Chrysler. There weren't really any Willard brothers in the business, or at least not any more. They started the business in 1929, but then during the Depression one brother wanted to leave, so Roger Willard continued on alone, but kept the name. The local story was that, at that time, he couldn't afford to repaint the sign, but that wasn't the case now. It was the biggest dealership for miles in any direction.

Roger Willard had done quite well. As for his brother, no one knew. Some said that he just drifted, and would occasionally ask his brother for money to get out of one jam or another, but finally Roger just cut him off. Roger and his wife Rena had one son. Even though their son, Bobby, was now in his thirties, he still lived at home. Everyone knew he wasn't too smart, and everyone wondered who would take over the dealership when Roger decided to retire. They lived the good life—with Roger working less and enjoying golf, not only at the Alexandria Golf Club, but also on their extended winter vacations to exotic places like Florida and Arizona.

After a somewhat poor Christmas season, Tommy's dad joined the company as their head salesman, and he was good. He was even doing the radio spots on KXRA—spots before and after the daily farm report, and one each morning right at 7:35. He closed each advertisement by saying, "This is Tommy Thompson, reminding you that at Willard Brothers we lose a little on every deal but we make it up in volume." The men just laughed, saying how foolish that was. Some even questioned the legality of saying something that couldn't be true. But they talked, and they came in to meet the man behind the voice, and they bought cars—lots of them.

Sales had gone up 50 percent, and the remaining Willard brother was beaming every Sunday as he sat up front in the parish church with his wife, both of them impeccably dressed. He wore a new tie every week. Mom once said that he gave 53 ties a year to the church rummage sale—and they were hardly worn. The women who worked at the sale always had first choice of the stuff, three hours before the sale opened to the rest of the public. Many of the best things were gone—including nearly all of Mr. Willard's ties—before it opened. The ties would show up on other men the following Sunday. It was possible to review Mr. Willard's previous year's entire tie wardrobe on the men as they walked back from communion. It also was said that some of the guys kept a close eye on the appearance of each new tie, and put their orders in early with their wives for next year.

Mr. Willard wasn't an usher, because he traveled a lot and didn't want to bother. But Tommy Thompson signed up right when he came to town. He also joined the Knights of Columbus and the JC's, and played on our church softball team that summer. Tommy Thompson had, in a few months, become a celebrity. And the son who bore the same name, voice, and deep dimples was the most popular kid in school his first day there. But unlike the other popular kids, whom no one really liked, he was both popular and well-liked.

Calling All Boys

Monsignor Ward gently tapped on the edge of the open classroom door. Sister Mary Ann walked over looking concerned. He said, in his restrained but vibrant voice, "I wonder if I might have a moment or two to talk with the boys."

"Certainly, Monsignor," she said as she stepped away from the door, nearly bowing, and announced, "Monsignor Ward would like to talk with the boys for a moment."

"We will be starting classes for altar boys next week. We are asking the good sisters to excuse you from religion class, so that you can work with Sister Gene and Father Reed to learn to be an altar boy. It is a lot of hard work, so we only want those boys who really want to do it. If you do become an altar boy, you must make a commitment to come to all the services that you are required to. In addition to the daily Masses, and the Sunday Mass, during Holy Week there are special services nearly every day; and you will need to serve at the Stations of the Cross, weddings, and funerals. We have had some problems with boys not showing up when they are supposed to, so we are sending notices home to your parents, and you will need to discuss this with them. They, too, have to pledge to bring you to church for these services. It is a big commitment. You will have to learn all the Latin responses and learn to do all of the practices of the Mass. In addition to coming during religion class, you will also need to come each Saturday from now until Easter."

He then handed Sister Mary Ann the forms to pass out. She reminded him that the boys were of various ages and that these boys may not be the right choice for being altar boys.

He said, "Well, why don't we give them to all the boys who are ten or older? If they want to be altar boys, and they can't learn the prayers, they can always just come on days when there are processions, and one of the other boys can help them walk. They will like dressing up in the cassock anyway, and it will be good for them."

Sister Mary Ann began passing out the papers, thinking carefully each time before giving one out. She passed by Stanley James without seeming to notice him. He raised his hand when she had finished, and looked not at her, but at Monsignor Ward.

"Yes, Mr. James," Monsignor Ward said with the same smile that had accompanied these same words years earlier. Monsignor delighted in occasionally calling Stanley James "Mr. James" because it reminded him of the first day of school. Monsignor was one of those men who never forgot small details like that.

Stanley quickly moved his eyes over to look straight at Sister Mary Ann, and said as politely as he could "Sister Mary Ann, I think you forgot me. I'm ten."

"Stanley, do you think your father would want you to be an altar boy?" Sister Mary Ann said, trying to sound gracious and concerned in front of Monsignor Ward.

"Well, I'll ask him. I know my mom would."

"Please Sister, give him a paper and we will see."

We entered the class of altar boys along with the regular boys—just three from the retard room, Stanley James, Dave, and me. Robert, Timmy, and Billy were old enough—but not interested—and the other parents didn't think it would work out. We had to learn all the Latin. We would say it in a chant as we walked home, with exaggerated inflections.

". . . Credo in unum Deum, Patrem omnipotentem, Factorem coeli et terrae, visibilium omnium et in visibilium . . ."

We had little idea what we were saying, but the sounds of the words were wonderful. I found that I didn't stutter when I shouted out the words; and Stanley James, well, he virtually crowed them.

On Saturday morning for six Saturdays we attended training in the church itself. We could not be late or miss a class without a really good excuse. Either of these breaches of our commitment could result in being removed from the class. We all arrived early for the first class; we sat in the front row and waited until Father Reed arrived. While we waited, we knelt, even though it wasn't required. We thought that it would make us look more pious, and that we would be considered a better altar boy. I pretended to be earnestly praying, but was more interested in listening to the women who were arranging the flowers for the church.

"Those are from my mother. She had a dinner party and used them on the table. She sent them in so that we wouldn't have to spend so much from the flower fund. I'm not sure if the money is going to last until we can start cutting spring flowers from our gardens."

The conversation appeared strange to me in two ways. First, I had never heard adults just talking in church—they were either speaking as part of a ceremony, or were correcting children in stern whispers. But these women were just talking—in church—like they were at the Red Owl store. Second, they were talking about things— not particularly holy things, just ordinary things—like the cost of flowers, and the need to economize. Economize! I had never even thought about things like how the flowers arrived in the church, or how the wine or the host that became the body and blood of Christ were purchased. Years later, the first time I saw the organist pick up his paycheck I was shocked. It was like finding out that Santa was really just mom. All the things I learned as an altar boy were both astounding and transforming. I was moving from being a spectator to a performer. I was both privileged to learn the inner secrets of the event, and disillusioned by the view behind the curtain.

The woman continued to talk. "Mother wanted us to use her flowers for the new Mary statue; she said to use the cheap flowers for the other places. These are the best roses and cost a lot. She thinks that the new Mary is working a lot better than the old one, and thought that maybe we should change them around—put the new one up on the high bracket and put the old one on the little table. But I told her that I didn't think Monsignor would agree to that, because the old one matches the St. Joseph statue on the other side better."

We had two Mary statues in our church. The original one, the St. Joseph statue, the Sacred Heart of Jesus statue, all the Stations of the Cross, and the Crucifix came from the old church, and were the typical painted plaster statues of late 19th Century Catholic churches. Then, as a dedication gift for the new church, the parish's wealthiest donor, Mrs. Norton, gave us a new white and gold porcelain Mary statue. This was also placed on the right side—that is, to the right of the priest when he is speaking to the parish. The right altar is always dedicated to Mary. The new statue was placed on a small wooden table. This Mary was favored by most of the women, both because of its closer proximity, and because of its brilliant new shine. Most of the men didn't really care much about it one way or the other. A special small bouquet was always placed at her feet. On the Feast of Mary, Queen of Heaven, she was the statue chosen to have the crown made of fresh flowers placed on her head; and she was the one that we prayed to the most to help the missionaries persuade the pagans to give up their worship of heathen idols.

The older woman working with the decorations thought that we should get a heart—shaped votive candle stand for the new Mary, like the one they have at the basilica in St. Paul. But then the woman who appeared to be in charge said it might get in Father's way during communion.

"There isn't much room here," she went on while arranging her mother's flowers in a vase on the small table.

Then she suggested that maybe if they just put a sign up on the large existing votive candle stand designating the four rows to the right for the new Mary and the others for the old Mary, that would work out just fine, and not take up any more room or cost anything. There was an equally sized votive candle stand on St. Joseph's side, which he shared with the Sacred Heart of Jesus statue, but only a few candles ever burned in it. Mary was much preferred when shelling out a dime to light a candle for a special request.

"Have you heard if Mrs. Norton is really going to donate a statue of St. Francis Xavier? You know, the patron Saint of Missionaries. Her nephew is a Maryknoll Priest in Vietnam working with those heathens there, trying to convert them away from those Buddhist gods."

The woman continued, "She sent him a beautiful statue of Mary—not this big, but good enough if you don't have any. But then she was thinking that if we had a statue of St. Xavier in our church, that might encourage more people to pray for the missionaries; and God knows there is work to be done in the world, especially in Asia before the Communists get them all. Mrs. Norton's nephew told her personally that so many of the people there are following someone named Hoe-Hoe-Ming or something like that."

"Is that the little fat gold god, like the one at the Chinese restaurant in St. Cloud?"

"No, that's Buddha. Hoe-Hoe-Ming—he's a real man, but a Communist."

"Oh, that's even worse, or at least I think it is." Then she continued, "You know, when we went to that Chinese restaurant in St. Cloud, the man at the cash register tried to get me to rub the belly of that fat gold statue. He said that it was good luck. But I told him I was a good Catholic woman who didn't believe in superstitions. So, I would be pleased to just stick with my four-leaf clover. After all, it got me through four kids."

She continued with the story of how she found the clover on her first date with Arnold, and how she preserved the clover by ironing it between sheets of wax paper. Occasionally she commented again on her near abduction into heresy by the cashier at the Chinese restaurant, and then again declared that her Christian principles would never be compromised. She was too smart to fall for such tricks.

The other woman looked a little frightened every time the Chinese restaurant was brought up and tried to avert her eyes. I wondered if she had fallen for the "just rub the Buddha's stomach" trick, and was now living in the deepest of sins. Just think, maybe she was a pagan without knowing it, and was in our church decorating the altar. Maybe she got all zombied at night and came back and lit those same altar cloths on fire. Yes, perhaps she looks innocent enough, but she could be a Buddha belly-rubbing, altar cloth burning heathen.

Before I could firmly establish the facts of the case, Father Reed arrived—late and looking all red and flustered, like he had run from the parsonage or the school.

He put his hands together and said, "Let's start with a prayer to St. Tarcisius. Saint Tarcisius is the patron saint of altar boys." He told us, "Altar boys should strive to have the same devotion and courage as Saint Tarcisius had. Saint Tarcisius lived a long time ago in the third century. He was trying to help prisoners by bringing them Holy Communion. One day the Roman guards grabbed him and viscously beat him to death, but he didn't waiver from his love, not for a moment. After he was dead, they searched his body but they didn't find the communion host."

"What had happened to it?" Joey asked. "God either made it disappear so that the guards could not abuse it, or as they were beating him to death, he ate it so that it would be safe from them. Either way, he died in the grace of God. His story was lost for almost 40 years after he died. Then a cook at the prison who witnessed the beating converted to Christianity. He was afraid to say anything at first, but finally told the story just before he died."

Stanley James asked, "Well, if they didn't find the host on him, what happened to the guards? If he wasn't bringing it, shouldn't the guards have gotten in trouble for killing him?"

"Nothing happened to the guards. In those days, those in power did whatever they wanted, even killed people, and the authorities wouldn't do anything. It's hard for you to realize how the world has changed. Let's hope that you will never be faced with the same situation that Saint Tarcisius was, but it could happen. Communists could take over the country and outlaw the Mother Church as they have done in other places. Then you will have to be brave altar boys, maybe giving up your own life for the church. But let us keep praying that it will never happen here," Father Reed concluded.

Then we were given a tour of all the secret places beyond the sanctuary, and shown how the electric bells were rung to produce deep thunderous tones by simply pressing a small white plastic button. Father Reed put on a surplice, so that we could practice properly lifting the back panel as he sat. Each Saturday we practiced the routine movements and the special procedures used for High Mass, funerals, weddings, and so forth. We took turns in each of the four altar boy positions. It was a combination of preparing for a play and a vocation, yet different from either.

First Mass

After completing our studies, we were assigned a Sunday Mass, or six weekday Masses—from Monday to Saturday—either the morning 6:00 AM daily or the 11:00 AM daily. The 11:00 AM Mass was the one that all the students from the catholic school went to. If you got the 6:00 AM Mass, you had to go twice, so the 11:00 Masses were the best. You didn't have to get out of bed early, and you got out of school 15 minutes early to dress and prepare the altar.

Candle lighting was the most exciting part of the preparation; placing the suborbeim, the golden chalice-like vessel that held the communion hosts, was the most solemn. Normally the suborbeim was kept in the tabernacle, but when it was filled with a fresh supply of host, then a boy carried it out to the altar; and when it was empty, a boy carried it back into the sacristy after the Mass to be refilled. To carry it, one must never touch the vessel itself. You can only carry it with a silk cloth. We thought that it was like the Ark of the Covenant, and that you would be struck dead even for accidentally touching it. Dave was so afraid of it that he would not even look at it. Stanley James asked Father Reed if it was true that we would die if we touched it, or if it were just a mortal sin, or both. Father Reed said it was neither. We needed to use the cloth because our oily fingerprints tarnished the gold plating making it really hard for him to polish. The practical aspects of ritual had never occurred to us. Hmm, God was smart after all, not just arbitrarily vengeful.

Two experienced boys always served with two new boys. The experienced boys were placed on the inside closest to the priest, and did most of the good stuff; the outside boys didn't do much—except the boy to the far right of the priest got to ring the bells. The boy on the far left was mostly there for balance.

My first assignment was a week of 11:00 Masses. And best of all, Stanley James and I were both on. The older boys were Jim and Randy. They were both well-versed in the Latin, so if we messed up or weren't loud, it would hardly be noticed. Monsignor Ward was the priest, so we had better not screw up. Stanley James was going to do the bells.

Right before we went out, Randy whispered to Stanley, "Now remember this is Saint Agatha Day, so in addition to the usual times, you have to ring the bells every time the priest genuflects, or turns left."

"What?"

"Ring the bells every time the priest genuflects or turns left."

We were all lined up, and the priest had already picked up the chalice. We walked out. The boys took their positions at the foot of the altar. Monsignor Ward walked up the three steps to the altar, turned to the left, and the ringing began. The two older boys tightened their shoulders, afraid to look at each other for fear of breaking into laughter, but their shoulders began to shake by the sixth bell.

Then just before the offertory, Monsignor Ward turned to Stanley James and said, "Cut it out!"

Jim and Randy broke into tightlipped laugher, but Jim wasn't able to keep his lips totally tight, and a fart-like chuckle blasted from his face. It was immediately echoed by Randy. Monsignor Ward took a deep breath, stared at both boys, and turned back. We had no idea what the reaction of the congregation was.

After Mass, as soon as we returned into the sacristy, it was the custom for the boys to kneel. The priest would then turn around, set down the chalice, and give the boys a blessing, touching each on the head. This day, however, the blessing was put on hold.

"That is the oldest gag in the church. Can't you boys think of something new? When I served my first Mass it was at the cathedral in St. Cloud for Bishop Lune. My parents invited all of their friends, and Bobby Martin told me at the last minute that because it was a Mass for a martyr, I had to ring the bells every time Bishop Lune took a step. Bishop Lune by that time was completely deaf. So I sat there, ringing those darn bells until my hand was ready to fall off. After that, they called me Ring-A-Ding Ward for years. Now, may the blessing of our Lord Jesus Christ be with you now and for all times."

He made the sign of the cross, and was unable to hide a certain kind of look that is more typically found on the face of a grandfather watching his grandchild getting into the same mischief he did. It held the assurance that there is continuity in the universe, and that no matter how changed the world appears to be, it really is the same.

First Funeral

Stanley James and I both got notes from the office on Monday. Sister Mary Ann first read the notes, and then called Stanley James and me into the hall. We had no idea what we had done, and the expression on Sister Mary Ann's face gave us no clues. She handed us the notes and said that Father Reed had assigned us to be servers at the funeral of Mindy Thomas' daughter on Tuesday. She calmly reminded us that while we would miss the morning classes for the funeral, we were expected to have our homework done and handed in after lunch. She also reminded us of the importance of exemplary behavior for altar boys during funerals.

We were surprised. Most of the time, boys served for at least three months or longer before doing their first funeral, and we had only been serving for a month. We assumed that the more experienced boys would do the important parts and that we would be able to just follow along. We also sensed that Sister Mary Ann had conflicting emotions about letting us go. She would have liked to remind Father Reed that these boys had work that was not completed, and therefore they should not serve. But she had already been overruled regarding this particularly masculine aspect of the Church, and therefore relinquished control over our time.

We heard our moms talking about the death of Mindy's baby the day before, after church, and had pieced together fragments of the story. We knew that Mindy was a girl who had suddenly left high school early in her senior year, like a few girls did each year—to visit an aunt or an aging grandparent—and then they returned in the spring. They looked different when they came back. Most often, their hair was cut shorter, and they preferred less girlish clothing, and wore older, somewhat bewildered faces. They didn't go to the prom, and the excitement of high school no longer seemed important to them. After graduation, they moved away to the Twin Cities, Fargo, or Eau Clair, and did not return to Alexandria very often.

Mindy was a farm girl, and did not quite understand the rules. When she returned, she returned with a baby, but no husband. Her father insisted that she could not live at home with two younger sisters. So she rented a trailer, as other such women did, at the High View Park on Highway 29. Bessie and George, the couple that ran the park for the absentee owner, often bought trailers from residents of the park when they wanted to leave in a hurry, and then fixed them up as rentals. They were suckers for sad stories from young girls wanting to start over, or from young couples down on their luck. Most often, the renters could not pay a deposit, but instead made promises of future payment. In such cases, the softhearted landlords were often disappointed, the rent was unpaid, and the trailer was left in shambles. The renters, their promises, and the last three months' rent were gone—along with the curtains the woman had made, and anything else that was not firmly attached. Never was there a forwarding address.

Mindy was different. She arrived looking small and scared with her mother and her baby. Her mother said that she could provide twenty dollars for a deposit, and that she would try to pay some more from her egg money each week, if the laying was good. Mindy had a friend at the park, Joy Jackson. Joy was married and also had a child. The Jacksons were good renters. Joy's husband had a steady income from working at the new 3M sandpaper plant. A plan was carefully crafted between the two young women. Mindy would get a job, and her friend Joy would care for the babies during the day. That way they both would make a little money. Mindy's mom would help out as she could. Mindy was actually a better risk than a lot of the sad stories that the couple had believed, so Mindy moved in that day.

The next day she got a job at Olson's Restaurant, one of the two sit-down restaurants in Alexandria. The other was Traveler's Inn, known locally as Travs. She was glad to be working at Olson's Restaurant, because Travs was the restaurant where the hoody boys hung out, smoked cigarettes in the bathroom, tried to pick up chicks, and told dirty jokes. She had been part of that crowd, but now she needed to move away from the parties and from the boys who still hung out there.

One of those boys was the father of her baby, Jamie. Which one? She wasn't sure. But if she worked there, she would look at their faces everyday—and at Jamie's—and wonder; she also would wonder if they wondered. She had never accused any of them. No, it would have been too easy for each of them to defend himself; they talked, and she knew it. At first, she liked that they talked, she was a farm girl who had never fit in. But because they talked, suddenly boys were calling her, stopping by, asking her to go to parties, giving her cigarettes and beer, and once even Black Velvet Whiskey. That was the police chief's son; he had stolen it from his uncle. She didn't like it all that much, but it was sophisticated, and she was the girl that all the boys wanted. The other girls for the most part didn't have much to say to her. Only Joy—who was her friend before she became so popular—still chatted with her. Joy told her to settle down, but she thought that Joy was just jealous. The only boy that ever called Joy was her not-so-handsome, not-very-cool, steady Jimmy, whom she married eight weeks after she became pregnant in the spring of 1960—after graduation.

Yes, she was glad that she was working at Olson's Restaurant, where the old people came in for breakfast after morning Mass, and ordered the 25-cent gravy on bread for lunch. The restaurant closed at 2:30; then it was time to clean up and go home to Jamie. There wasn't enough of a dinner crowd in Alexandria to stay open late—except the young crowd, the crowd that Olson's didn't want anyway. That's the kind of restaurant the Olson's had run for over 40 years.

Old man Olson opened Olson's Restaurant in 1926, a date that seemed ancient to the children of the 1950's. Of course, he wasn't old then. In 1926, he was twenty-eight, and the town was already booming. Tourists were driving up the new Highway 52, or Highway 29, which crossed each other just a block from the location of the restaurant. The structure originally was built as a feed store in 1881, but by 1922, the feed store was closed and just waiting for an enterprising young man to transform it. Now he was 62 years old, but still came in every day. His oldest son, now 40, worked with him. His son cooked and ran the kitchen, and the old man took payments from the customers and sold the cigars, cigarettes, and candy that filled the glass case on which the register sat.

Mindy wanted to work as many hours as she could. She had arranged with Joy to give Joy a third of whatever she made for watching Jamie. That left two thirds of her earnings for everything else she and the baby needed. Her mother said she would try to help out, but she knew that her mom made at most three dollars a week selling eggs, and that money was never enough for the unexpected needs at home.

She worked hard, and the customers seemed to like her, but she got fewer and fewer hours, until she was working only the late lunch and clean up hours. She didn't like this much, because after that last diner left, she and old man Olson were alone in the restaurant, and the doors were locked during clean up. She could sense him watching her. At first, she thought he was concerned that she might take something; but then she began to realize that he was just watching her. One day he calmly approached her and asked, in the practiced way of bosses who know their power, if she wanted more hours. She understood at once. She had been the "popular" girl in high school, the town knew it, and so did old man Olson. Three days later, old man Olson's son decided that he would stay to lock up. She knew that they talked, just like the boys in high school did. On some days, they both stayed to lockup. Mindy got more hours, and the older women at Olson's—who were also desperate for more work—found their wage-earning opportunities dwindling. But no one said anything; everyone just smiled at the ladies coming in after Mass, and the men who ordered their 25-cent lunches.

After leaving work, Mindy rushed to Joy's trailer to pick up Jamie. She smiled and laughed, and all the worries, shame, and fears vanished. She got a report from Joy, shared her tips, and reported the hours that she was scheduled to work the next day. The number of working hours never quite matched the length of time that Joy cared for Jamie, but Joy never asked why. Mindy then carried Jamie to their own house next door, so Joy could complete her chores. Then, on Sunday morning, May 14, 1961, Mindy went over to Jamie's crib—a crib that she bought at a rummage sale, painted pink, and tied pink ribbons on—and found Jamie cold and blue. Just lying there—uncovered, not breathing, lifeless. She screamed and screamed until it sounded like someone else, some other woman in a far away place screaming. Then Bessie, whom everyone simply called Bess, came running over from the office, after getting a complaint. She started banging on the door, but Mindy didn't hear her. The woman—the far away woman—wouldn't stop screaming. She couldn't hear anything with that woman screaming, not even the sound of her little dead Jamie. Bess used her key, ran into the bedroom, and began repeating, "Oh my God, Oh my God," over and over, in rhythm with Mindy's screams.

Joy and the other neighbors soon gathered. Joy called the police, then Mindy's mom, then the priest, then Nelson's funeral home, and then the Catholic Women's Church Auxiliary for the funeral lunch. Father Reed wrote a note to the school, selecting the three boys to serve at the altars. It was not a big or important funeral; some new boys could be included so that they would get some practice. On Monday, the notes were delivered from the office, and I was assigned to be a funeral altar boy for the first time.

I polished my shoes that night and got up early the next morning, carefully adding another layer of Brill Cream to my hair and combing it in a wave. I remembered not to eat breakfast because the funeral would be in the morning, and a three-hour fast is required before communion. Once you had been required to fast from midnight, but that changed a few years earlier. Now, we could eat before school and still have fasted for three hours before the normal 11:00 AM Mass.

The altar boy's dressing area was on the second floor of the bell tower. The stairs to it were through the sacristy where the priest dressed for the service. By the time I got to the room, Stanley James was already there; the other server arrived almost immediately behind me. It was Billy Johnson. Billy was two years older than us, and from the regular classroom.

"We're gonna get gypped, I know it," he said.

"What do you mean?" Stanley James asked. I just looked dumb.

"But not as bad as if Father Reed was doing the funeral," Billy continued, as if he hadn't heard Stanley James' question.

"What do you mean?" Stanley again asked.

"Ain't you ever done a funeral before?" Billy asked.

"No, neither of us has." Stanley answered for both of us.

"Well, most of the time the family gives the priest an envelope with a twenty for him and one dollar for each of us. On a really good one, there is two dollars for each of us, and thirty for the priest. When Old Man Norton died, that was the best; they requested Tom, Jon, me, and five other boys. It was a High Mass. We each got five dollars, and I'm not sure how much Monsignor Ward got, but I bet it was a bundle. Poor families don't give anything; they either don't know no better, or they just ain't got it. So Monsignor will give us a quarter. Father Reed, he doesn't have so much, so he just gives us a dime—so that we don't feel so gypped, but I still do. So, even if we don't get anything from the baby's mom, because it's Monsignor Ward, we will at least get the quarter," Billy concluded.

By this time we had put on our cassocks. We would have guessed to dress in the black ones, but Monsignor left us a note on the step, saying to use the white cassocks. It was a Mass of the Innocents, not a Requiem. Billy told us that was because Jamie had not reached seven, the age of reason. Before seven, even if you are really bad, you don't go to hell. After seven—then you can do mortal sins and be damned for eternity. If you die before you're baptized, then you just go to limbo. It is just like heaven, but you can't see God. But you don't know that there is one, so you don't know you're missing out on anything.

"What about Purgatory?" I asked.

"Oh, that's just for people over seven who have only venial sins. You've just got to burn for a while—unless someone buys you some Masses, lights candles for you, that kind of stuff," Billy concluded.

We went down, and Monsignor was waiting. He said that because Stanley James was the tallest, he would carry the cross. The cross was on the end of a fancy pole, the same one we used for the Stations of the Cross during Lent. Billy would serve on the right, and I on the left. He went over how to hold the incense box with me, and reviewed the holding and the lighting of the incenser with Billy. Billy was confident—this was his ninth funeral—and there was hardly anyone out there anyway.

"Oh, the family has decided not to have the Women's Auxiliary prepare a lunch, so we will have to get you boys back in time for school lunch. We will still go to the cemetery, but it shouldn't take long. There will only be a few for communion, and it is a low Mass." Monsignor then ended his briefing with, "Any questions?"

We walked out into the sanctuary with Stanley James leading, carrying the cross. There were only nine people in attendance—Mindy's family, two pallbearers, and two nuns from the hospital where Jamie and Mindy had been taken so that the baby could be pronounced dead. They stayed with Mindy until her mom was able to make it in from the farm.

Mindy didn't cry; she just stared blankly, like she wasn't really there. Her mother looked worried. Her sister and father looked very uncomfortable, but not as much as the two pallbearers did. Actually, the family hadn't asked them; they didn't really have any friends to ask, so Monsignor Ward asked them. One was Officer Beecher, the young policeman, church usher, and Boy Scout leader. It was not a problem for him because he was one of only a few men on the police force that was not married, so he was usually assigned to work night shifts anyway. The other was Mr. Thompson, Tommy's dad. There wasn't much business at the car lot on a Tuesday morning anyway, so getting away was no problem.

Because this was our first funeral, we made lots of small mistakes; I stood on the wrong side of Billy, and forgot to close the cover on the incense box. Billy rang the bells twice in the wrong spot, but no one noticed. The little coffin was white. It looked like it was covered in wallpaper, white wallpaper with small gold squiggly lines running in various directions. It was closed. Stanley James led the procession out of the church. First him, then the coffin with the two men, one on each side, then the priest flanked by Billy and me, then Mindy holding on to her mom, then her dad and sisters. The nuns came last.

Just as we reached the center of the church, a terrifying cry came from the soul of the baby's mother—a cry like a wild animal screeching in pain, then inconsolable tears, then wailing. The hair stood up on my neck. Billy kind of smiled, not because he was cruel, but because the sound was unbearably painful. Monsignor put one hand to his forehead for a moment as if to block the sound, but quickly recovered and slowly continued to walk. I couldn't see the nuns, the family, or the face of Stanley James. I could hear beneath the echoing sound of sorrow, a softer noise of feet collapsing, and then legs dragging, and I knew that Mindy was being held up and moved forward. I hoped that her dad was helping her mom, but I was afraid to look, afraid to deviate from how things should be, must be. I could feel my own toes curl and felt a tingling numbness with each step I took.

We reached the hearse; the coffin and the pallbearers got in. We got into the next limousine from the funeral home. Neither Stanley James nor I had ever been in a limousine. We sat on pop-up seats facing the priest. The family followed, and the nuns went back to the hospital. Monsignor did not talk most of the way out. Then, as we rounded the corner before the cemetery, he again gave instructions and went over the plan, much like I suppose a football coach or director does. The graveside service was short. We waited by the car afterwards while Monsignor Ward went over to the family, held Mindy's hand, and talked to her. He came back and we got in the car.

He looked at his watch and said, "We'll be able to get you boys back in time for 11:00 Mass." As soon as we got back into the sacristy, we knelt down in the customary way and he blessed us, placing his hand quickly on each of our heads. Then, in an uninterrupted motion, he reached into his pocket and pulled out three quarters. He handed one to each of us and said, "Thanks boys, for serving today."

We hurried up the stairs, slipping off our surplices and unbuttoning our cassocks on the way. We quickly hung them up, and raced down. Monsignor Ward was already gone. We ran back over to the school.

When we arrived, Sister Mary Ann looked confused about why we were there. Stanley James said quietly that the family decided not to have a funeral lunch, so Monsignor Ward told us to come back to the school. Sister Mary Ann replayed this in her head several times to determine if the situation somehow was the boys' fault, but at last could not determine any guilt.

"Well, I wish you had let us know, now the lunch count will be off. Children, get ready for Mass, line up and don't make a sound."

Sister Mary Ann then walked down to the kitchen to announce the situation. We knew there would not be a problem—the lunch ladies always made more, the first kids to finish got seconds.

When Sister Many Ann returned, Stanley James said, "Sister Mary Ann, we took communion at the funeral. We can only take it once a day."

"Are you asking me or telling me? If you're telling me, I know that; and if you're asking me, you should know that," was her reply.

"No, I just wanted to tell you," he said.

The real reason he wanted to say it was so that Sister Mary Ann wouldn't think that we were in mortal sin. There are only three reasons you can't take communion: one, you broke your fast; two, you already did; and three, you committed a mortal sin. If you didn't go to communion, people thought that you had done something really bad. So, he just wanted to tell her so she wouldn't ask what we had done.

Just as the offertory began, Sister Mary Ann noticed that George Ann and Melinda were whispering, and then Melinda giggled.

She reached ahead and pulled on their arms and said, "You owe me one hundred 'I will not talk in church.'"

It was a light penalty, but Sister Mary Ann didn't want to forget it, so she reached under the apron of her habit where there were three pockets. In one of the pockets she always kept her little book. It wasn't there. A cold, sick feeling like the dampness in a basement slipped across her face. She remembered picking it up, or did she? She knew it was there when the boys came back, because she was looking at it when they walked in. Did she put it in one of her other pockets? Discreetly, she checked them all. Well, she must have dropped it.

She tried to tell herself that she could find it after church, but after a few minutes of imagining it blowing in the wind, she couldn't contain herself. She got up, walked to the side aisle and walked outside. She hurriedly looked on the sidewalk, on the steps of the school, and then back in her classroom. Had one of the kids taken it? Hidden it somewhere? But how? It was in her pocket. Could it have fallen in the trash? Oh, God what to do? She was a nun, she couldn't be looking in the trash. She closed the door and stood to the side, so that no one would see her if they happened by, and looked in the small rectangular window in the door. Not there. She looked all around her room. They had not left the classroom today—only gone to church. It had to be recovered, but now she needed to get back to church.

She hurried back, looking all about her along the way. She retraced every move in her mind for the rest of the Mass. Even walking back from receiving the Body of Christ, her eyes quickly swept the floor of the church. Could she have dropped it when she reached for it to write down the names of the girls? Then did the children steal it when she went out to look for it? She should have looked better in the church first.

She decided not to let her class join the other students in the lunch line, but to take them back to the classroom. She told Sister Rose that her book was missing, that she suspected one of the students had taken it, and asked her to please tell the kitchen staff that her class would be a little late coming to lunch. As they walked back, she kept her eyes on the ground and on the children.

When they reached the door, she said, "My class is to return to our room before lunch." This had never happened before, and something new was never good. We returned to the room, and all the children sat down.

"I know one of you took something from me, and I know who it is, but I'm going to give that person a chance to come clean. They will feel so much better about themselves, and while they will still have to confess this sin, God will love them more for returning it."

As she made this announcement to the class, her eyes tried to read every small face in the room. All but the dumbest of us knew she didn't have a clue. Whenever they said, "this person," it meant they didn't even know if it was a boy or a girl. But what was gone? Man, I hoped it was not money. Jesus, if she found the quarter on me she would kill me.

"MMMMMonsignor ggggave me the qqquarter; hhhe hhe gave one to Stanley James too. Ask him, he will tell you. I I I d di didn't steal it," I blurted out, forgetting to raise my hand.

"No, it is not money that is missing, as someone knows," she coldly replied, trying to look at the class and me at the same time.

By this time, someone usually started crying and the jig was up. But everyone just looked scared. Sister then asked each student to take everything out of his or her desk and pockets, and to put it all on top. She walked to the first desk, flipped through each book and dropped it on the floor, then opened the pencil boxes, dumped out the crayons, opened the desk, then had the student stand against the wall while she tipped the desk and chair over in case something had been taped to the bottom.

She glanced back at the children standing along the wall with pockets pulled out. To make sure that we were not passing it from one to another—making a fool of her—we stood apart from each other with our arms straight out. As she came to the last five desks, she had already decided that Mr. Pearson needed to come and take the boys to the bathroom, where they could be thoroughly searched. She was sure that one of them was hiding it, where, they knew she dared not consider. She and Sister Rose then would search the girls if need be, but the book would be found.

Yet she was still uncertain. What if they had not taken the book? None of the usual tricks had worked to get a confession. She remembered picking it up, didn't she? What if she had dropped it after all?

Then Sister Rose came to the door and said, "Sister Mary Ann, we think your book has been found."

Sister Mary Ann slowly walked to the door and started walking away with Sister Rose, but stopped after a few steps and said, "Children, you may go down to lunch. You can clean this up after we come back."

When we reached the cafeteria, some children were laughing, some were saying, "Oooh, yuk," as they pulled small bits of paper (pages from Sister Mary Ann's little record book) out of their chili soup. Most of the kids were dumping their soup in the trash, and they were not being stopped or admonished for wasting food.

Mary, the red-haired girl from the other class, whispered to the cook by the trashcan, "They said it was all right to throw away your chili if you wanted to."

The cooks were busily buttering bread, so that the children would have plenty to eat, and they cut up more carrots.

Sister Mary Ann stood in amazement, like God had betrayed her. She was the only one who went to the kitchen to tell the cooks the altar boys needed lunch. None of the children in her class had been to the kitchen. Could she have picked it up before she went down to the kitchen? Could it have fallen from her pocket? Could she have dropped it in church, and could one of the kids have taken it out of church while she was gone, snuck into the kitchen and put it in the chili? No, one of the other nuns, the cook, or someone would have seen.

She couldn't find a guilty party and she could not even convince herself that a crime had been committed. But what was she to do about the penalties recorded in the book? Could she trust her memory to recall them all? She could not forgive them without forsaking justice, but she could not impose penalties without certainty.

After school we started walking home past the church, "Does anyone know how much it costs to light one of the candles in the church?" Stanley James asked.

Dave's mom lit them quite often, and he said, "Well, mom said it is a donation, so you can give any amount, but it has to be at least a dime, so that the church can make some money off of it."

"I think I want to light one," Stanley James said, "with my whole quarter."

We walked into the church, and our voices automatically changed to whispers.

"Why do you want do that?" I asked.

"Because of the funeral," he said.

"You don't light candles for babies; that is a waste of money, they are already in heaven," Dave instructed.

"No, I want to light it for the baby's mom, Mindy. I want Mother Mary to help her," Stanley said very softly.

"Joey told me that his mom said that she is a tramp. It might be a sin to light a candle for a tramp," Dave said again, pleading against this waste of good money.

"But Mary Magdalene was a tramp, too, and Jesus didn't care, so it's gotta be ok," Stanley James said as he walked up to the votive candle stand and slipped his quarter into the slot on the metal box.

It clanked with a loud sound, much louder than the thin dimes that women placed in the slot before Mass. He then reached for the matches and pulled one out of the box. They were wooden matches. Someone glued a picture of Mary over the advertisement that originally decorated the box, so that it would look churchier, and then continually refilled it. The sand paper on the sides was worn with all the use, but Stanley James found a small spot in the corner to strike it. The best candles, those in the center top next to the cross that decorated the stand, were all lit.

So he picked one in the center and prayed, "Mother Mary, please help Mindy. I don't think she is really a tramp. I know she loved her baby and feels real bad; make her feel OK."

He knew it wasn't a real prayer, it was kind of a retard prayer, but it felt right and it was, after all, his quarter.

As the boys walked out of the church, they looked up, and there stood Monsignor Ward in the balcony choir loft. He was standing there with his hands clasped in front of him, and had the same big smile on his face that he normally reserved for the arrival of his new Cadillac. When he first heard them come in and walk to the votive stand where the matches were kept, his heart collapsed into a dark sick pain—he feared they might have been the ones who lit the altar cloths on fire. But he waited, withheld his judgment, and when he saw the motive of their visit, the joy that consumed him was like that of Lazarus's sisters seeing their brother emerge from the grave. When we saw him, we quickly looked down and walked fast. We did not run, that would have been a sin. We emerged from the church to the bright outdoors.

As we walked home, Stanley James separated first heading south; then as we walked further, Dave would peel off heading south on Cedar Street. Yeah, he was now one of the boys who lived on those wonderful streets named after trees. Cedar Street headed south just before I turned to walk between the two lakes on Willow Drive. On this day, just before Dave separated, Tommy joined us. He was just there, walking with us, talking to us, just like we were regular kids. As we walked and talked about the events of the day, a glint of silver caught my eye, and I looked at the dead center of his chest where he had zipped his blue spring jacket. There, attached to the end of his zipper, was a round silver ring. Was it always there? It looked just like, just like the one on . . . no, I couldn't even think it.

Dave departed and Tommy said, "See you."

The next day he was still sporting the silver ring on his jacket zipper, so it couldn't be one of the rings from Sister's little book. Why did I ever even think that? Tommy wouldn't have had anything to do with that!

Right after the morning prayer and Pledge of Allegiance, Sister Mary Ann announced that we would each be required to say one complete rosary, all the mysteries. This was in lieu of any punishments that might have been recorded in the lost book. If we didn't have any punishments in the book, the rosaries would provide us with additional grace and reward in heaven. It was either payment or reward depending on our state of grace, and therefore of benefit to every child.

The Summer of the Great Dugout

Finally, summer arrived; and summer for a ten-year-old who doesn't live on a farm is perhaps as close to heaven as a boy can be. The farm boys had chores all summer, and even at this age their bodies were useful in the field during haying season and on a daily basis feeding the pigs and chickens. They—the farm boys—had other advantages; they belonged to 4-H, and raised animals, which they took to the fair in the fall. They cared for the animal everyday, feeding it, brushing it, loving it, and placing their hopes on the rabbit or pig to win a blue, red, or white ribbon. The final event of the fair was always the auction. They hoped that their animal would sell high—which they usually did—often for two to three times the market price. The animal was then left for slaughter, and the child went home from the fair with cash, sometimes as much as twelve dollars for a rabbit or thirty for a pig. The boys cried in the back seat of the car—and in their beds for a few nights; but for some, the feeling of loss faded, and each year the hurt was less. They learned through 4-H the hard realities of attachments and sale, caring for an animal, but letting go. They were farmers; and farming was a business, not a hobby. They didn't talk about the pain. They bragged about the cash.

Every business in town picked up in the summer. The hospital had a lot more admittances with folks getting sick—probably due to the unsanitary condition of some cutting boards or toilet facilities. The emergency room action was always way up. The increase was usually due to fish hooks in the eye or butt, broken bones, fight wounds, or cuts from drunken tourists trying to fillet fish like their shirtless teenage fishing guides had done the day before. The boys' dexterity permitted them with a flick of their wrists to fillet a sunfish in mere seconds with such flair that it was both utilitarian and entertaining. The ladies, having drunk a considerable number of beers, whispered to each other during the entertainment, and then giggled and smiled. Their giggles often created a sense of emasculation in their husbands, but generally made for good tips for the guide boys. But their husband's attempts to imitate the actions of the skillful natives generally resulted in even more laundry at the Douglas County Hospital, and longer working hours for Eva.

Us city kids—we were carefree, or almost. In the summer after fourth grade, Stanley James took up the stain pre-treatment duties at the dry cleaners, and by the end of the summer he was running everything except the presser. He was not tall enough to reach the equipment, or skilled enough to produce the flawless creases demanded by the clients. I, too, began working in the mornings at the gas station. In those days, gas stations provided service with the sale of each gallon of gas. Windows were washed all around, oil checked, and even the headlights were debugged, all when the price of gas was 21.9 cents a gallon. I was too short to reach the windshields, so I had a box that I dragged to the side of the car to help me reach across and polish the glass to perfection, then quickly jumped down to complete the headlights, side, and rear windows. Unlike the fishing guides with their filleting knives, never once was a tip offered for this service; but occasionally tourists commented that the gas was jacked-up in price to gouge them. Dave's dad sold the dairy that year and bought the town's gem—the A&W Root Beer stand. Dave began working there. His job was not nearly as glamorous as Stanley James's or mine; he washed the tall glass mugs and put them in the freezer. He did, however, get all the root beer he wanted to drink.

Daylight in Minnesota lasts over eighteen hours in the summer, so the days seemed endless; and even with chores there was time off for young boys to dream and play. This summer was the summer of the great enterprise. We saw a movie the winter before about a space invasion from Mars in which the invaders built an immense underground complex. From this underground complex, they implanted devices in humans so that someday they could control the world or something like that. We thought that the underground complex was very cool—so we started drawing up plans for one. It had secret tunnels that led to a big meeting room, and each of us had our own room with more secret tunnels. Eventually the complex would spread beneath the entire city, and we would be able to go anywhere in winter without going outside. We might even make a tunnel over to the school, and have it come out somewhere near the playground. Then the kids would all wonder where we went to or came from.

The enterprise was enormous, and we believed that it would take us several weeks to complete. We decided that the entrance needed to be somewhere very secretive and safe. Once underground, we would be able to dig unseen. But the entry—that had to be carefully selected, out of adult sight. We found the perfect place. On the Northwest side of Lake Winona there was a hillside that was completely hidden from Mr. Lane's, the landowner's, view. We began our digging there. We had to be careful that Mr. Lane didn't see us, but he was an old man who seldom came out of his house and we were well out of sight and perhaps as much as three hundred feet from his back door. We all brought shovels and Dave dragged over a rusty pickaxe that might be handy when we encountered boulders. We began early in the morning, continued until it was time for us to go to work, and then reconvened that evening. This was a real commitment, with all the passion that ten-year-old boys could generate.

The ground on the side of the hill was soft and the digging proceeded well. We were strong boys and used to hard work. By the second day, we had created a hole about five feet long, six feet wide, and two feet deep. The progress was somewhat slower than we had anticipated. We checked the schedule, and discovered that we had planned to be working on the big meeting room—ten feet underground—by this time. Yet we were making progress, so much so that we decided to have a cigarette break. Hard working boys had to have a break. Stanley James's mom and dad both smoked over a pack a day; they usually had more than one pack open at a time, and they left them lying about. They both smoked Winston's. It was easy to slip two or three cigarettes out of a pack—they would just think the other one had taken them. They bought them at the Clark station by the carton. Occasionally, Stanley James would even take a whole pack when the carton was about a third empty. If it was too low, then the pack would be missed; and if it was new, taking one would leave an obvious hole.

We laid down in the hole; it was just big enough for us to lay down side-by-side, hidden from the horizon in the dimple of the earth. We lit up, and Dave said, "Remember when Robert asked Sister Mary Ann if God could make a rock so big that He couldn't lift it?"

Janie had asked that one too, but I never told Robert about it. It just must be something kids talk about in big cities. It happened about a week before the end of the school year. Rather than answering Robert, Sister Mary Ann told him to step out into the hall and that she would be there in a moment to give him the reply he deserved. From the calm thrill of her voice, we all knew something bad was about to happen. A chill rolled down my spine; it felt like a frozen Brillo pad, and my toes curled and tingled. We all felt it, we all knew. Robert knew it, too. He did not go out to the hall, but instead slipped into his chair as silently as a knife drawn into folds of velvet. Sister Mary Ann, without any expression, ever so coldly strolled over to him, gently reached out, and put her hand on his thick golden hair. His beautiful hair was so thick that it stood straight up several inches before rolling into waves of oiled wool. He slowly reached for and grasped the edges of his unbreakable melmac chair. His body then hardened like Plaster of Paris does in a rubber mold. She slowly tightened her fingers in his hair and lifted him, chair and all, and dragged Robert, the chair, and unspeakable fear out the door and into the silent corridor. Once outside the door, we heard the chair hit the floor, then the familiar sounds of a child being taught the ways of unquestioning obedience. Jimmy, whose eyes had disappeared deep into his secret place some time earlier, now seemed alert, and asked Stanley James what Robert had done.

Stanley James said, "He asked if God could make a rock so big, he couldn't lift it."

"Can He?" asked Jimmy.

"I don't know," Stanley James said quietly, "I will have to think about it."

We never talked about the things that happened in the hallways of St. Mary's. We all knew; but when school was out—like the veterans of the war camps—we never spoke of it. Would we grow up to be like them, I wondered, like the war prisoners? Everyone in town knew which men had been in the camps. Both the adults and the children understood the washed looks that came over these men's faces, and they knew never to ask. Stanley and I asked Robert after school, not about what happened in the hallway, but why he had asked Sister Mary Ann that question. He said the boys at the projects always talked about it, because it proved that God is just made up.

"What do you mean?" Stanley asked.

"Well, if God can't make a rock so big that He can't lift it, then He can't make anything He wants; and if He can, then He is not all strong because He can't lift it. So, either way He ain't real." Robert confidently explained.

He sounded as sure as Janie had sounded. Man, the kids in the cities sure are smart, I thought. Then I said, "Sister Mary Ann must have heard the question before." But then I immediately fell silent, because I was getting very close to talking about what we didn't talk about. Stanley James didn't say anything, but the look in his eyes was like wheels turning—the same look he had that morning when he was looking across the field and envisioning where we were going to dig all the tunnels.

"Yeah, I remember," said Stanley James.

"You told Jimmy that you were going to think about it. Have you figured it out yet?"

"I think so," said Stanley James.

"Well, can He?"

"Yep," Stanley said, taking a long drag on his cigarette and looking many years older than he was. "He is God, so He has to be able to do it."

"But then how can He lift it?"

"Oh, that's easy. If He is God, He just makes himself over—even stronger than when He made the rock. After He does that, He can lift it. Then, when the next boy asks Him the same question, He makes a bigger rock, and then He again makes Himself even bigger. Kind of like a weight lifter."

"That must be how God got so big—always making bigger and bigger stuff." Stanley James's answer came from his own understanding, not like the memorized answers in the Baltimore Catechism, where the carefully composed questions are followed by carefully composed answers. But the Baltimore Catechism didn't have the most intriguing questions—like God's Big Rock.

As we lay there in the freshly turned dirt, un-bathed (it was a Wednesday and bath day was Saturday), with cigarette smoke hanging over us and filling our young bodies, the sweat running down our stomachs, we were truly in the boyhood garden of paradise.

We went home exhausted, agreeing to gather in the morning to continue our project. The next day did not go so well. We just began digging and were all talking all at once when we heard a screen door slam shut and an old adult voice yelled, "What the hell is going on?" Running toward us was Mr. Lane, the man who owned the land on which we were digging.

We ran in two different directions—I ran with Stanley James and Dave ran the other way. Mr. Lane chased us, and we ran down along the edge of the lake until we came to the barbed wire fence where old man Jones kept a "wild horse." He bought it after he came back from Korea, but hadn't ridden it for three years. No one ever went in the pasture because the horse would trample you to death. But now—what choice did we have—death by Mr. Lane, or death by Jones's horse? We ran into the pasture; Mr. Lane stopped by the fence. The horse saw us and started running at us. Just when it looked as if we were going to make the second fence and be free, I fell. Not a full flat-on-your-face fall, I just stumbled. Stanley James circled back in a kind of slide—like a baseball player sliding into home—and grabbed me by the back of my shirt, swinging me forward in front of him. The horse reared up—not fully, just a few feet—and his front hooves came smashing down on Stanley James's side. Stanley slipped out from under the blow, and, protecting us with his shovel, continued running and pushing and pulling me until we leapt over the second fence. He caught his pants leg on the barbed wire, and even with all the action, the sound of the tear was clearly heard.

Once over the fence we continued to run. We looked back to see Mr. Lane with his arms up in the air, not yelling, but almost like he was glad that we had made it. He then shook his head and turned back to the site of the dig. The horse was still rearing up, and on we ran. We went over to Dave's house. He had already arrived and was hiding in the garage in his dad's wooden fishing boat. It was his spot, his secret spot away from humanity. We each had our own, but this was his. Dave lived right next door to the nuns, so he had to be particularly discrete. There was a wooden fence that separated his back yard from the nuns. Dave lived on the corner and faced Cedar, and the nuns' house faced 9th Street. So, the fence was at the back of Dave's house but on the side of the nuns' house. It was made in the new basket weave style where boards are woven between the posts in a very modern fashion. Dave sometimes crawled out the side door of the garage and listened to the nuns through the open windows of their convent house. He said that he once heard Sister Rose swear. And he thought that Sister Gene once told Sister Allen a dirty joke—but he didn't hear all of it, and didn't understand it. She started by saying, "What do you call a naked priest in a convent?" Then he heard an even lower whisper, and then laughter—the kind that you don't want your mom to hear, because she will ask you what you're laughing about. But today there was no laughter, Dave was hiding, crying, shaking.

"Dave, are you all right?" Stanley whispered.

"Oh, man, I'm glad to see you. I'm all right, are you?" Dave whispered back.

"Yeah," I said, "Stanley got trampled by Jones' horse."

"Can I see?" Dave asked.

I pulled his t-shirt up, and there was the bloody U-shaped mark of the horseshoe.

"I'll be all right," Stanley said, without even a hint of a tear.

Then we saw that blood was dripping—no, actually flowing in thin pulsating sheets—from his leg, where the barbed wire had caught him.

"It's ok, really," he insisted.

"I'm sorry," I whispered, knowing that he would have gotten away if I had not been there.

"Hey, we need a smoke," he said.

He produced a cardboard pack of Winston's in the flip top box. We all broke into the brand's popular theme song. "Winston's taste good like a . . . clap, clap . . . cigarette should." Stanley James flipped the cover of the box with his dirty fingers each time we clapped, and the tears and dust mixed with our grins, relieved that we were safe and hidden in Dave's secure secret place. We lit up, sucked the smoke deep into our soft lungs, and took inventory of the situation. We would have to dig elsewhere, but maybe we could tunnel over to Mr. Lane's later. We got away with all the shovels, but where was the pick?

"Oh crap, it's still there," Stanley realized.

We planned to look tomorrow, but the next day we didn't see it from the fence. While Dave worried for weeks that his dad would need it for some purpose or other, his fear faded in time—as did our plan for the great underground complex. We never dug again, and soon the summer, too, had faded away; and it was time for school to start again.

Fifth Grade 1961-62

The Master and His Pupil:
And it told of the demons, how many of them there were, and what
were their several powers, and their labours, and their names, and
how they might be summoned, and how tasks might be imposed on
them, and how they might be chained to be as slaves to man.

English Fairy Tales
by Joseph Jacobs, 1890

Second One Found

The door to the school was already unlocked because the Boy
Scouts were meeting and Mr. Larkins, the janitor, was still cleaning.
He stayed late on Wednesday night because of the scouts, and also
because Father Reed was teaching a class of converts. Men or women
who wanted to join the church had to take six weeks of classes. Of
course, if there was a need to speed things up, then the converts
could schedule private sessions with Father Reed, and at a rate of
two lessons each night, the whole thing could be completed in three
days. There were four men in the class and there didn't appear to be
any hurry, so Father Reed decided that they would all meet together
on Wednesday nights when the school was open anyway.

The first boys to arrive for scouts saw it. Stanley James and I joined
scouts because we heard that they went to Camp Willabee every
summer. We were usually the last to arrive. Mom picked Stanley James
up at the dry cleaners, and if there weren't any customers in the store,
she and Eva would talk. Then suddenly mom would say, "Oh, I gotta
get the boys to scouts," and then we had to rush, and still we were
the last ones. So, we didn't see it, but we heard about it.

On Thursday morning, everyone was talking about it before the
school opened. It was another drawing, but this time it was taped to
the Blessed Virgin herself. Right in her hand, like she was holding

it. From what the boys who saw it said, it sounded like the same kind of picture as before—all drawn in black lines, except this time the man had his pants pulled down only to the knees. Inside the black lines, his pants were colored blue and so was his shirt. The man had a really big wiener and big balls, but this time it was pointing up. In the other drawing it was pointing sideways. There was something else in the picture—it could have been another person—but it was hard to tell for sure. Maybe it was an animal, or just a ball with a mouth, or maybe just some lines. Anyway, they said these lines were red and so was the mouth on the man.

The boys looked at it for a long time because they were afraid to take it down. At first they thought they might just pretend that they hadn't seen it. Then they decided that they should tell the first adult who came along—otherwise they might get blamed. Father Reed got there before Officer Beecher or Mr. Johnson, so they told him.

Father Reed took it down and calmly asked if anyone had seen Mr. Larkins; but the boys hadn't. So he looked himself and found Mr. Larkins cleaning the girls' restroom. They talked and both walked over to the statue. Mr. Larkins said that he'd better clean off the tape residue, or it would collect dust and form a dirty spot that would stain the statue.

The boys were questioned about who got there first, but they all got a ride from Joey Turner's mom, who was heading over to play bridge. That was why she dropped them off so early. The door was open, so they came inside.

Mr. Larkins opened the office door for Father Reed. Father Reed wrote a note, put the note and the drawing into an envelope, and left the envelope on Sister Rose's desk. The boys whispered about it during the meeting, but no one mentioned it to the leaders. But the next day, everyone was talking about it. Who was leaving these drawings? Was it the same Protestant boys who were trying to burn down the church—the ones who called us Cat-Lickers?

Re-capper Lost and Found

Dave was bragging about a cool bottle opener that his dad bought at the State Fair. It not only opened pop and beer bottles without damaging the cap, but it was able to re-cap them. The man demonstrating them re-capped a bottle of Coke-a-Cola, shook it, and then aimed it at the crowd—but the cap held, held in carbonation, flavor, and freshness. Worked well for beer, too. If you only wanted a few swigs, the re-capper kept the rest fresh for later.

"In one week, this investment will pay for itself," the man exclaimed.

And it came with four reusable attachable handles for your beer bottles. No more cold hands or warm beer from holding the bottle. These handles kept hands warm and beer cold—the way it should be. They looked really cool, too. I tried to figure out how long someone needed to hold a beer in order to make it warm, but such a calculation was beyond the grasp of a fifth grader. I only knew that my uncles and my dad tossed them back so fast the foam didn't have time to settle. There was never any danger of them becoming warm.

The best part was that this new device provided Dave with an opportunity to get beer anytime he wanted it, or at least a little, sometimes. His mother sometimes only wanted half a beer—so his father finished it for her. But now, she decided that she would use the re-capper and put the rest of the bottle in the refrigerator for the next day. Dave could then sneak into the kitchen during the Ed Sullivan Show's boring parts—when the singers were on—reopen the bottle with the re-capper, take a tiny sip and re-cap the bottle. The thrill of getting caught might well have been more exciting than the actual effect of the beer, but Dave was on top of the world. He talked about the re-capper every chance he got. He told us he was going to bring it to school the next day for us to see. We could even touch it.

Sure enough, the next day he pulled the re-capper from his pocket. Dave, Tommy, Stanley, Robert, and I gathered off to the side of the building—a little way down the sidewalk, because this was clearly contraband. The rules were that any student who brought a "dangerous" or "nuisance" item to school—that is, anything kind of fun—had the item taken from him, and placed in a box in the lowest drawer of Sister's desk. On the last day of the year, your mom could come to school and collect the item(s) from the teacher, along with a long lecture about why she should have prevented her child from bringing the item to school in the first place. To avoid this, we generally considered items placed in the bottom drawer lost forever. We occasionally got a peek at them as new items were added. These nostalgic glances only served to deepen our loss.

All possible care was taken; we glanced over our shoulders, and then back at Dave as his hand reached into his pocket to produce the re-capper. It wasn't that complicated. It was just a plastic opener with a molded circle on the side in the negative shape of a bottle cap. The opener had a few more points of contact than normal—these were to prevent damage to the cap while opening. When the cap was placed in the circle and simple pressure was applied, it re-capped the bottle.

Then, like magic, Sister Mary Ann was there. She appeared out of nowhere—right behind Dave. Tommy warned him with a gentle nudge, just in time for him to slip the re-capper into his pocket. But instantly, we knew that the jig was up. Or was it?

She walked up to us, and simply smiled and said, "Good morning, boys."

"Good morning, Sister Mary Ann," we responded, with guilt-covered faces.

I did not get past the G-sound in good morning, but she didn't seem to notice, so I dropped back to an uncomfortable silence.

"What are you so busy with here?" she asked. She was engaged in the long, slow entrapment—the one where you start to play the game, just in case she doesn't know—but the down side was, to play the game you had to lie to cover-up, and then you got into even more trouble.

Before anyone else could answer, Tommy said with his usual carefree style, "Oh, Dave was just showing us something."

We were stunned by Tommy's betrayal. But Sister was very pleased, and suggested that Dave might like to show her, too. Dave reached into his pocket—but the re-capper wasn't there. He pulled out his jackknife—the one with two blades and a screw driver—a piece of string that the egg man used to tie egg cartons shut, and a folded up piece of paper. He laid them on the sidewalk and automatically pulled his pockets inside out—this was always the procedure when a kid was asked to empty the contents of his pockets. Which item could it be? The knife warranted no special scrutiny; all boys were expected—nearly required—to carry a knife, and the sisters often asked a boy for the use of his knife. If a boy didn't have one, while it was not a punishable failure, it certainly was a lapse of preparedness. No, it could be the carefully folded paper, but that only proved to be the note sent home the day before—with his mother's signature, just as requested. Was it forged? No, it was unreadable in adult cursive.

Tommy spoke again, "Dave was showing us the string. He said he would teach us to play Cat's Cradle at recess, but we all thought that was kind of a sissy game."

"Well, if that's right, then I guess you won't be needing it," she said.

As she reached out her hand for the string, Dave stooped down to get it in a kind of genuflection. She rolled it into a neat ball, somewhat disappointed that she did not discover something more sinister, and wondered if she would have gotten a better indictment had she separated the boys and interrogated them separately. Perhaps, but they would commit other infractions, and next time she would be more careful. The doors were open now, and we followed Sister back to school in complete silence as we looked around on the ground for the vanished re-capper.

About half an hour before the end of each school day, we walked in two rows down the hall to the restroom. This was the second of the only two opportunities we had each day; the rest of the time we learned to control our bodily functions as tightly as we controlled our thoughts. Upon reaching the bathrooms, the first two students in line held the doors open. Sister stood in the hallway looking in through the open doors—doors that the architect had foolishly designed into the floor plan for privacy. The first two to finish relieved the door holders. Only five boys could enter at a time—one for each urinal and the two toilets. We were the last class of the day, because some of the retards had a hard time holding themselves on the way home, and parents had complained. Most of the time the regular class was gone by the time we arrived, but on this day the timing was off—so the first two boys took control of the doors from the regular class and one boy was sent in to report how many boys were still in the bathroom.

"Three, Sister," came the count.

So, only Dave and I were permitted to enter. Dave took his place to the right of the door at the first urinal—next to Tommy from the regular class—and I took the last place on his other side. Without even looking down, Tommy pulled a white plastic object from his fly—the re-capper—and while maintaining every nuance of urinating, placed it into Dave's pocket without even moving his head or looking at the pocket. It was as if his hands were a wholly separate body, functioning without Tommy's awareness. Then he jerked his crotch backward in the familiar action of retracting one's dick into one's shorts. He zipped up and as he turned, he winked—but without winking—only somehow causing his eyes to sparkle. He washed his hands with soap and water—counting to 20 and rubbing fingers into fingers, just as we had been instructed but seldom did—wiped, crushed the paper towel into a small wad so it took up less space in the trashcan.

He walked out saying, "Good afternoon, Sister Mary Ann."

The Miracle of the Trailer Park

Mindy continued to work at Olson's Café, but her presence there weighed like a dark cloud on the customers. The ladies who came after Mass shook their heads and said, "She has to get over it. I lost two children, and I survived."

At first, the Olson men were relieved when she returned and said nothing when they asked her to stay to clean up, but she was like a corpse. It was always clear that she hated them, hated their power over her, hated their fat hands and their self-satisfied demeaning attitude, but now she simply didn't care. She was like a walking dead woman, without the ability to feel anything. Her lack of fear, loathing, or even contempt made her worthless to them, but they didn't know what to do with her. They didn't have the courage to toss her out with the trash the way they wanted to, so they moved her to the early shift and asked Tammy to return to clean up.

Tammy asked, very matter of fact, "Will I get more hours?"

"Sure," said Old Man Olson, and Junior grinned.

Joy stopped over and tried to talk to Mindy, but Mindy just sat, not responding. Then one day Joy said, "You know how you said that you wanted to paint the little bedroom and fix it up for a sewing room? Let's do it."

Actually, Mindy had planned to paint it pink, use it for a sewing room for a little while, and then it would be Jamie's room. Joy only talked about the sewing room.

"I ain't got money for that." Mindy replied. At least she answered Joy. Joy hoped this was the beginning of Mindy's return.

"Bess—the landlady—she'll give you the paint. She does that for everyone if they're willing to do the painting," Joy responded with certainty.

Joy knew that Mindy would never get around to asking Bess, so she stopped by and the two women devised a plan to help Mindy paint the room. It was not so much that the room needed to be painted, as that Mindy needed to do something—to change something—and the room could be the start. Bess brought over primer paint, a roller, and a paint pan, and told Mindy how important it was to first coat the walls with white primer over the dark blue paint. Then, when that was dry, she could put on the final two coats of whatever color she wanted. Bess left a paint chip card with her and told her that she could get the color that she wanted, as long as it was one of the standard colors on the card.

Bess stopped over at Joy's to let her know how it went. Joy called Mindy and told her she would be over the next day to help paint, so Mindy needed to pick a color and get the primer on.

Mindy hung up the phone and walked to the small room at the end of the hall. Without much, if any, thought she opened the can. The primer was, of course, white, so no decisions were needed. She didn't cover the floor; she didn't tape the windows. That would have taken too much effort. She simply poured the white creamy paint into the paint pan and rolled the roller into it. It was like a movie—not really her, just some woman painting, dipping the roller, and painting some more. When she finished two walls she sat down in the uncovered chair, right on top of the fabric and bags that she had put there months ago but had been incapable of moving, and began to cry. This was the first time she cried since that time in church, at the funeral that now she could not even remember. This time she wasn't only crying for the loss of Jamie. She knew deep down that she was also crying for the loss of herself. She had faded away and she knew it. The road had become nearly impassable. It was like walking waist high in the mashed potatoes and gravy that she served the lunch crowd. She couldn't move, she couldn't finish, couldn't wash out the roller like Bess had instructed her to, she wouldn't be able to go with Joy to get paint. No, everything was far too much of an effort. Even weeping, sleeping, eating were insurmountable tasks. She just sat with her eyes open. God, Mary, and Jesus had all abandoned her.

Then as she sat staring at the badly primed wall, she began to see—slowly at first, but then more and more clearly—the shape of the Virgin Mary in the drying primer. Clearly, it looked like our Lady of Fatima, only all in white with the blue undertones of the original paint. She just looked at it, and as the paint dried it became even clearer. Mary did love her, and she was being given a sign. She only had to let Mary love her. She had believed that she wasn't worthy of being loved, and that is why God took her baby, but that wasn't right. Mary loved her enough to give her a sign—a sign that she never dared to hope for.

God had not taken Jamie from her; God gave her baby a home in heaven. In the drying paint she could see Mother Mary holding Jamie, holding her in Heaven. Slowly, like water seeping into small cracks, she began to fill with the grace of God. His life entered into her as Mary smiled at her from the painted wall.

That entire night she stared; and then she began to pray. Not memorized prayers, but poetry that flowed from her heart.

The next day, Joy came over with her baby, barely able to hope that Mindy might actually have looked at the paint chips, and fearing as she did every time she went over that she might find Mindy dead. She still had the key Mindy had given her when she first started caring for Jamie, just in case she needed to get anything from the trailer. She kept it because she feared that someday Mindy would not come to the door—even when Joy knew she was home. She knocked and waited. The day was windy, and she felt vulnerable standing on the metal stairs that shook. She knocked again, and Mindy opened the door—wearing the same clothes she had on the day before. That was not unusual, but what was unusual—what was like a miracle—was the life that now filled her body. She was not dead, not confined in the white darkness of some hellish wasteland; she was present in the very moment.

She said, "Come in and see, see what has happened."

They went to the back room and Joy saw that there was primer on the wall. Joy thought, "So, the walls have gotten primed; is that all it took?"

"Do you see it?"

"Yes, you did an excellent job." But all the while Joy was thinking they would have to give this another coat; this primer didn't cover the dark blue so well.

"No, do you see the Virgin Mary?" Joy looked on the table, on the dresser for a small statue, the kind that is common in Catholic households.

"No, look at the wall," Mindy said, then pointed to the outline of Mary, her arm holding Jamie, and her legs and even one foot clearly shown. "She is surrounded by blue white clouds. She is in Heaven."

After Mindy pointed out the profile, Joy could kind of see it.

"Mary wants me to know that she loves me; and wants me to love her. She is taking care of Jamie in Heaven, where she is happy. It would have been a hard life on earth, with all the boys and men, and, you know, everything. So, now she is safe with Mary, and she sent me this picture—like a photo—so I would know."

Joy didn't know what to say. She could see the profile, kind of, but she had also seen lions in clouds even more clearly. But to see Mindy—yes, that was a miracle. The change was so dramatic, it was like turning on a light in a dark closet and finding a diamond ring.

"We must take a picture of it."

Joy thought that was a good idea, and said "Yes, let's take a picture before we paint the room, so you can show people."

"Paint the room?" said Mindy. "This is a sign from Mary; we can never paint the room."

She found her Brownie camera, the one that she got for her 16th birthday that had a flash attachment, got real far back in the room, and took three pictures, since that was all the bulbs she had. She had one photo left, however, so she asked Joy to step outside with her little baby and she took a picture of them in front of the trailer. They drove down to Trumm's Drug Store; the pictures would be ready in three days.

As they started driving back Mindy announced, "I think I will quit working for the Olsons. I don't like it there." Then, without thinking, she turned left at the light onto Highway 52 rather than right toward the HighView Park. She drove past the electric plant, between the lakes. There, next to the Lakeland Motel, stood Lakes Café—with a sign in the window that read "Help Wanted."

The woman who ran the café was a Protestant, but didn't belong to any church. She was divorced and had a son in the Navy. They did a good breakfast business with folks from the motel, and had a good lunch trade. She was known for big portions and low prices. The café was only a few years old. It had fluorescent lights, a plastic counter, metal chairs, and big glass windows. It was very inviting to the blue collar workers, and even to the few office women that worked at the Land O' Lakes milk powdering plant. It was close enough for morning coffee, and they stayed open for early dinner, but closed by 6:30 PM. Neither the after-mass ladies nor the after-church crowd from the protestant churches frequented it, so it was closed on Sundays.

Mindy went in while Joy waited in the car, and was hired on the spot. Then they went over to Olson's Café. At first Old Man Olson thought that Mindy had forgotten that this was her day off, but he quickly noticed something was very different about her. Before he could say anything, she said, "I am very sorry but I can't work here anymore. I won't be coming in tomorrow. I know it is wrong of me not to give notice, but I just can't do it anymore."

"Well, if you expect us to give you a reference, you are out of your mind," he automatically replied before it even occurred to him that he didn't want her there either.

"Oh, I would never ask you to give me a reference, I'm sure I don't deserve one," Mindy said as she turned and walked out.

The other waitresses were both amused and proud of her. In their hearts they wished that they could just walk out, but whatever chains held them there were fastened tightly, and they quickly went back to work.

When they got back to the trailer, Mindy said, "I have to do some wash so I'll be ready for my first day of work. But first, Joy, will you say the rosary with me?"

Neither of the women had ever been much for saying the rosary—they weren't even sure of the names of the various mysteries that each of the ten beads represented. They decided that it wasn't important to name the mysteries; they would just say a plain rosary. Mindy knew where hers was—she had carried it at the funeral—and so she led, and Joy recited the responses. The two women knelt before a badly primed wall, in a small room in a trailer park on Highway 29 North in Alexandria, Minnesota, and all of Heaven smiled down on them—one certain that Mary had touched her, and the other grateful that her friend had miraculously risen from the dead.

Where, O Where Have You Gone

Sister Gene was helping Father Reed with the preparations for Holy Week. Holy Week is the week before Easter and every day there are special services; the favorite among the altar boys was on Holy Saturday night. That is when the holy water and the baptismal water are made in a special candlelit ceremony. There was a lot more Latin than we heard the rest of the year, but our responses were fairly simple, and all the altar boys took part—so even if you messed up, it didn't matter much.

All the altar boys went down to the music room each Wednesday, to learn the new parts. Even though I was older now, I remembered being in that room with Sister Gene as some of my best times at the school, and I looked forward to being there with her again. Each classroom had a double locker inside the room that was for the teacher only. She kept paper and supplies on one side, and then had a place to hang her coat and put her boots on the other side. Because this was the music room, Mr. Larkins built wooden shelves on the coat side of the locker for more storage. Sister Gene kept the Holy Week books in the locker, and when we arrived, we were each to take one out and review the prayers. On the first day, she diagrammed on the blackboard where we were to walk and when each of us was to do particular things. Later, we went over to the church to practice it. The cross bearer would be Billy Johnson, but Stanley James would carry the campanile. While not as dramatic as being the cross bearer, it was a good job. The campanile was an umbrella-like thing with the pole coming off at an angle. The boy who carried it needed to be really strong and steady. He carried it behind the priest—but the center of the umbrella needed to be right over the center of Father's head while the priest carried the monstrance containing the host around the church. If Stanley did a good job, he might get to do it for the bishop's next visit, too. We all wanted to do a good job. This was the All-Stars of altar-boying.

The following Wednesday we had to draw the diagram. When Sister Gene called on us, we needed to remember what came next, and where we were supposed to be. We were very nervous, and kept whispering to each other.

"Is that right?"

"Yeah, I think so," was the most common, noncommittal answer.

As we got our books out of the locker, we saw another drawing on the inside of the door. We could see it, but Sister couldn't see it from where she was standing. Because we were lined up getting out books, we saw it for a long time. This one was very different. It was drawn in pencil, and everything was very clear. It was really bad. It was a picture of a priest with his cassock unbuttoned and a nun with her habit pulled way up showing her boobs. The priest's wiener went over and into the nun, right in her private parts. It even had the hair drawn in, the naughty hair. It looked like the artist started to draw a beard on the priest, and then tried to erase it, so only a dark smudge remained on the lower part of his face. The nun looked kind of fat, and had freckles all over her face and even on her boobs. She was wearing socks and shoes, and the artist drew straps just below her knees with tabs that buttoned into the tops of her stockings. I didn't know that was how nuns kept their socks up.

We were really scared during class, and didn't know if we should tell. No one did, and when we put the books away, everyone was very careful to do it quickly and not look at the picture. We were afraid that Sister Gene would see us look at it. It wasn't a sin to look at it the first time because we didn't know it was there, but if we looked at it again, then it would be. Even at the age of eleven, we understood these ethical distinctions. Sister Gene must have noticed that we were behaving strangely because she walked over to the locker. She turned bright red and her hands started to shake. She took the picture down, stared at it for a few seconds, and then folded it up and put it under the apron of her habit, into one of the three secret pockets that we all knew they had.

She looked up at the clock and said, "Oh, it's time for you to go back to your classes."

Actually, it was two minutes early, but we didn't care. We wanted to go back.

We thought that sometime that day another envelope would be delivered to our room, so that Sister Mary Ann could add the new drawing to the mounting collection. Why she was assigned to archive the sealed envelopes, I was never sure; we only knew that the other two were in her right hand drawer in a file folder without a label. But the envelope never came.

The next day Sister Gene wasn't at school; she was sick, and she didn't get any better during that whole week. Mrs. Beasley, the lady who started the tutoring program, substituted. In addition to her tutoring duties, she filled in from time to time. She wasn't a nun of course; she was a regular teacher and taught at Washington School before her son was born. It always seemed strange, when she substituted in his class, to have a mom for a teacher. Sister Gene wasn't better the following week, either. The adults said she had a nervous condition and couldn't get to sleep, maybe even had a nervous breakdown.

"Well, she always was very excitable and really active. That's what happens to that kind, you know," we heard the adults say.

"Oh yeah, you betcha," was the automatic response.

In the middle of the second week, a note went out to the parents of the third grade. We all heard about it the next day while we were waiting for the doors to open. Sister Gene's condition was worse, and she would not be finishing out the year. There wasn't another nun at the convent in Little Falls to take her place, so Mrs. Beasley agreed to stay on as a fulltime teacher until summer.

As for the Holy Week rehearsals, Monsignor Ward ran us through them himself. Father Reed was also gone. He had to go to Saint John's Abby for some very important projects of some kind that couldn't wait. Monsignor Ward said that we would do fine, and if we made any mistakes, not to worry. Jesus loves children, and thank God, we still qualified. In our innocence we never connected the simultaneous departures of Father Reed and Sister Gene and the pencil drawing. Nor did we realize how different this drawing was from the others.

Lent: the Season of Hope

Until Marcel Breuer designed St. John's Abby Church in 1958, Catholic churches for five hundred years included fourteen images of the Passion of Christ hanging on the walls. These are known as the Stations of the Cross. Each image depicted one of the stops along the Via Dola Rosa in Jerusalem, where the final events in Christ's life unfolded. They are a kind of meditative storyboard leading the worshiper from the condemnation of Jesus to his final burial in the tomb. Several times each week during Lent, the altar boys and the priests walked from one image to the next. The tallest boy carried the pole that is topped by a cross. This he held facing one image at a time, while the priest recited the story displayed at that Station, and the prescribed feeling that the parishioner should experience. One of the other boys carried an incense burner and the other a reserve supply of incense. While the ritual appeared to focus on death and sadness, the faithful knew that it was just a prelude to the hope that Easter brings. And in April of 1962, we had hope.

The Organization of American States ousted Cuba from membership—good, the no good Commies. Then Castro issued the Second Declaration of Havana, telling all Latin American people to rise up against imperialism. By imperialists he meant us. What a liar, we should blow him up. He ain't got no right to say bad things about us. Well, at least that guy the Russians shot down, Gary Powers, was home for Easter safe and sound.

But the reason Catholics were beaming that spring was because of our Catholic First Lady—and I don't mean Mary. I mean President Kennedy's wife Jacqueline. She just returned from India, and she stopped off in Rome to have a private talk with Pope John XXIII. The women all looked at the magazines, and this Easter they all looked just like her, piping on their jackets and pillbox hats on their heads. They wished that they all could be married to a good Catholic man like John, too. Of course, we didn't know then that while she was in New Delhi, J. Edgar Hoover was having lunch with her husband. He told John that the Bureau had 70 recordings of his telephone conversations with Judith Campbell. Judith Campbell was sleeping with him and two mob bosses, Sam Giancana and Johnny Roselli. Hoover also told John that these two guys—the two mob bosses—were helping the CIA in its efforts to kill Fidel Castro. But, of course, we didn't know any of this then. Then, the world was Technicolor perfect.

And soon it would be an even more perfect world. We were finally going to kill those Communists in Viet Nam—the ones I first heard about in church. Now they called them Vietcong guerrillas. I guess like King Kong, only he was kind of good, but these guys were just bad guys. They were Buddhists—Communist Buddhists—that's the worst kind of bad guy, you know. So, President Kennedy launched "Operation Sunrise" to kill all the Vietcong. He sent over two thousand of our guys, money, and lots of guns to do it, and planned to send a lot more. Yep, times were good, soon all the Commies would be dead—Castro, too. Then everyone would just be good guys, and elect good Catholic presidents, and be just like Americans. That would make them happy, you know, to be just like us. Because we were the best and we protected everyone.

The other thing that we didn't know, and probably would not have been alarmed by even if we knew, was that our missiles near the Soviet borders in Turkey became operational that Easter. Three years earlier, President Eisenhower warned that it would be a "provocative" step to put missiles there, analogous to the deployment of Soviet missiles in Mexico or Cuba. But he wasn't president anymore, and why should we care what the Russians thought? We were powerful and we had God on our side, and Jesus and Mary, too.

At the Wednesday service for the Stations of the Cross, two weeks before Easter, I carried the incense burner and Stanley James carried the cross. I loved it when we served together. I think Monsignor knew it, too, so he often put us together. I felt safe with Stanley James. If I didn't know what I should be doing, he was always able to cue me. Some of the other boys thought it was funny if someone didn't know what to do; they would never help you. You felt like you had swum too far out in the lake, and no one would give you a hand.

My mom and Aunt Eva were talking outside the church after the service when Aunt Eva showed mom some dark areas that had formed on her hands. She said that at first she just thought that she had bumped herself at the laundry or at the drycleaners. They had been so busy, what with everyone getting ready for Easter and such; and the hospital had been unusually busy for this time of year, too. But they didn't go away and she had always been a fast healer. They had actually gotten bigger, Eva said.

"Well, I think you ought to go to the doctor. You know, it could be something—you just never know," Mom said.

"Well, I'll ask one of them doctors at the hospital what he thinks. Maybe I'll ask the one who left the arm on the table that we found that time in the laundry. That way I can kid him about that, too. He will never live that one down," Eva chuckled, liking the idea that she had something on a doctor.

The last week of Lent all the statues in the church were covered with violet cloth, even the cross above the altar. It was a week of sorrow and no delights—like music or art—should be enjoyed. Those are things of this world, and we were to concentrate on the things of the next.

On Holy Thursday, the day of the last supper and the betrayal of Christ by Judas, mom asked Aunt Eva if she had seen a doctor yet about the spot.

"Yeah, he said I should come in, he might need to run some tests. I'm not really sure about it. You know the hospital has insurance for the nurses and the management staff, but we're not covered, so I need to find out how expensive it will be," she said, somewhat suspicious of whether she really needed "tests" or not.

"No, you need to go in right away, it will only get more expensive if you leave it. You remember what happened to Mrs. Elma. Because she let it go, she had to have an operation that cost over a thousand dollars. The doctor said if she had come in right away he could have just given her some pills, you know. So you'd best not wait."

The Sunday after Easter, Monsignor Ward had interesting news. Father Reed was assigned to St. Upsola parish, beginning immediately. St. Upsola was a very small parish that had been without a priest for over a year. A priest from Melrose drove there each Sunday to say Mass, but they had been praying that Bishop Bartholomew would soon assign a priest as a pastor. St. Upsola must have heard their prayers, because Father Reed was ready to take on this new challenge. The need was so great there that Father Reed was not coming back to Alexandria to say farewell. He was leaving right from St. John's.

Father Manner, a retired Benedictine priest from St. Johns, would fill in on a temporary basis until a new assistant was assigned from the graduating class of newly ordained priests. We all said a prayer for Father Reed at the end of the service.

Camp Willabee, Here We Come!

After nine Boy Scout pancake breakfasts, served after all three Sunday Masses, our troop finally had enough money for the trip to Camp Willabee. We each still had to pay $6.00, but most of the other costs were covered. On Sunday, July 8, 1962—the date that we had waited all winter for—we at last boarded a rented bus for the Boy Scout camp way up north near Brainerd. Most of the guys from the regular room were already on the bus by the time Stanley James and I from the retard room made it. About the only ones missing were Tommy Thompson and Dave. I'm not sure why Tommy didn't come; he was in Boy Scouts, but maybe he just decided not to go. Dave was really pissed. He had worked really hard, but couldn't go because he got the measles and was quarantined. His mom let him call us once a day—not at camp, of course, that would have been long distance, but at home before we left. We had a party line, so we were only supposed to talk for three minutes, to be considerate of everyone; but we talked for nearly ten minutes the day before we left. I suppose that was a venial sin; but Dave's mom didn't stop us, so I think it was probably her sin, not ours.

Anyway, now we were on the bus. Doug Anderson, a boy from the regular room, had a Japanese transistor radio with a little speaker that was playing "Itsy Bitsy Teeny Weenie Yellow Polka Dot Bikini." The song was considered a little off color three summers ago, but we rapidly became conditioned to the new music. Now, it was a summer classic that even the adults sang along with. Doug was sitting with his four really cool friends Robert Baker, Gary Boyd, Joey Turner, and Randy Hicks. Stanley and I couldn't hear the music real well, but we knew all the words. We weren't really sure if it was an impious song or not, but the adults were singing it, too, so we decided that it was O.K. It still made us giggle a little, and we held our fingers very close together saying, "I think it was this teeny weenie," and then laughed as we had naughty thoughts of how that might look.

Edward Woods was leaning over the seat by them, wanting to be a part of the group. But we knew they didn't like him. He was fat.

I remembered the first time I saw him. It was from our classroom window just before last Christmas. I was watching the parsonage when a black Caddy pulled up. It looked almost like the one Monsignor Ward drove but had out of state license plates. I later learned that the Woods moved here from Princeton, New Jersey. His dad was the new administrator at the Douglas County Hospital. His mom once taught journalism to undergraduates at Princeton University, but now she was just a mom. When I first saw him, I thought, "Now there's a retard, I suppose he will be showing up by the end of the week, and then we will have two fat kids in class." Peering from the window, my visual comparison still gave the fattest kid prize to Dale by 10%. But, to my surprise, he wasn't one of us after all. He was a regular kid—a fat regular kid. That just didn't seem right.

Terry said to him, "Get back, you stink," as he tossed himself back against the seat.

There were lots of other boys on board, 17 in all. This was the biggest troop ever. Some of the boys were a year older than us, so we didn't know them very well. Stanley James and I were sitting on the other side of the bus from the cool kids. Some of the kids looked a little scared, some were quiet, but most were talking. Officer Beecher moved over and sat in the seat in front of the cool boys. He started talking to them about the camp. He was a really great guy. I thought, "Gee, I wish I had a dad like him." My dad had never been to scout camp. He wasn't the kind of man to be a scout leader, or an usher in church; he just worked and then drank beer at night until he fell asleep on the sofa. He didn't even come to parent night at school. Mom came with Eve. While Stanley's dad was cooler than mine, he didn't like Catholic stuff. I think he was afraid he might catch it or something. But Officer Beecher was a policeman, a scout leader, and an usher in the church. He could talk to a guy; he knew what was cool, and what was stupid. You could probably even ask him stuff; you know, stuff that you couldn't ask a priest or your dad. Stuff you think you need to know, but no one really tells you. We couldn't really hear what they were talking about, and we didn't want to stare. I didn't want one of them to look at me and say, "What are you looking at retard?" That would make me feel really dumb, especially in front of Officer Beecher. We all wanted him to like us.

We didn't get to ride on a bus very often, so this was really neat. The scouts rented it from another troop. We were all talking about how great it would be if our troop had a bus; we would rent it, make lots of money, and then we wouldn't have to do all the pancake breakfasts.

Mr. Turner, Joey's dad, was only staying for the night. His wife was picking him up early Monday morning, so he could still get to work. Officer Beecher, our scout leader, was going to be with us all week. We didn't know the bus driver—he was from the troop that owned the bus, and was heading right back. Next Saturday our parents were coming up for Camp Day and they would take us home.

When we got to the campgrounds, Officer Beecher went inside the office to check in and find out where our campsite was. He soon came out with a small map, and we drove to the Crow Ridge site. It was one of the furthest sites from the lodge house; that meant it would be a real hike to swim, and for the meals that we didn't cook. But that was O.K.—the hike would be through the woods. We got to the campsite; the operators had already dropped off the tents. Time to set up. The two leaders showed us how to set up the tents by setting up their own. It didn't look that hard, just a big pole at each end, then staking out the sides. The tents didn't have floors and were sized to hold two cots.

"O.K., one tent for every two boys. Pitch them on the ridge so that if it rains you won't be in a puddle," Officer Beecher instructed.

We eagerly grabbed the remaining eight tents. Stanley and I grabbed the second to the last one, and Robert and Gary got the last one. We all rushed to get what we thought were really good spots. We started setting up the tents when we saw Edward still standing around, that lazy fat bastard. We knew that the scout oath prohibited swearing; but at camp, every boy used all his best words—the ones we could never say at home. It was kind of a guy thing to do, and I didn't even feel bad about it. Surprisingly, I also discovered that I didn't stutter when I swore.

It was a lot harder pounding in the stakes than it looked when Officer Beecher and Mr. Turner did it. I looked up and saw Officer Beecher coming out of his tent. He went over to Edward. Now the lazy ass was going to get it. Edward looked worried, almost like he was going to cry. He should, too. What a fat butt!

I couldn't hear what Edward said, but I heard Officer Beecher say, "Why didn't you say something before the bus left," then something else, but I couldn't hear it. Officer Beecher went back in his tent. Edward just stood there next to a folded cot. What do you know; he still wasn't going to help. Soon all the tents were up. The leaders called us together.

It was about four o'clock, and we were going to hike to the lodge. The first night we ate dinner with all the other scouts from the camp, and then afterwards we had a presentation of the camp rules by the operators; then back to the campsite. The next morning would be swimming. But before we started walking to the lodge, Officer Beecher said, "We seem to be a tent short, or a scout long. It seems that Edward has a cot, but no tent. Who wants one more in their tent?"

"Not us," I thought. "Not Edward, he had always treated us retards like shit." I was glad to see him standing there.

I heard a voice behind me trying to sound low, like a man's whisper. "Stinky Edward," it said. I wanted to laugh, but was too scared.

Then, damn it, Stanley said right out loud, without even asking me, "He can be in our tent."

Shit, shit, shit! Stanley, you asshole. How could you do this? You butt hole. Now the cool kids would never like me. I didn't say it out loud, but I thought it. Edward didn't look at any of us; he just carried his cot to our tent. He seemed to know right where it was.

On the hike to the dining room, one of the older boys started telling us about chores. "The worst is latrine duty. Two boys get that, and you have to clean the outhouse, but we don't call it an outhouse, at camp it is a latrine. Then there is fircwood. That is pretty cool. Camp clean up is not real good, but not that bad, just make sure everything is picked up and no trash is tossed around. The best part about that is if you catch a boy tossing something on the ground, you can report him, and then he has to do your job and his job, too, for two whole days. There are a bunch of other things, too. The best is camp record keeper. That boy hangs out with the scout leader and writes stuff down. He gets to carry a book on a strap that fits around his shoulder."

"That's what I want to do," I said.

"It don't work that way. All the jobs are written on little pieces of paper, and put in the scout leader's cap, and you have to pick one, but you can't look. Don't reach way down when you pick. That's where the latrine duty was last year."

We arrived at the dining room, which was kind of like a big garage building. It was something like the school cafeteria, and even had two ladies. I had to look twice to make sure they weren't the same two ladies who were at St. Mary's. We had sloppy Joes, green beans, and chips. It was better than school. We had Kool-Aid to drink instead of milk, but just one glass.

By the time we got back to our campsite, it was getting dark. We went to our tents. I wasn't sure what we were supposed to wear to bed, and no one really told us. At home in the summer, I just wore my underwear, but I didn't want to be the first to take my pants off, so I just waited to see. Edward finally just got into bed with his clothes on, so Stanley and I did the same. We didn't say anything that night. If fat ass Edward hadn't been there, we would have talked all night—talked about cool stuff, maybe even farted, and then laughed about it. But with fat ass there, we just closed our eyes and pretended to be asleep. In the night I heard him; he had the sniffles, and was sucking snot up his nose and then breathing in short silent gasps.

Yeah, he's probably too fat to breathe right at night, I thought. I knew Stanley was awake, I could tell by the way he was breathing—you know, pretend-to-be-asleep breathing. Stanley, why did you do this to me? Why, why, why? This was supposed to be fun! These thoughts kept playing over and over in my head.

The next morning, as predicted, chores were assigned, but not in the same way as last year. A list was posted on the message tree. We always had to check the tree before leaving camp and upon returning. The list was carefully written in perfect fifth grade cursive. I quickly looked for record keeper, but that was Doug Anderson. Oh well, I didn't write very well anyway. But, oh shit! I got latrine duty, and so did Edward and Stanley.

Stanley James asked, "Officer Beecher, why didn't we draw for chores like last year?"

"Are you questioning my authority, Stan? A scout never questions his scout master; is that understood?"

"Yes, I guess so," Stanley said.

"What did you say?" Officer Beecher snapped.

"Yes, sir," Stanley rephrased.

Before we could go swimming, we had to do our chores. For latrine duty, we had to mix one-half cup of bleach with a pail of water and wash the inside of the outhouse. There were only two brushes. The outhouse—I mean latrine—had a door in the center and then a shit hole on each side, so two boys could use it at the same time, facing each other. There were little turn knobs on the wall by each hole that you turned to read "Occupied." That way, if both the holes were taken, another boy didn't come in. This was different from most outhouses where the holes are side by side on the same bench.

On the outside, there was a metal trough with a pipe—that let the pee drain to the same place as the poop. It was all right to pee anywhere—well, not right in camp or by a tent, but just off a little in the woods—but if you wanted to pee at the latrine, that trough was the place for it. We had to wash the trough, too. We decided that we would take turns and rotate each time. First, two of us did the shit holes; then we gave the brushes to the third boy, and he could use one or both to wash the pee trough. While the trough was cleaned, the others would add new toilet paper rolls, if they were needed. A little sign hung on the inside of the door that said, "The job is never done, until the paper work is complete." We laughed every time we read it. We knew what it meant.

We ran back to the tent to put on our bathing suits. With all the cots in the tent, it was really crowded. We put our stuff under the cots at night, and then on top of the cots during the day. Edward's cot was the middle one. He sat at one end to put on his bathing suit, and Stanley and I sat at the other end of ours—that way he didn't see our wieners. When Stanley and I came out of the tent, most of the boys already had their trunks on. I had forgotten my towel and had to run back. Edward was still sitting on the end of his cot with his back to me.

"You'd better hurry up," I said. But he just sat there.

I ran out and got in line. Officer Beecher counted. "Who's missing?" he asked.

"Edward," I said. "He's still in the tent."

"Get out here, Edward," Officer Beecher called.

The boys were all in line. I had never noticed before—because most of the time it was just Stanley and me who went swimming together—but our trunks looked really dumb. Doug had a real cool swimsuit. It was solid black, and wasn't like our badly fitting shorts. It was made of a stretchy, shiny material. It looked like it was made out of the same kind of stuff his mom wore—expensive. His mom always looked kind of like a movie star. Even when my mom looked like one of the women in the magazines, she looked like the ones in the coffee advertisements. Doug's mom looked like the ones in the cigarette ads. She wore tight skirts, blouses with the collars turned up, and silver jewelry and sunglasses. Her hair was black and down to her shoulders, sometimes with a scarf in it, but not around it like the girls wore. She always wore high heels, even at the Red Owl. His dad was cool, too. He wore sunglasses. They had a boat and lived on Lake Carlos, where the rich summer people lived. But they lived there all year round in a big house with a screened-in porch. I saw Doug there once, with his mom, when I rode my bike past. She was sitting in a wooden chair on the screened-in porch, with her sunglasses on and wearing a black swimsuit, made of the same material as Doug's. That's how I knew. I think they must shop down in the Twin Cities. I had never seen that kind of suit in Alexandria.

Of course, mom bought mine at the church rummage sale—no reason to waste money on something I would just outgrow. I wondered if I was wearing one of the other boy's old suits, and if he would recognize it, and if so, would he say anything?

Officer Beecher walked to our tent. He pulled back the flap, and Edward was still sitting there. I don't think he had put his suit on yet.

"Get it on now!"

Officer Beecher stood there holding the tent flap open as we watched Edward pull his pants down and put his suit on. We could see his huge butt and I heard the boy who was trying to make his voice sound low like a man's whisper, "Edward has a shiny, stinky butt."

Everyone laughed; that is, everyone but Stanley. Stanley was being such a shit. Why did he like stinky butt? I was supposed to be his friend. I thought the only reason we got stuck with latrine duty was because he let stinky butt stay in our tent.

Finally, he came out. His swimsuit had a cloth belt on it. Maybe that was the way all fat swimsuits are made, I thought.

We started hiking for the lake; it was by the lodge dining hall and other buildings. As we walked, Edward was behind me, and further behind him I could hear the kid who was still trying to sound like a man, saying every few minutes, "Edward has a shiny, stinky butt," in a whisper so low that it sounded more like a thought than words. After a while it wasn't funny anymore, but he kept saying it anyway.

During our week at camp, we were supposed to complete the work needed to advance to our next level badge, or on merit badges if we were already First Class level. The first year boys at camp could move from Tenderfoot to Second Class this year, and then next year on to First Class. Someday we might even be Eagle Scouts. Well, maybe; but not many boys made it that far. To earn the Second Class badge, we had to do a whole array of things, including camp improvements, knot skills, basic first aid, and cooking. Then on Friday we each had to pass a test of our knowledge of scouting rules, history, goals, pledge and motto. This was a verbal test.

Each boy was called into Officer Beecher's tent. I was the third boy to be called in. Doug sat next to Officer Beecher on his cot. I sat on the other cot. It was carefully made up, and everything in the tent had been carefully placed at right angles. After ten questions, Officer Beecher marked "passed" after my name, and laid the clipboard on the cot. I looked down at it and saw that all the other boys tested so far were also marked "passed." But then I noticed that Doug was last on the list, and had not yet been tested.

Without thinking, I said, "Doug shouldn't hear all of our answers before he takes the test."

Immediately I knew that I shouldn't have said it.

"What do you mean?" Officer Beecher said, not appearing to be upset at all.

"Oh, I just thought that it might be better for him not to hear what the other scouts say, before he is tested."

"Are you implying that Doug would cheat? That he would let your answers influence what he says? I can tell you right now that Doug is an honorable scout. He's the kind of scout you can only hope to be."

I had one last chance to save my badge. "Yes, sir, I know that, sir. I was completely wrong. That was a really un-scouting thing to say. I hope that Doug will forgive me."

"We will discuss it later. I will leave it totally up to him to decide if you will pass." He had not raised his voice like my dad would, if he were mad. No, I guess he knew he was right, so he didn't have to. I had to think hard whether I had ever been mean to Doug. Gee, I hoped not.

As I left the tent, I heard the falsely deep voice whisper, "Hey, are you going to stinky, shiny butt's tent?"

I turned. It was Joey.

"So you're the whispery voice. That's really cool. How do you do it?"

"You like sleeping with stinky, shiny butt?" Joey asked with a look of both puzzlement and distain, which prepared him for several possible responses.

"Hell, no. I hate it. He farts and everything." He didn't really, but I needed to dramatize my dislike of the loser.

"Why did you want him in your tent?" Joey continued the inquisition.

"I didn't. Stanley asked him. I wish he would get the hell out," I responded, feeling that I had gained some credibility.

"Why don't you move? You could bunk with me. Doug has to stay in Officer Beecher's tent, because he is the record keeper and has to write down anything that might happen at night. You know, like tent stake pulling, and shit like that. So his cot is free."

That would be really cool. "I have to tell Stanley, but I don't think he would mind; after all, he would still have stinky, shiny butt Edward."

"Yeah, the two losers together," Joey said with a sneer.

"O.K. I'll be back," I said, filled with both hope and excitement.

I ran off thinking, what the hell, they'll have more room without me. And what the hell, he chose to let stinky Edward in the tent. What choice did I have? I can get away from these losers—and maybe the cool kids, the kids from the regular room, will like me. Maybe if I start hanging around with them, who knows, they might even put me in the regular room. That would be so cool—to be a normal kid, not a retard—I thought as I walked with brisk steps to our tent.

When I got to the tent, Stanley was alone, sitting on his cot, reading up for his test. There was one more scout scheduled, and then Stanley at 2:30.

"Stanley, I know who the voice is. You know, the cool whispering man voice. It's Joey. He is really cool. He just does it, makes it low and kind of almost impossible to hear, but you still do," I started the conversation, thinking that this jewel of information would impress Stanley James and assure him that even as I became more a part of the in-crowd, that I would still toss him tidbits of cool stuff. He could start admiring me for a change.

"How did you find out?"

"I was talking to him. He did it for me. He is really a cool guy."

"I don't think so. I think I'm going to let Officer Beecher know, so he will stop him."

"Stop him? No!" I said, alarmed.

"Edward is in the shit house right now crying," Stanley said, looking at me with one of his God-dammed frowns.

"He's always in there; and he puts up both signs when he is in there. I think he is afraid that someone is going to see his little wiener, or his stinky, shiny butt," I said, panicked by his stubbornness.

"No, he's in there crying; he's afraid. I need to tell Officer Beecher. Joey has to stop," he whispered, half talking to me, and half to himself.

"No, you don't get it. Joey said I could share his tent, and I want to. If you tell Officer Beecher, you will ruin everything! Joey will know I told you. I didn't tell you so that you could snitch on him. Don't be an asshole. I want those kids to like me. I don't give a damn about what stinky butt thinks. No one likes him, and if you tell, no one will like me either."

"I'm sorry. I have to. He just has to stop."

"Damn you, Stanley James. I hate you. I hate you! I hate you!!"

It was Stanley's turn; he went to Officer Beecher's tent. I ran to the latrine. Sure enough, both "Occupied" signs were up.

"You're an asshole, Edward," I shouted. "I wish you would fall in that hole and die. I wish you were dead like the frog Randy smashed yesterday."

Then I went to Joey's tent. I thought if I told him first, maybe I could still be his tent-mate. Maybe his friend Doug would still let me get my badge.

After I told Joey, he said, "Why in the hell did you tell him?"

"I'm sorry, I didn't think he would tell. I'm really sorry."

"Well, no way are you going to be my tent-mate. You had just better watch it. Maybe, just maybe, you will drown or something."

That night was the big bonfire and the badge ceremony. We put on our scout shirts and went to the dining hall. I didn't tell Stanley that I told Joey; and he didn't tell me if he had really told Officer Beecher, or not. We didn't say anything. We just walked, and as we were walking up toward the lodge I heard Joey's man whisper.

"Stinky butt will be the first to die, then his tattle-tale friends." Then he repeated, "Stinky will be the first. Stinky will be the first. Stinky will be the first." I didn't sit with Stanley or Edward; yet no one would sit with me. After dinner, the director of the camp stood up and talked to us about the history of the American Boy Scouts. It was started by Lord Robert Baden-Powell. He was British, and Mr. Baden-Powell wrote the first Scouting book. He was a war hero from South Africa. He killed a bunch of black natives and Dutch people and made sure it was safe for the English. Then, a millionaire from Chicago, William Dickson Boyce, was visiting London in 1890, and a boy carrying a lantern guided him. When he offered the boy a shilling, the boy said, "No, sir, I am a scout. Scouts do not accept tips for good deeds."

I guess he thought he could save a lot of money if he didn't have to tip anymore, so he started the Boy Scouts in America. I'm not sure why we have Boy Scout Camp, he didn't really say. But after he was done, we marched down to the big campsite by the edge of the lake. No one camped there; it was just for the ceremonies. Tonight, we got our badges. That is, if we passed everything. Man, if Stanley told, then Joey wouldn't get his, and he would want to kill me. Our moms and dads were coming the next day, and any boy who didn't have a badge to show for the week—well, he was just a loser.

It took a long time to start the ceremony. We raised the flag of the United States. I tried to see if it had fifty stars, or if it was the old one, but couldn't tell. Then we raised the flag of Minnesota; then the Boy Scout flag. The logs were carried in, and each of the older boys placed a log on the fire and said something.

But I was just worried, thinking, will Doug let me pass? Why did I say something so stupid? Why would I care if he used my answers? Scouting was what was important, not whether Doug was cheating. Scouting is more important than worrying about asshole stinky Edward. If he wants to stay in the shitter all day, that's his business. Stanley should be thinking about scouting, not some stinky butt. Oh damn, if Joey doesn't get his badge my ass is grass. Why did I tell Stanley? "Please God, let me and Joey get our badges. I'll never tell on a Scout again, and I will never accuse a Scout of anything, not even murder."

At last, they began to call the names for Second Class badges. Later would come the First Class, the Merit Badges and then the Star, Life, and finally the Eagle, if any, would be given out. They began calling our troop for Second Class. Robert Baker, Gary Boyd, Joey Turner, Randy Hicks, Doug Anderson; and at last I was called. I didn't notice, but Stanley James was not called.

When they handed me my badge, the camp leader said, "We understand that you have some problems, but Officer Beecher asked us to give you a chance. I hope you will not forget this important lesson. Learn to respect those in authority. They have been placed over you to guide you on the right path. Do you understand?"

Nothing had been said to any of the other boys. I quickly said, "Yes, sir," and was grateful to God for sparing me the shame of not getting a badge. I even remembered to thank God. "Thank you God for giving me the Boy Scouts, and Officer Beecher, and for making Doug so cool as not to flunk me. Thank you, God. Thank you, God." It was important to remember to thank God, because if you didn't, He would get you when you least expected it.

As I walked back to my place, I glanced down at my badge with the Scouting slogan, "Be Prepared," embroidered on it. Then I saw Stanley James sitting alone, trying to look like he wasn't hurt or ashamed. I didn't want to look at him. He must have told on Joey. What an unScouting thing to do, trying to get a good Scout in trouble. He didn't deserve to be Second Class until he learned what honor was, I thought. Man, I just made it, and I wasn't going to blow it now.

That night, walking back, I was hoping that Joey would ask me to stay in his tent, but he didn't say anything, so I went back to mine. Stanley didn't say anything either. I felt like I didn't fit in anywhere.

That night I hated Stanley James with all my heart, because I was still sleeping in the same tent as stinky butt Edward. I wished he were dead.

The next day, Saturday, was the last day of camp and Parent's Day. The Scouts' moms and dads would drive us home. Mom and Eva came; our dads had to work. Mom wasn't real sure if Eva was going to be able to make it. She had been to the doctor, and she was really sick. The spots on her arm were cancer. The doctor told her that he wasn't sure what they could do. Sometimes it just stopped—went away by itself. Sometimes people thought that was a miracle. But he said they didn't know why, it just happened. They could try to amputate her arm, but she didn't want that. She wouldn't be able to work. Anyway, she was here today and it was going to be a fun day.

There were all kinds of water games—first canoeing, which we had really only done once, but now we were racing. I was glad when we picked teams by drawing colored balls. Gary Boyd and I were together. We didn't win, but we didn't lose. Then the swimming contests started. Matches were made by drawing names and while groups of scouts raced, the rest of us could swim over by the floating raft, the one with the diving board. Stanley and I seemed to have silently made up in the water. The day was sunny, and all that had happened seemed to have evaporated. Maybe it was because Edward was not around. Then I heard his name called. Who is he going to race against? I thought. Whoever it is will beat the heck out of him.

They called his name again. Where was he? Probably in the shit house, I thought, probably crying. After the third time he was called and there was no response, we were ordered out of the water to line up for a safety check. We had done this many times before, but always at the beginning or at the end of a swim. We counted off. He was gone.

"Has anyone seen him?"

The leaders ran off to check the restrooms. Edward's dad and mom ran forward.

"Edward," his dad called out loudly. "Edward! Edward! Edward!"

His mom, now almost in a panic, started screaming, "Have you seen him?"

"Life guards in the water. Start the cross search," the scout leader said, loudly but trying to maintain his calm.

He kind of sounded like the sergeant in an army movie, just when they are about to attack the Japs, but they know that they are not going to win. The older boys, who had earned their lifesaving badges moved into action. The criteria for the badge included successfully completing practice searches. Now they knew that they were actually searching for a person, or more likely a body. They walked three feet a part. When the water became deep, they began to swim very slowly—together in a row, with their heads underwater, and their eyes open.

Edwards's mom began to scream. "No, no, Edward," and ran into the water. Neither she nor Edward's dad knew how to swim. He ran in after her. They stood there, thigh high in water. He held her and she slumped. She knew what they were looking for; she knew that every summer boys died in Minnesota's lakes. Not at camp, but in the lakes when no one was looking. There seemed to be an evil spirit in the lakes that stole children when no one was looking. It took but a moment of inattentiveness, just a fragment of conversation, and a boy or a girl was gone; only a wet body and a drenched soul remained.

Then the voice of a boy—not more than fifteen—broke the silence. "I found him. He's hiding under the raft. He's OK. Just hiding."

A scoutmaster swam out. There was a conversation, and then on shore some boys started to laugh. Just a little laugh—kind of like when a joke is told and only one person gets it, then it is repeated or explained, and then the laughter flows like a ripple.

"What, what is it?"

"He's OK. Some boys depanted him underwater, and now he is hiding."

The scoutmaster came ashore with a grin of relief and that "boys will be boys" look. He told Edward's parents that he was fine. Then he picked up a towel and swam back out, handed it to Edward and swam back to shore with him. As Edward started to swim back, all the boys started singing, "It was an itsy bitsy teeny weenie yellow polka-dot bikini, that HE wore for the first time today," and then breaking out in wild laughter as we competed the line "from the blanket to the shore."

Edward's mom and dad put him in their car. His mom looked back at us. The look on her face was just like the one worn by a fat Jewish Polish woman that we saw in an old newsreel at school about the war. You know, the one about the Germans invading Poland or something. She looked at us, just that way, like we were Nazis or something. We weren't Nazis. We were Boy Scouts, American Boy Scouts. Someone should have run right up to her and told her, but no one did, we just kept singing. I made my voice real high to be funny, and Joey made his real low. I felt like part of the Scout Pack. At last, I was fitting in like a real kid.

We never saw Edward again; they moved to New Jersey. I thought that New Jersey was where all the communists lived anyway. I think we heard that on Hubert Humphrey's "Report from Capital Hill," which we sometimes saw the end of on Saturday mornings as we waited for the half-hour of cartoon broadcasting. Yeah, that was it; they were communists that had come to Minnesota to infiltrate us. He ran the hospital, too; maybe when the Russians bombed us he would have hidden all the medicine so that we would all die. You could never be too careful, those communists were everywhere. It was better just to trust good guys, guys like Scouts that you knew were good Americans. I guess we showed them. But now they were back in New Jersey, maybe meeting in their communist cells making new plans to invade us or something.

Recapping

The rest of that summer rolled by slowly. Dave recovered, and as none of the cool kids invited me anywhere anyway, I fell back in again with Stanley James and Dave.

August 24th was a wonderful Friday morning. The day was bright, but not too hot. Stanley got all his chores done at the drycleaners; there weren't a lot of clothes brought in. The new Viking Cleaners was getting more and more of the town's business. I was kind of glad, because Stanley could hang out with me more. The rush at the gas station would pick up tomorrow when the tourists got ready to start their long journey home—cars packed with dirty clothes, fish, memories, and exposed film. Most of the tourists didn't like to have their film developed in town. It was cheaper, and they believed more reliable, in the city. We decided to go over to Dave's house. Maybe we could sit in the garage, in his boat, and smoke cigarettes and talk—talk endless hours of talk—as we tried to understand the world that we were discovering each day.

Dave was home; we sat on the porch first and talked. We talked about how Marilyn Monroe was found dead in bed.

"I heard she was naked," Dave said. "Totally naked."

"I heard that wasn't her real name—just a made up name. Her real name was Norma Jean."

"In Hollywood you can just make up stuff and be anybody you want to be. It's kind of a pretend place," Dave said with a lot of authority.

I wished I lived there; a place where I could just make up stuff and it would be that way. If we lived there, we would have cool names, and we would tell everyone we were in the regular room, and that's where we would be, not retards anymore at all.

Then we talked about maybe walking down to the park and hitting a softball; then about going down to the Red Owl and getting some baseball cards. Then when we were sure that no one was listening or watching us anymore, we walked back to the garage. Just as we got there, we saw Tommy—walking as carefree as anyone. We didn't even notice that he was carrying something—our eyes were fixed on his greeting and his pleasant smile.

"Hi, guys. Do you want to drink some beer?" he said, just like he was asking us if we wanted some bubble gum.

Only then did we look down and notice that he was carrying a six-pack of Hamm's Beer.

Without waiting for our response, he walked into the garage by the side door. We followed, grinning with mixed fear and joy. We were fortunate that no one saw us enter the garage—our bodies were bent and we were glancing over our shoulders and every cell in our bodies shouted guilt and delight. When we got inside, Tommy was already sitting in the boat.

"Dave, get the re-capper," Tommy ordered.

"OK." Dave crept back out, looking like a thief planning to steal the royal crown jewels. He returned out of breath.

"Did anyone see you?" I asked.

"No, I don't think so; Mom is in the basement doing laundry."

Tommy just smiled. I think he was smiling at our innocent clumsiness. Not in a way that suggested he was superior to us, but more like a smile of envy. I think he envied our naive innocence, the thrill of our fear, and most of all, our ability to tremble.

"Hey, where did you get the beer?" I asked.

"I took it from the Sisters' refrigerator. They pay me 50 cents to mow the lawn. I just got done when they came back from the grocery store, so I went to the back door to tell them I was done, and they said, 'Oh come in, we're in the living room.' I walked in, and Sister Rose handed me three quarters. I knew it was three because they weigh more than two, but I didn't look at them. After all, if I looked at them, that would mean that I didn't trust them, wouldn't it?"

"I guess so," Dave agreed.

"So, I just put them in my pocket. They wanted me to look down so that I would notice the extra quarter tip. Then I would say, 'Thank you so much,' and all that. But I didn't, and they couldn't say, 'Why don't you count it?' I mean why would they cheat me?" Tommy continued.

"I know they were disappointed when I didn't look. Like in a restaurant, when people leave a good tip, they will look back over their shoulder to see if the waitress notices when she starts clearing the table. They want to see the gratitude on her face and feel powerful. They hate it when the bus boy just tosses it into a box to be shared at the end of the day. That's what the nuns wanted, to make me grateful. I thanked them, but not for the tip. Then as I walked back out, I opened the refrigerator door, just to see what nuns eat, and I saw the beer, so I took it. I didn't think about it. I wasn't sure what I would do with it. But see, it all worked out—I saw you guys. Now we can all have a beer or two."

He calmly opened the beer, just like my dad did when offering a beer to a friend, and we all clicked the bottles together and began drinking. Drinking in the shade, sitting in the boat in the garage, with spiders crawling up the glass of the dirty windows and the faint smell of gas mixed with oil for the outboard motor accenting the air.

"Man, it was some year at school," I said.

"Why do you think Sister Mary Ann is, well, the way she is?" Tommy asked in a way that you could tell wasn't just casting about for a topic. He wanted to know, wanted to understand, and he thought we might be able to give him clues to help him later decipher this mystery.

Dave responded reflexively—before the last syllable even left Tommy's mouth, "That's easy, because she's a bitch."

We smiled, but the question was not a casual one, and deserved more than a cliché in response.

"No, I don't think that's it," said Stanley James. "I think she is like the old God—not the pagan gods that the heathens worship—but like the Jewish God, the one in the Old Testament. He never just says, 'Ok, that's ok,' when something goes wrong. I mean you can't just say 'Excuse me' to Him. I think He likes to punish people, but He can only do it if they do something bad, because He's God, and to punish someone who didn't do something bad, that isn't right."

Stanley James then looked at the dirt covered window. The layers of encrusted grime filtered the light so that it descended evenly across his face. He looked like a young Dionysus, or Plato sitting under the holy oaks in some ancient time. Of course, we weren't even outside, we were just sitting in a filthy garage in a fishing boat with peeling blue paint. He began, "Suppose, I mean just suppose that in the beginning, before there was even a world, there were a lot of gods? I know it is heresy to really think that, and heresy is a sin, a really bad one. But just suppose that there were lots of gods, and suppose some of them didn't like each other very much because they were made in different ways and believed in different stuff, kind of like we don't like the Protestants and they don't like us. Suppose that one of the gods was named Jehovah and another was named Jesus. Maybe they didn't really have names yet, but just pretend they did. Suppose Jehovah believed in justice, and that everything had to be paid for, so that if you did something wrong—even a little something—you had to pay the price for it. Then suppose there was Jesus who just loved, who was just love, and he didn't charge anything, and if you hurt him he just filled the hurt in, and didn't make you pay the price for what you had done.

"Now, if Jehovah didn't like Jesus because the other gods liked playing with him better, he might come up with a plan. Jehovah might say, 'Look here Jesus; I'm going to make people. I'm going to make them in our image, I'm even going to give them free will like us, because if they didn't have free will they wouldn't be able to chose how they want to live. How could they? And that wouldn't be fair.'

"Jesus would think that was a good idea—the more beings in the universe, the more beings to love. He might really like the idea and think, that Jehovah is a really nice god, and that they could be good god-friends—love and justice—that even sounds like a couple of pals. I think a lot of people would like to see that on earth, too.

"So Jehovah made man and put him in the garden and everything was cool. Jesus would come by every now and then to look at them, but they didn't belong to him so he couldn't touch them or anything—

just looking—like at a store. He asked 'How long are those people you made going to live?'

"'Forever, unless they chose not to.'

"God waited for them to do something bad so he could punish them, but then he realized that he had forgotten to make up the rules. So he decided to make a rule against eating the fruit from just one tree and told Adam. Adam then told Eve, 'God said that if we eat of that tree we will die, so keep your hands off it.'

"Then nothing happened. God watched and watched some more, but nothing happened. So he said, 'Well, I can't make them eat it, but I can send a little temptation, that's fair. That way they are still choosing.' He thought, 'I will send the snake, they're real good talkers.' Nowadays snakes can't talk, but back then, all the animals talked, and the snakes were the best because they had two tongues. Talkers are good at getting people to do things, you know."

I thought of Tommy's dad. He was a good talker, and he got people to buy cars. I wondered if the snake had dimples like Tommy. That would have helped, he could have talked them into eating it.

"The snake decided to talk to Eve because if she got mad at him, she wouldn't smash him. Adam was a man, so he might have said, 'I'm not listening to you,' and just stepped on him. But ladies are polite and will listen to sales people.

"Well, it worked, and she ate it and didn't die, so she gave some to Adam. She said, 'God lied, I didn't die.'

"Then Jehovah said—kind of mean but pretending not to be—'Oh my, what have you done? Now I'm going to have to punish you.' He sent them from the garden and sent bad weather so that they would have to work, and they had to die, too. Then he said, 'I like these rules,' so he made up a whole bunch more. He made up rules like you can't eat meat on Friday, can't mix milk with meat—all those rules that don't make any sense. Then he set up kings and popes and told them to make up even more rules. With all these rules, men were getting punished all the time. Sometimes they couldn't even keep track of all the rules, so God would send a flood to kill most of them, but not all. If he killed them all, then he wouldn't have anyone left to punish, so he always made sure a few lived.

"Then Jesus came by again and saw how sad the people were. He started to cry and said, 'What are you doing?'

"'I'm only being just. I made these people. They're mine.'

"'Yes.'

"'I gave them free will, didn't I?'

"'Yes.'

"'So they owe me their lives, don't they?'

"'Yes.'

"'They owe me everything, so they have to do what I say, even if I tell them to kill their own sons. They have to do it, because I'm their boss.'

"'I guess so.'

Stanley James took a swallow from his beer, a ray of light hit the edge of the bottle and it sparkled in the light. He continued, "Jesus couldn't find any mistake in the way God was thinking, so he had to admit that he wasn't doing anything wrong. He looked at the people and he was still sad, so he made a deal with Jehovah.

"He said, 'What would it cost me to get those people?'

"'Well,' said Jehovah, with the kind of a smile that someone gets when they know you really want something. 'First, they have free will, so you can only have the ones that choose you for a god rather than me. Second, they owe me their lives, so you would have to die for them.'

"Jesus looked at the people and said, 'I'll do it. But how? I can't die; I'm a god, and we don't die.'

"'Well, you will just have to turn yourself into a human, and then you will be able to die.'

"'How would I do that?'

"'You will have to be born, but then you will also be one of the guys I made. So, you will have to follow my rules, too. So I'll be your boss. I'm fair, so I'll tell you exactly what they will do to you if you turn yourself into one of them—they will kill you. That's how you will pay the price for those ungrateful beings, you will be killed by their hands. Besides, it wouldn't be right for a god to kill another god.'

"Jesus of course still did it.

"He became a man, and sure enough, we killed him. Then after he was good and dead, Jehovah looked down and couldn't believe what he saw. Jesus was dead, but he was living in some of the people. Deep inside them they didn't care about justice, they would rather have love. And Jehovah couldn't do anything about it, because of the deal. Not everyone chose Jesus, but everyone could if they wanted to. Sure, sometimes they get killed and stuff, just like Jesus. But just like Jesus, the most important part of them continues to live in other people, and so they never really die."

We sat there real quiet for a while and just drank our beer. Dave got out the cigarettes from the secret hiding place behind a roll of insulation. We lit up. I didn't want to talk about God anymore. I wanted talk about something that wouldn't make my head hurt. "What kind of a boy do you think drew that dirty picture of the nun and the priest in Sister Gene's room?" I asked.

"I think it was the same kid that drew the other ones. I think it is some Protestant boy who sneaks into the school at night," Dave said.

"Man, what a dumb kid he must be," I said.

Tommy, who up to now had only been listening, took a long drag on the cigarette before passing it to Stanley James, and said, "I don't know about the other dirty pictures, but I think that the pencil one was drawn by a smart boy—the kind of boy who sees things, who notices things that other people don't see. Things like buttons that aren't all buttoned on a priest's cassock, and wrinkles in a nun's scapular. Or the way people look down and check themselves to see if they have dropped something on the front of themselves, and then kind of brush with their hand as if there was lint, but there really wasn't—as if they had been just checking, but didn't want anyone to know. A boy like that, he might have drawn that picture, but not the other ones. He might have drawn it just to see."

"To see what?" Dave asked a little harshly.

"To see what would happen, to learn how adults react, what they do," Tommy said.

"Why would he want to do that?" Dave asked again.

"Well, you see, someday I—we are going to be like them. When we are, we're going to have to be smarter than them, or they'll become our bosses, they'll have control of us. That's what they all want, you know. They want to be bosses, have power over each other, the same way they boss us kids around."

"Why can't we all just be the bosses of ourselves?" Dave asked.

"I don't know, maybe it can be that way. I don't want to grow up and still be bossed around. So, that's why I watch, so I don't get caught when I'm big," Tommy said, talking differently than I had ever heard him. He wasn't the happy boy I thought I knew. He sounded like a man in a sad movie—the kind grown ups watch, and kids hate.

"Caught by whom?" Dave asked expressing the confusion that we all now suffered—confusion brought on not only by Tommy's conversation, but also by the beer and the cigarettes.

"By the adults—the ones that want to be my boss. Haven't you been listening?" Tommy said, a little pissed off.

"Sure, let's never get caught. Not for drinking beer, not for smoking cigarettes, not for talking about stuff that we're not supposed to. Let's never get caught," said Dave.

Then Dave said, "I have to pee."

Tommy handed him an empty beer bottle and said, "Pee in this."

Dave did. In fact we all did. We talked and drank and peed in beer bottles for the rest of the afternoon, and the conversation dissolved into even more confusion.

Finally, Tommy opened the door and grabbed the garden hose. He started mixing the pee like a chemist, mixing dark honey-colored smelly pee with the light nearly clear pee. Then he topped off each of the beer bottles with the hose, picked up Dave's re-capper, and sealed each bottle, carefully placing them back into the six-pack.

"Time to return the nuns' beer," he said.

He stepped out; we looked at each other, crawled out the door, and lay in the grass next to the fence that separated Dave's house from the nuns'. We were afraid to look. But we could hear the back screen door open and then Tommy's voice calling, "Sister."

Oh crap, he's going to confess. Shit! He's going to tell on all of us, just to save his soul a few days in purgatory, I thought.

"Oh yes, Tommy," said a woman's voice. I think it was Sister Rose.

"Sister, you paid me too much. I know I only had a dime in my pocket when I came over here, but now I have eighty-five cents. You must have made a mistake, so I came back."

"No, we meant to give you a tip. You work so hard, and do such a good job. Please, we want you to keep it," she said.

"Thank you," Tommy said. "I've been hoping that I can earn enough so that I can give ten dollars to church this year, and I think I'm going to make it."

He left, and we heard him walking down the street whistling. I thought he knew we heard him, too.

We were afraid to move, afraid that Sister Rose was still in the kitchen. Then we heard her say, "I found the beer. It was sitting right here on the back porch. Sister Marie's sweater fell on it."

Another voice said, "And Sister Mary Ann was so certain that she had put it in the refrigerator. She is always so sure."

"Well, we'll just put it there now, and it will be cold by dinner. I do like a good cold beer on a summer's night."

We were sure now that the voice we heard was Sister Rose's. Our eyes were bugging out of our heads. We were too terrified to laugh. We hurriedly crawled back into the garage and said repeatedly, "I do like a good cold beer on a summer's night," and laughed our heads off until it was time to go home for supper. But even during supper, I broke out laughing, knowing the nuns were enjoying a good summer's dinner with a nice cold beer.

Sixth Grade 1962-63

God grant me the serenity
to accept the things I cannot change;
courage to change the things I can;
and wisdom to know the difference.
                    The Serenity Prayer—Reinhold Niebuhr

Our Last Year at St. Mary's

School started as usual on the day after Labor Day, September 4. This year was different; first, it was our last year at St. Mary's School. While we were in what was called the Ungraded Room, most of us advanced each year to a higher grade level. After this year, we would move to the public school, to Central Junior High School. We looked forward to this adventure, and to being free of Sister Mary Ann, but we were also a little afraid. At Central there would be new dangers—dangers that were the focus of much of our Catholic school training. There would be "bad kids" who would subject us to "peer pressure." What sinful acts would they try to lure us into? We didn't exactly know, but we hoped to find out.

It was also different because Tommy left suddenly two weeks before school started. In fact, he left later the same night that we drank the beer. We didn't know him very well. No one really did. But he was always there with a smile—a knowing smile—and he wasn't like a lot of the other kids in the regular room. He seemed more like one of us, a reject, who had learned to pass himself off as a regular kid. We liked that about him.

We heard that his dad got an offer to be the head sales manager at the Cadillac dealership in Minnetonka—a growing suburb of the Twin Cities. He didn't give any notice, he just came in and said he was leaving. They put their house up for sale a few weeks earlier and, wouldn't you know, it sold two days later. The price was cheap; I guess

144

they didn't realize how much real estate prices had gone up. Everyone thought that they would be looking for a new house—a bigger one, on one of the big lakes, where new houses were already starting to replace the fishing resorts that boomed a decade earlier.

This put Roger, the owner of the dealership, in a really bad situation. He had made his son, Bobby, the president of the company with a big salary, knowing that Tommy's dad would bring in the sales. Bobby began dressing a lot snappier and attracted a girlfriend—a good-looking one, too. Her name was Marla Anderson. She was from Garfield, and worked as a waitress at the Hillside Inn Supper Club. That was a pretty swanky place. Anyway, they went out a few times, and then she told him that they needed to get married. The wedding was planned for November 3. We were all hoping to be the altar boys. That one should pay really well.

No way could Bobby really run the place, and Roger didn't trust anyone but Tommy's dad. Roger asked Tommy Thompson if it was because he made Bobby president, and gave his son a bigger salary. Then he offered to change all that. We heard he really begged him to stay. Roger even started to cry—not like at a funeral, more like when guys get into a panic. They don't want to, it just starts. But Tommy Thompson just said that it was time to move on; their time in Alexandria had come to an end.

I was looking out the window and I saw Mindy leaving the parish house, talking with Monsignor Ward. As she drove away, I saw him walk over to the school. Just then, Sister Mary Ann got a note from the office. She read it carefully, and then looked around the room. She was judging, evaluating risk, trying to determine her best selection. Finally, she asked me to go to the office and bring something back to the room. I knew it had to be a box or something heavy—otherwise she would have asked one of the girls. Asking a boy was always risky, but had to be done sometimes. Robert had already moved on to Central, so now just Stanley James and I were big enough to carry the heavy stuff. She wrote something on the bottom of the note, and sent the note with me down to the office. I got there just after Monsignor Ward; he was already in the office talking to Sister Rose.

"It would be impossible to have her volunteer here," Sister Rose said in a very authoritative voice.

"But there must be something that she can do," Monsignor pleaded.

"She can't work around the children, she doesn't have a high school diploma. She dropped out, and you know why," Sister Rose snapped back.

"But there must be something. She, well, she is thinking she might want to join a convent." His voice dropped, trying to avoid conflict.

After a very long silence, Sister Rose said, "Well, I hope she is not considering our order."

"Why not? I understand from the history of the Franciscans that they have always been very receiving," he replied.

"History? What about her history? And besides, I think she is unstable. This Madonna appearance, and the way she has been running around with a scarf around her head and tied under the hair at the back of her neck. Who does she think she is? I think people might mistake her for a novitiate. She is a freak. She wouldn't make a very good nun. I would never recommend her; and, in fact, all the nuns here would speak against her entering the order. We don't want her in our school or in our convent," came the retort.

"You forget, my good Sister, this is not your school. It is St. Mary's school. It belongs to the diocese, not to you." He was hot; I could tell he was clenching his teeth.

"Fine, you try to get teachers to work here for thirty-five dollars a month. If we leave, you wouldn't get any others to come," she said calmly, but defiantly.

It sounded like they were fighting. I had never heard nuns and priests fight before.

"I will try to find something for her to do over at the church," he ended.

I was afraid, so I walked back out into the hall, waited until he left, and then pretended to be just arriving. The package was less exciting than the fight—just a new box of lined paper for penmanship class.

The next day, there was a lot of gossip at the front door of the school. There was a big sign on the door of Willard Brothers car dealership: "Temporarily Closed." The factory sent trucks to pick up all the cars. Susan knew all about it—her dad worked at the bank, and she had heard him talking on the phone and to her mom.

"Remember how Tommy's dad always said, 'We lose a little on every deal, but we make it up on volume.' Well, as sales manager, Roger trusted him to order the cars and to make the bank deposits. His son Bobby had no idea what was going on and Roger wasn't even coming in most days. Well anyway, Tommy's dad sent the checks to a bank in St. Cloud. He told the bank here that they wanted to switch banks, and Bobby signed the papers closing the account and transferring the money. Only Tommy Thompson could sign checks on the new account. He sold lots of cars, sent the bank loan checks to the new account, and then wrote out checks to himself and cashed them. Sometimes he just cashed a lot of the other checks, too. Now Willard Brothers owes the factory for all the cars they sold, but they don't have any money. Roger is ruined. They might lose their house."

Man, she knew all the details. I always liked Tommy's dad; this just didn't sound like him.

"Gee, I thought he was a really cool dad," Dave said.

"Wait, there is more," she continued. "I also found out why they sold their house really cheap. The Thompsons told the Joneses that they didn't owe anything on it, and gave them a great deal. But it turns out, they had a mortgage from State Bank down in Glenwood, and another one from a bank in Sauk Center. The Joneses gave them the cash that they got when her mom died, and thought that they were getting such a good deal that they wanted to close right away before the Thompsons could find out that they were selling way too cheap. Everything happened so fast that they didn't do all the checking and stuff. So they might lose the house now."

"What does Tommy's dad say about all of this?" I asked.

All the kids surrounded Susan as she continued, "Well, when they called the Cadillac dealership down in the Cities, they never heard of him. And the place where he worked before he started at Willard Brothers, well, they don't know him either. No one even knows if that is his real name. He is just gone. They checked with the school to see if Tommy's records had been sent anywhere, and they haven't, yet. Sister Rose is going to check today to see if the records they got on Tommy were even real. Who knows, they might not even have been Catholic! And they were going to communion and everything."

This was some revelation, but more shocks came throughout September. Apparently, Mr. Thompson was also the treasurer for the Knights of Columbus, and the JayCees. Both groups were wiped out St. Mary's parish always published everyone's name in the annual report with the amount that they gave the Church that year. Even the children's names were always included. Monsignor was afraid to do that this year. He had noticed that the collections were a little thin, and was planning to start preaching a few sermons on the importance of giving. Now, he could not be certain why they were low. He decided to send out private statements that year; that way, if there was any discrepancy, he could handle it privately. He would be glad that he did.

But, what really stunned the women of the parish was that the cash from the Women's Auxiliary was also gone. It wasn't the thousands of dollars that was embezzled from the Willard Brothers—it was only $137.50—but the box was gone. Mrs. Thompson was such a wonderful treasurer, making detailed reports at each meeting. The kids all tried to think whether anything of theirs was missing, but heck, we didn't have any money to start with.

While the students gossiped and tried to recover from the shock of the Thompsons' disappearance, all the nuns could talk about was the Second Vatican Council that Pope John XXIII called. It opened on October 11, 1962. We all went to the gym to watch it on a TV that was loaned to the school and set up on a section of the portable stage. Pope John XXIII read an address entitled *Gaudet Mater Ecclesia* ("Mother Church Rejoices"). In it, he rejected the thoughts of "prophets of doom who are always forecasting disaster." He said the church should teach Christ's words in a modern ever-changing world. He said to use "the medicine of mercy rather than the weapons of severity."

Last Hopes

Aunt Eva got worse through the month. Most days she couldn't get out of bed, so mom spent a lot of time there. Stanley worked in the dry cleaners as soon as school got out until bedtime. I never got to see him anymore, except before school. We sat along the wall, catching the first rays of the fall sun.

"Did you hear? The Pope's going change the Church so there aren't so many sins anymore," I said.

But Stanley was too busy trying to finish his homework. He didn't want to fall behind, but he was spending as much time as he could at the dry cleaners so his Dad could take care of his mom. Fall is a busy time, with lots of people getting their coats cleaned and stuff. I looked down and saw that he hadn't even started his math paper. I took it, and started copying the answers from my paper. I never made mistakes in math. It was really easy for me—not like writing, where I always got the letters turned around. He didn't see me until I was done. He saw me put the paper back in his book. At first he started to frown, but then he didn't. The bell was ringing so we headed inside. Sure, I knew it was wrong, but it was just this one time, so he wouldn't fall behind.

Four days later John F. Kennedy called together his advisers. The CIA had photographs showing Soviet nuclear missile installations under construction in Cuba. Cuba lay only ninety miles off the Florida coast. I guess the Russians were mad after all, about the ones we placed in Turkey. On Monday, October 22, there was a special broadcast on TV. Everyone watched as President Kennedy announced the threat of the missile bases in Cuba. Not only that, there were 43,000 Russians in Cuba, too. We were a nation held hostage. They could kill us at any time. Yes, we believed that every last man, woman, child, and dog could be dead within three minutes if they pushed the button. This was a real crisis, and we were glad that we had a good man at the helm. Even his wife wasn't afraid. She was right by his side, not hiding in a bomb shelter or anything. Kennedy proclaimed an air and sea "quarantine" of Cuba to prevent any more shipments to Fidel. Some of the men thought we should invade, take those suckers out, and string Castro up by his balls—but that wasn't what the President wanted, so we all hoped that the blockade would work.

I asked mom, "If we are going to be dead before the end of the week anyway, do we still have to go to school?" But she said we did.

The next morning I completed Stanley's math homework again. By now any small residue of guilt had faded. It was my way of helping out. He didn't resist. Then at 9:30—the moment of crisis came—not off the coast of Cuba, that I wouldn't have cared so much about. No, Sister Mary Ann called Stanley James and me up to her desk. On it were our two worksheets, side-by-side, and on each question 8 was wrong—and wrong in the same way. I wrote 96, not 69, on both sheets. I knew I had to act fast.

"I copied Stanley's," I said. "When he wasn't looking, I took his paper out of his book and I copied it. But I only copied half of it; the first five I did myself."

I added the last part not because I thought it would lighten the punishment, but because the detail made the lie more plausible. For the briefest moment, I wasn't sure if Stanley James would go along with my confession, but then he knew. He knew that I wanted to do this. This was my way of saying I cared, kind of my gift to him.

Men don't say things like they love someone. They don't even say that to their sons. So, boys learn early and they don't say dumb stuff like that either. What they do tells how they feel. In the war, a man once jumped on a hand grenade and died so that his friends would live. That was his way of telling them he cared. This was my gift, and Stanley knew that it was important that he accept it.

"Stanley, how do you feel about your friend stealing your answers?" Sister Many Ann asked.

"I feel real bad, because it's a sin. I will say three Hail Mary's for him, so that God will forgive him."

He was fast. That might work. The Hail Mary's might get me some relief, and how could she counter that one? If he said he didn't care, she would have trapped him. She would have made him write a hundred times, "I will care if friends cheat, because cheating is a sin." If he said he was mad, then she could punish me. But feeling bad that I sinned? What a good scam. What could she say now? He was so cool. I felt good deep inside, but still had to look guilty and scared.

"Your fingers must learn not to sin," she said, and with that I placed my right hand on the table and the familiar pointer stick swung down sharply, making contact with my knuckles. It hit really hard. I told Stanley later not to say the Hail Mary's. She didn't deserve any.

I knew Stanley James would have done the same for me, but I was proud of myself. Even though I would backslide many times into spineless boyish ways, at that moment I understood what it was to be a man. I defied the rules, earthly authority, and Heaven itself in the name of—well, I don't want to say it—but in the name of love. That knowledge was Stanley James's gift to me.

Today I have a condition known commonly in the medical profession as Catholic school knuckles. I have bone chips around nearly all my knuckles. The largest one is on my right ring finger—it's the one I got that day. A doctor once asked me if I wanted it removed. At first I said yes, but then instantly changed my mind. I'm glad I have it, because it is a reminder of that day, the day that I wasn't afraid.

The next day our United Nations Ambassador, Adlai Stevenson, said that the United States was prepared to present proof that Moscow had missiles in Cuba. He said the weapons had to be removed, and asked the Soviet Union's delegate, Valerian A. Zorin, to admit that the missiles were in Cuba.

That night there were special prayer services at all the churches in town. At St. Mary's, we said the rosary and some other prayers. A lot of women and children were there. Most of the men stayed home to keep an eye on the news, just in case something happened. I saw Mindy there. She was very peaceful. She wore her white scarf and a white dress; the other women never wore white after Labor Day. It was kind of an old-fashioned dress, not like one that Jackie would wear. More like something Mamie Eisenhower would wear. After the service, several women talked with her and she told them not to worry. Mother Mary had told her that the Russians would back down. We weren't going to die. She said that before the end of the month, the crisis would be over and the missiles would soon be leaving Cuba. After that, things would slowly start to get better with Russia, and we would never have a nuclear war with Russia. Some were reassured. Some looked a little skeptical. But all wanted to believe.

The Russian ships headed for Cuba did stop, and the Russians did remove the missiles. We took our missiles out of Turkey a year later. We said we did it because they were obsolete.

I had heard about the Madonna of the Trailer Park, everyone had. Now there was proof, or at least enough proof for a boy desperate for a miracle. If Mindy's Madonna could resolve a missile crisis in Cuba, she certainly could cure a sick woman in Alexandria.

So, when mom came home late on Monday night, I said, "Is Eva going to die?"

"I don't know," she said.

"Why doesn't she go to the trailer park and see the Madonna there. It ain't so far as the ones in France, and it might work just as well," I said.

"I don't think so," she said. "It's not really approved, at least not yet."

"But when the first people went to Lourdes, it wasn't approved either. Things only get approved after enough people get miracles. She stopped the Russians. Please take her there. It might help. Stanley and I were good altar boys for Jamie's funeral, and now Mary is holding her, so maybe that might count more. Maybe little

151

baby Jamie will tell Mary to make Eva well. I know the doctors will just say she got better on her own, but we will know it's a miracle. We could promise to say the rosary everyday forever, or something," I pleaded.

"I will ask her if she wants to go," Mom finally said.

Stanley James wasn't in school the next day. I wanted to tell him about my idea, maybe he could tell his mom to go see Mary and baby Jamie, too. I raced home after school and waited for mom to come home. It was dark that Tuesday night, there was only a sliver of a moon in the night sky. At ten o'clock, dad came in from the gas station and told me I had to go to bed. I did, but I waited—waited and prayed one Hail Mary after another. When I heard mom come in at 11:00, I ran out of my room.

"Is she going to the Madonna, the Madonna of the Trailer Park?"

"I don't think so; she is really very tired and can't get up right now."

I knew this was serious and called for drastic measures, so I went back to my room and prayed to the Madonna and to baby Jamie. I told them that if my Aunt Eva lived, I would become a priest, and build a church right there in the trailer park in their honor. It would have a gold ceiling, just like the one in St. Paul, and marble floors and all kinds of good stuff, the best stuff. I started praying the rosary again. I wanted to say all 20 decades again before I fell asleep, but I didn't last that long. The phone rang about five in the morning and I could hear mom crying. Dad got up, and I could see that he was holding her. That didn't happen very often, so I knew. I knew that Aunt Eva was dead.

I thought, if I hadn't fallen asleep, if I had said the whole thing, maybe Mary would have believed me.

The next day Stanley James didn't go to school again, but I did. Mom went with Uncle Bill, and made the arrangements with the church and called the women's auxiliary. The funeral was medium size. Dad closed the gas station for a few hours—just put a sign on the door. I was one of the mass servers along with Dave and Gary. I told mom to give the priest three dollars for the altar boys. I would give her mine back, and I would give her all the money I earned until it was paid off. I just didn't want Dave and Gary to think that they were gypped, because we were poor. But mom said not to worry, and that I could keep my dollar, too.

No one from Bill's family came, but a lot of relatives from mom's family were there, as well as a lot of hospital people. Even some of the doctors and nurses came, and one of them wasn't even Catholic. I wasn't sure if he knew that he was not supposed to come up for communion, and I didn't know what I was supposed to do if he did. I didn't know if Monsignor knew who was Catholic. But in the end, he just sat there like he was supposed to. I reckoned some adult told him all about it. I saw Stanley crying, and his dad just put his face in his hands and cried the whole time. He didn't even look up when Monsignor talked. He just grabbed Stanley and held him. He didn't let go at communion, so Stanley James didn't come up, but he didn't seem to worry about it. Bill didn't know all the pallbearers—a lot of his friends weren't Catholic—so mom asked most of them. The funeral was on a Friday, so the ladies served tuna casserole, cooked carrots, and buttered bread, with pudding for dessert.

On Sunday, Stanley James came to church with mom and me. It was the first time that anyone could remember Roger Willard wearing the same tie that he had worn two weeks before. His wife Rena and his son Bobby were with him. Bobby's girlfriend decided that she didn't want to get married after all, and was hitched up with a new guy. After church, Mr. Willard decided to go fishing alone on Lake Le Homme Dieu. I guess he didn't know fishing season was over, and you can get a $50 fine for fishing out of season. He must have fallen overboard; they found him floating at five o'clock.

Rich's dad sold insurance in town, and he heard his dad talking on the phone. His dad said that it seemed a little odd that he drowned just one day before his next insurance payment, but he couldn't prove anything. Taking it to court would really hurt his business in town, so they arranged to pay Mrs. Willard the full amount.

Paul, Gary and Joey served at the funeral for Mr. Willard on Wednesday. They were a little worried about whether they would get anything, but Mrs. Willard made sure that they each got two dollars, and that Mr. Willard was sent off with a new tie. Monsignor made a point at the funeral to say repeatedly that this was a tragic accident—an accident—just when Mr. Willard was embarking on a happy retirement. No one said any different.

The Mission Quest

Our Bishop, Bishop Bartholomew, reestablished his friendship with Bishop Gonzales, from the diocese of Lima, Peru, at the council meeting in Rome. He had met him years before at the workshop for North and South American missionary partnerships. Then the two dioceses were linked in a cooperative relationship and participated in a few two-year exchanges of priests. They were only modest successes. Finding a Spanish-speaking priest, or one who wanted to learn Spanish in Minnesota in the 1950's, was nearly impossible, so interest was low. Now the spirit was different. Now, with the world changing rapidly and the church determined to step out into it, the two men decided that this decade would be committed to Peru. The focus of the plan was to eventually, perhaps in as little as two or three years, establish a school in Peru supported primarily by the St. Cloud Diocese. They hoped that this would become the core for a national Catholic school system for poor children.

Bishop Bartholomew met with a priest from each parish. Each parish was to establish a program to raise money for the Peruvian diocese, and the program had to involve children. It was important for children to become a part of the work of the church early. In the future, involvement of the lay community needed to be widespread, and the only way to insure broad participation was to get the children involved early. So, in the typically bizarre blending of Christianity and pagan secularism that the church had long ago perfected, Monsignor and Sister Rose decided that as part of St. Mary's participation, we would have an Olympic Day.

Sister Rose called the whole school together and told us that every class that collected fifty dollars by May 14, the feast day of Our Lady of the Most Blessed Sacrament, could participate in St. Mary's Olympic Day. The Olympic Day would be held Monday, May 27. The following day, Bishop Gonzales would arrive in Alexandria as part of a tour arranged by Bishop Bartholomew. But before arriving in Alexandria he would meet with the Franciscan Mother House in Little Falls in the morning. All the nuns from the diocese—including the nuns from our school—would be attending, so there would be no school at St. Mary's that day. There was a possibility that the Franciscan Sisters from Little Falls would staff the new school in Peru. After arriving in Alexandria he would say a Mass at St. Mary's where a special collection would be taken up for a new mission school. It would be a Solemn High Mass and all the altar boys would serve. We would have several practices beforehand, just to make sure everything went right. This would be the biggest event in the church since it was dedicated thirteen years ago. Bishop Gonzales would also speak at several events in town, including a special lunch for the Knights of Columbus. Bishop Bartholomew and Bishop Gonzales would then fly to Rome for the summer session of the council. On their return flight, they would travel to Lima, for a tour of the Peruvian diocese. While there, they would choose a location for the new school and develop a detailed plan for its operation. We were excited to be a part of this new explosion of energy in the church, but even more excited about our own Olympic Day.

Stanley James raised his hand.

"Yes?" Sister Rose asked.

"Can we have softball at our Olympics, even if the Roman ones didn't?" Stanley James asked.

"Sure, why not?" Monsignor said. Then, turning to Sister Rose he added, "I think we can do that, don't you?"

"We can have softball for the boys, but I think we should have groundball for the girls. Softball is not very ladylike," she softly replied.

"Yes, I meant for the boys, of course. And I'm sure the girls will enjoy groundball," Monsignor confirmed.

During recess, we made plans for the Ungraded Room to come up with the cash.

"That's over two dollars each, and some kids won't raise any, so that might be four dollars for some kids. We can't raise that kind of money," Dave said.

"Sure we can," insisted Stanley James. "We just have to find ways to do it."

In the afternoon, Sister Rose came to the door of our classroom with a large manila envelope. Sister Mary Ann stepped out in the hall; they talked in low tones for a few minutes. Then, Sister Mary Ann slid the paper halfway out, looked at it briefly, pushed it back in with an audible sigh, and sealed it. She walked back into the classroom, and visually inventoried everyone in order to be sure that no one had been watching—which of course we all were. We had become very adept in the use of peripheral vision. We could all watch out of the corner of one eye, while appearing to be staring straight ahead, paying full attention to the sentence we were repeatedly writing. We were also very adept at writing without much thought, like the kind of skill a concert pianist develops. His hand movements are controlled directly by sight—without traveling through or interference from the central brain. So too, we were able to copy the letters without ever really concentrating on what we transcribed a hundred times.

Sister Mary Ann wrote the date in the corner of the envelope with a pencil, as she had done with the others. She then placed the envelope in her lower right hand desk drawer. Had she received the one Sister Gene found in the music room—the one drawn in pencil and not in black crayon? I didn't think so. This must be a new one. Who was drawing these pictures? It must be someone in the regular class. They were drawn too well for one of us, and besides, they weren't showing up in our room.

That night at the dry cleaners, Stanley asked his dad if he could put a jar out for people to donate to the missions in Peru.

"Well, maybe it would be all right. But don't say Catholic. Just put something like feed the kids on the jar," Bill responded.

So, Stanley cut out pictures from Bishop Sheen's mission magazine, pasted them on a jar, and put it in front of the cash register. He wrote on it: "Kids collecting money for the children of the world." The pictures looked really sad. He intentionally picked out all the skinny starving kids. Then he put in two dimes—just to get things going.

Every afternoon when he got to the dry cleaners, he had to put it back on the counter. Bill didn't want to answer questions about it during the day, so he put it under the counter. Even so, after a few weeks Stanley collected $2.25; by that spring he collected $27.58. At recess, we added up how much everyone had, and, little by little, we soon had fifty dollars for the class. In fact, we had $51.38. We wondered if the regular classes did as well.

Now that we had the money, we started worrying about the weather. Should we pray to St. Clare of Assisi for good weather, or to St. Medard of Noyon?

"I like Medard of Noyon; Clare is a sissy, and this early in spring we need Medard to send his great eagle to protect us from rain and bring good weather," Dave said. He was always cool on St. Medard, I think mostly because he liked eagles.

"I think we should pray to both. St. Medard only protects us from bad weather, but St. Clare brings good weather; we need both," said Stanley. That made sense; we were covering all the bases, just like in softball.

"Well, O.K. You pray three Hail Marys to Clare—and make sure that it's to Clare of Assisi, we don't want them wasted on some other Clare that can't do anything. I will pray to St. Medard of Noyon. I saw a holy picture of him with his eagle overhead, and he was laughing. He is the only saint that I ever saw laughing. I like him," insisted Dave as he divided up the prayer tasks.

"In France, they pick a virgin and crown her with roses in church on his feast day. I think she is then his girlfriend for that year," George Ann chimed in. "I wish we did that here."

"Saints can't have girlfriends," I said. I didn't really know that, but a saint with a girlfriend just seemed dumb to me.

"If Jesus can have lots of wives, why can't a saint have a girlfriend?" she countered.

"I don't know, let's just get the praying done," I said, knowing it wasn't smart to argue with girls.

"Do you think boy saints like Hail Marys? Or should we do Our Fathers for Medard? Let's do three Our Fathers and one Apostle's Creed for extra measure. I think he will like that really long one. Then let's tell him that if there is really good weather, he can have Mary for his Alexandria girlfriend," Dave said.

"Do we need to ask her?" I asked.

"Nah, we'll just tell the other boys that none of them can pick her for their girlfriend for a year," he said.

Olympic Day

Dear Commander at the Roman Emperor's Court, you chose to also be a soldier of Christ and dared to spread faith in the King of Kings—for which you were condemned to die. Your body, however, proved athletically strong and the executing arrows extremely weak. So another means to kill you was chosen and you gave your life to the Lord. May athletes be always as strong in their faith as their patron saint so clearly has been. Amen.

Prayer to Saint Sebastian

Memory

In a man's life there are only a few days that are burned into his memory with such indelibility—with such intensity—that every frame can be enlarged and examined decades later without the slightest pixilation. While wives hope that such clarity is reserved for his wedding day, and his children hope their births are one such occasion, the workings of our minds are not regimented, and so such days cannot be freely selected. Instead such days—these few segments of our lives—choose themselves. May 27, 1963, was such a day for me.

Stanley James and I looked forward to this date with unwarranted expectation. It was only St. Mary's Olympic Day. But in our boy-minds, it took on a grandeur and heroic proportions exceeding the 1960 Games in Rome, or even the ancient games in Olympia. We talked endlessly about it. Perhaps it was a diversion for Stanley James, a way to focus his life on something that he could control—as the foundations of his world were becoming perilous. Perhaps my excitement was simply due to his powerful personality sweeping me along, as it had so many other times.

He and Bill came over for Sunday dinner the day before the big event. Bill's face had changed so much. His famous grin and white teeth were gone. His teeth were darkly stained from coffee and cigarettes, and they were no longer straight. They became long as his red gums receded, and his face was lifeless. Now, the width of his mouth accentuated his sagging lips. His face took on the look of an old rag that has been washed far too many times.

Mom tried to engage him, but he hardly spoke. What was there to talk about anyway? His business that was failing? Or Eva's death and the haunting suspicion that if only he had more money, maybe, just maybe, something more could have been done? Could they talk about the phone call that he made to his mother, begging for money to see a doctor in Chicago who might have helped? Eva overheard it, told him not to worry, that she didn't want to go to Chicago. An easy choice, since his mother flatly refused his request. Or maybe they could talk about Sally, the drunken slut that had already replaced Eva in his bed?

Sally owned Sally's Lounge. Bill started working there part-time as his business began to fail. The plan was to work nights bartending, and then at the dry cleaners during the day, just until things picked up. What actually happened was that Stanley tried to work at the dry cleaners after school and in the evenings, and Bill never got it opened until noon. Sally was well known in town. Her bar was once called Sam's Place, and she was once a hot young waitress there. She didn't waste much time replacing Sam's wife, Donna, and then managed to toss Sam out, too. How she ended up with the bar no one ever knew for sure, but she did. After that, every young buck in town hung out there for the next few years. But over time, the young bucks got older, and so did Sally. As she did, her skirts got shorter, her blouses got lower, and her makeup got thicker. Now, she mostly looked good after midnight—that is, if a man started drinking by nine. There is something about neon lights that can really make a woman look attractive, particularly a woman who can give you one on the house. Apparently, Bill had been there too long, had too many on the house, or just didn't care. He didn't care about anything anymore.

No, none of these topics made for a lively conversation. The topics—the safe topics—were the always-pleasant talk about the weather, which was indeed pleasant, and the boys—the boys and the games. But Bill wasn't really interested in these either. So, thanks to the television, the evening was saved by this still new intrusion—this wonderful electronic device that freed us from conversation, and permitted shared isolation to pass for a pleasant visit. With only one channel available—channel seven—even conversation about what show might be preferred was avoided. The adults stared at the flickering light and listened in a silent stupor—passing time that passed for time together. But not Stanley James and I. We were sitting in the little entryway by the back door, talking about the games that were still growing in importance.

First, who would be the captains? For the games, the sixth grade kids from the Ungraded Room were to be combined with the regular sixth grade kids; and the fifth grade kids would be combined with the regular fifth grades, and so on. Each grade had two boy teams and two girl teams. The boys and the girls each voted for two captains. All of the boys in the retard room used at least one of their votes for Stanley James—but did any regular kids vote for a retard? Maybe, because it was important that the two captains be really good, because no one knew who would be on which team. Stanley James had two things going for him. First, he was the fastest boy at the school. No, that wasn't really right; he was probably the fastest boy in town—maybe even the county. Second, he could hit a ball without fail. On Saturday mornings, Bill told him that he didn't have to go to work at the dry cleaners until noon—he needed some time to play. So Stanley James went over to the park on Elm Street—a park built when the new houses were built. One day some of the older boys were short players for baseball—not softball, but real baseball—and they asked him to play. At first he wasn't that good at hitting, but he could run—run like they had never seen. So, they let him keep on playing, and soon he could hit, too, without ever missing. If it was in strike range, he hit it—hit it hard—and then ran like a BB shot from a rifle that had been pumped ten times. He ran like his life would stop if he didn't make it home.

Sometimes I went over and watched him. One time I got to play with them. I wasn't very good, and they laughed at me, and said I caused them to lose. After that I resented Stanley James for spending so much of his time with them—the guys that thought of me as a little kid. I resented him, and yet I coveted what he had—his skill, and his acceptance by the big boys.

That didn't matter now. Now I was glad that he was first-rate, that he could run and hit. I was glad that tomorrow he might be captain, and that I would be on his team, and that we would win all the gold medals. Well, maybe not all the medals. I looked out the window and the moon was just a sliver, beginning to make the shape of a "D." I asked Stanley James if that meant the moon was beginning to get full, or if it was almost gone. He wasn't sure. We thought that we should know, but didn't. We decided that we would look tomorrow, and if it was fuller we would know, and we would not forget. Yes, tomorrow, that would be the day.

A Day for the Gods

At last, tomorrow arrived. The weather was perfect—thanks to all our saints and all the praying we did. We were told that we could wear tennis shoes and old clothing, so that we wouldn't have to worry about getting dirty—but no shorts. It would not appear proper for Catholics to wear shorts. The ladies in the kitchen packed us bag lunches of peanut butter and jam sandwiches, with an apple and carrot sticks. They put them into brown paper bags and drew the Olympic circles on them. They looked really cool. All the circles were perfect; they must have drawn them around something, maybe a small glass. No one could draw that good.

We were ready to go by 8:05, but Jimmy wasn't there. Sister Rose brought a note down to the room; Sister Mary Ann read it, then we all went down to the gym. There we were given the usual instructions about how Catholic boys and girls must behave in public. We were using the facilities over at the Central Junior High School. They were out of school already. It was a mild winter and they didn't need to use any of the seven snow days built into their school year. Because St. Mary's didn't have buses and most of the kids lived in town, we didn't have snow days. The nuns walked from the convent, and most of us walked from home. But we did have Holy Days off, so that made our year longer than the public school year.

At first we weren't sure if we would be able to use the public school facility—because we were a Catholic school and all. But then the Knights of Columbus said that they would rent it for a day. The church softball leagues—including the Protestant groups and the Knights of Columbus—had rented the softball field for years without any problems. So the Central School principal decided to take the thirty dollars and let us use it. Sister Rose said that it would be better for the Knights to give the money to the mission, and we could just do something on our own playground. But the Knights said they had given plenty to the missions, and the kids needed to have an Olympics.

In the gym, they announced the two captains: Joey Turner was the captain of the Blue Team; and, yes, Stanley James was the captain of the Red Team. The team captains were to take turns choosing the members of each team twice: once, late in the morning, for the team relay event; and then again in the afternoon for softball. No one knew who would win the softball game. Stanley James was good at hitting, but he needed more than that to win. He also needed a good pitcher. Doug was the best pitcher, but, would Joey get him? Dave was pretty good, too. Well, we would just have to wait and see.

The team relay races were another matter. Everyone knew Stanley would win all the individual races—even if he ran backwards he would win; no one could beat him. But in the team relay, each boy ran half the track's distance and handed off the baton at mid-point. We didn't really have batons—we used the plastic ball bats that the little kids played with instead. The strategy was to get the lead, then put your slow guys in the middle, and then choose someone really good at the end—someone who could really pile it on. That guy, well, he was the hero when you won. Would Stanley be good enough to bring the whole team in? That depended on the picking. As long as he didn't get too many of the really slow kids, he was sure to win.

We started walking in a straight line down the sidewalk on Washington Street until we reached the school. The first event was ball toss. Five kids at a time lined up to toss softballs. A little flag was placed by the longest toss, the second longest toss, and the third; then five more kids lined up. If they tossed the ball further, the flags were moved; otherwise they stayed. When the first event was finished, the first ribbons were handed out. Joey got the gold medal. It was really just a yellow ribbon with a cardboard circle covered with gold foil at the top. Sister Vincent made them. Dave got the Silver; it was gray ribbon with tin foil. Bill got the bronze. That one was just a brown ribbon and didn't have any foil on it. I guess they didn't make bronze foil. But it did have a gold star pasted on it. We thought they were neat and the winners showed them to everyone. The girls did everything after the boys. The individual events continued through the morning and then the last two events came before lunch. These were the big ones.

The fifth grade had their team relay race first, and everyone was really excited about it. As the sixth grade boys were about to start picking their teams, Mrs. Langley drove up—she had Jimmy in her car. He didn't want to get out. But when Sister Mary Ann started walking over to the car, he got out. He looked scared. He didn't want to be there and I guess, even then, I knew why.

For boys, such days are more than games; they are an assessment of their potential manhood. Jimmy was weak and frail. For him the day would be one of rejection—being picked last, and coming in last in every event. He might even have one of his stupid staring-off things, or his nervous shaking thing. Hell, he might even get so scared that he would pee in his pants. Yeah, it had happened before. We never said much, but sometimes there were drips on the front of his pants, and I think one time he even shit a little. Sometimes the regular kids pointed and snickered behind him. Sure, he heard it; but us retards learned early on that it was better to pretend not to hear it. And you know, after a while, you really didn't hear it anymore. You learned to pull yourself in so far that there wasn't a real world out there, only your world. You made your world any way you wanted it, and went there when you needed to. Sometimes when Sister Mary Ann hit my hand with the pointer stick, I just pulled myself in so far that I didn't even feel it. I didn't even know she was doing it. Then when I came back, I saw what had happened and was glad that I wasn't there. But with Jimmy, I think it was different. I think he just wasn't anywhere sometimes. No, this was not his day. This was a day of mandatory humiliation, so that other boys could be crowned with bright shining ribbons.

Joey Turner and Stanley James stood side-by-side, and waited for Sister Mary Ann to return. They had already flipped the coin, and Stanley James won. He would pick first. As they waited, they sized up the boys, looking them over like the cattle judges at the Douglas County Fair. I looked at Stanley James, with a "you-gotta-pick-me" look. I knew I should have gotten his commitment last night, but I thought that might make him feel like I didn't trust him. No, he would pick me, I thought. But as I looked around, I wasn't sure if I was the best pick. He knew how degrading it was not to be picked first, or second. Not being picked up front announced to the world that you were not, well, not very masculine—that you wouldn't be much of a man. As I watched, suddenly and without warning,

Stanley's face—no, his whole body—changed. I don't know if he straightened up and stood taller, or if the sun simply changed to a slightly different angle. He appeared to me to almost glow, to radiate. Sister Mary Ann returned. I think she sensed it, too, but didn't see it.

"Now boys, when the captains pick, you are simply to get in line behind them and don't say anything," instructed Sister Mary Ann.

"Stanley."

The tone of her voice saying Stanley's name clearly communicated that he was now to pick.

Pick me, not Doug, I thought.

"Jimmy."

His voice was radiant, but pierced my heart. What? What a creep, I remember thinking to myself. I flashed back to Camp Willabee, when he let Stinky Butt Edward stay in our tent.

Without a moment's delay, Joey picked me. Wow, saved by Joey; but now I wouldn't be on Stanley James' team. Well, I would show him.

Stanley James called, "Thomas."

Good pick. He was fast, too. I wish we had him, I thought.

Joey called, "Doug."

Great, I knew he was fast. Stanley called Dave, and the picking continued until the last boy was chosen. The captains lined up the boys in order for the relay. For our team, the Blue Team, Doug was first, I was second, then the others. Joey placed himself at the end, for the strong finish.

Stanley James started the Red Team off with Thomas, but rather than putting himself last, he put Jimmy last. If they got a big enough lead, Jimmy would be the one to cross the finish line and he would be the hero. Now, some forty years later, I understand what Stanley James wanted to achieve. But in the mind of a boy, such a plan appeared insane. Putting Jimmy last risked everything. And even if Stanley's team won, he would have risked everything just to allow someone else to seize the moment. Someone who might not even be aware of the importance of the victory. Yes, that was insane. Even today for most people, such a risk—such a sacrifice—was out of the realm of possibilities. But on that day, on the Central Junior High School field in Alexandria, Minnesota, that decision was made by a boy, a boy who had only his moment of glory to give.

Right from the start the Red Team was ahead; with each round they ran faster. Our boys just couldn't seem to get the speed they needed. What was Stanley's plan about? Did he pick Jimmy to motivate his team, to make them so afraid of losing that they pushed it every step of the way to win? Was this super coaching? No, I decided. He got to pick first. If he had not picked Jimmy, then the Blue Team—picking last—would have been stuck with Jimmy, and been certain to lose.

As the race moved toward its conclusion, Stanley ran faster than I had ever seen him run. They were almost a full lap ahead by the time Jimmy got the bat. He started running. He only had to finish the last half lap. He was a sight as he comically flailed about—taking clown strides. His hands swung over his head; his feet landed at odd angles. But on his face, his desire not to let Stanley James down, not to let his team down, was overwhelmingly powerful. First, just the Red Team was cheering him on. Then the girls and the fifth graders joined in, and then like the spread of a germ in some sci-fi flick, everyone began cheering for him—even the guys on the Blue Team, our team. Even Joey, who was our captain and would be our last runner in a few moments, was cheering. The girls jumped up and down and clapped, the boys shouted. I, too, felt something enter me. It was like a ball of light and warmth, penetrating my shoulder on the left near my neck, and then spreading throughout my body. It made me feel energized.

It bubbled inside until I, too, was shouting, "Jimmy, run! Jimmy, run, run, run, run . . ." without even the slightest stutter.

Joey took off and was now closing in on Jimmy; the finish line was only a few yards away. The two runners were so different. Joey was totally unaware of the actions of his body—like a racecar driver who simply pushes the accelerator, but doesn't think of the movement of each piston, or the firing of each spark plug. He knows all these things are happening, but a driver is so "at one" with his car that it is an extension of his mind. So it was with Joey. His body was simply an extension, a tool of his mind. He pushed faster without thinking about it. Jimmy was a total contradiction. His body was out of control; it had to be told every movement. He was both afraid of it, and discovering its power. I could see Joey's lips mimicking the chant from the crowd: "Run, Jimmy, run!"

Then, unexpectedly, Joey crossed the finish line first. The look on his face was one of confusion. It was the same look men have when they want to loosen a tight bolt, and then find that they have applied too much pressure and snapped it off. Sure, he wanted to win; but even in those last seconds, he wanted Jimmy to win more. But that wasn't his choice to make. He was captain of a team—and wining the game, well, that's more important than what any member of the team wants. He was out of breath, bent over breathing.

Jimmy looked scared, but Stanley James ran right over to him.

"Great race,'" he said. "We got the silver." Of course, he knew there were only two medals.

Jimmy said, "Did I do OK? Did I do OK?"

"You did great," Stanley James said as he and the other boys all slapped him on the back.

He was, for the first time, one of them—one of the guys—and his face beamed.

I stole a fleeting look at Sister Mary Ann; she appeared to be pleased that Stanley James's plan had failed. She was gratified that Stanley James was taught an important lesson. His hubris at choosing Jimmy first—just so that he could prove that he could win, even with the slowest boy in the school on his team—caused him to lose. That kind of ridiculous display of strength verged on sin. No, it was sinful. Pride—the greatest of all sins—goes before the fall. And the fall had justifiably come. But look at him, jumping about, not displaying any remorse, she thought. He used Jimmy for his own shameful plot. Jimmy, while happy for the moment, would soon see how callous everyone really was.

The sun was now higher in the sky, and its brilliance illuminated the scene with the innocent quality of warm spring light. The light paired perfectly with a tender cool breeze. The breeze was of just the right strength, enough to cool, but not strong enough to affect the race.

The next event was the all-sixth grade boy's race. Then the sixth grade boys would help set up lunch, while the fifth graders and the girls finished their races. All the boys ran one lap around the high school track to determine who was the fastest boy. All the boys knew that there was really no reason to even run this race. Stanley James had won every race on the playground since second grade, and over the years he only grew stronger and faster. Now, he was the tallest boy in school. This was not a race as much as an event to honor and crown him. The boys lined up, still glowing with the excitement of the last race and Jimmy's near win. Then, much like before the team relay, something like the light touch of an angel's wing fell over our shoulders, and somehow we all seemed to understand the same thing. I remember the knowing clearly, but no one ever understood it.

It happened in the seconds before Sister Vincent said, "On your mark, get set, go."

We knew.

Jimmy charged forward. Stanley James reached out, moving like a true Olympian athlete—in perfect form, but in slow motion. We all followed suit, each boy taking the position that he knew he deserved, but all behind Jimmy. It was a bizarre sight to behold—Jimmy in comedic form, followed by Stanley James, in the shape of the man he would be. It was a near perfect form that was already discernable in the boy. A young Labrador that is no longer a pup still has large paws that predict his future form. So, too, Stanley James's large feet and hands did not appear ill proportioned, they looked perfect for his aspiring shape. He was a statue in motion—slow motion. Behind him were Doug, Joey, Rich, me, and on down. Any boy could have chosen to race ahead, but all surrendered the "win" for their proper place. We were all filled with an incredible joy seeing this boy—Jimmy, who had arrived in paralyzing fear only an hour ago—now running, gaining strength, and being free. I never again in my life felt that level of oneness with other human beings—the un-restrainable exuberance when I ran that single lap in complete timelessness. It could not have happened on an earthly cinder track. We must have been transported through some miracle plane. Humans—even boys—are not capable of such grace.

This time Jimmy crossed the line first—to the cheers of all the fifth graders, all the sixth grade girls, and—most importantly—the sixth grade boys. Stanley James and Joey picked Jimmy up on their young shoulders, and Sister Vincent, all smiles, handed him the golden ribbon. Our faces were bright red. The expressions that they bore I have seen only dimly reflected on the faces of the men who now win the Super Bowl or the World Series. Because on that day, that very special day, we did not win the competition; we conquered the rules that dictate how men must struggle for conquest. We were victorious over the laws of the universe. Such was our triumph.

But unknown to us, there was an angry God watching these events. One who was not pleased. We had violated the order of His creation. We had not acted in accord with the rules that hold the universe in its place—and man in it. By His order of things—Jimmy had not won, and therefore deserved no golden reward. We had placed a false crown upon his head, one that insulted the God that demands that everything must be earned in order for it to be justly deserved. It was clear that this euphoria, this drunken state, this ecstasy, was a device of Satan, just another way of distorting boys and stealing their souls from the Just God. And he, Stanley James, had revealed his true nature. He didn't even restrain himself from using an innocent child like Jimmy to swindle other boys out of justice. But, thank God, not everyone was taken in. Sister Mary Ann had the strength to end this madness, and try to save the boys. Yes, all the boys, she would even try to save Stanley James—if it wasn't already too late.

She rushed over, grabbed the ribbon from Jimmy's hand, and said, "Put him down. You have made a sham out of these games. We wanted to do something enjoyable, but you boys don't deserve it. Sister Vincent worked hard making these ribbons and they were meant for boys who won them fairly—not to be used as some kind of joke. We will not be ridiculed. Line up, these games are over."

The other nuns looked stunned. At first, they considered arguing, challenging her perceptions. But a division between the sisters in public would not be pious. What could they do? Would the completion of the games be worth the complete humiliation of one nun? Perhaps they did not see everything that Sister Mary Ann had seen. It was true that Jimmy could not—did not—win the race by defeating the other boys. No, the boys had chosen him to win. Did they plan this ruse in advance? Why did they want to do it? What were these boys thinking? The other nuns suddenly had a sinking feeling, that perhaps the boys were always part of some kind of conspiracy, and now in their final days at St. Mary's, used this day to announce it. What else were they doing? Were they all part of the dirty pictures, and altar cloth burning, and all the other unsolved crimes—everything that had occurred under their noses? They loved these boys, had given them their lives. They had become nuns to teach these boys and girls; and now, maybe, all of them had been deceived.

Return to Reality

We walked slowly back to school. We went right to our rooms, and sat quietly. The lights were off, and the shades had not yet been lifted, so the light was cool and filtered. The time was 10:51. We did not plan to attend the eleven o'clock Mass, because of the games. Monsignor Ward arranged for two seventh grade boys, already out of school, to serve. By now, they had fastened the long rows of buttons on their cassocks and were putting on surplices, so they could race down stairs and be the first one to claim the long brass candle lighter. That was the fun part; the other server took out the water and wine to the side stand, and then only the missal needed to be placed. Not a lot of preparation for a low mass.

"Take out some work!" Sister Mary Ann demanded, not wanting to see unoccupied hands.

Should the children attend Mass after all? The nuns should have talked about it on the way back, but with their spinning thoughts, all was trapped in the vortex. Should she leave the room to ask the other nuns? Leave these children alone? She stood by the door. One of the other nuns would surely be coming by, she thought. Time was running out. We could get there late, but what were the other classes doing?

Jimmy started one of his rocking modes. Then he made his sound, kind of an "urrrr, urrrr," a sound that was a cross between a dog's growl and a cow's moo.

"Quiet, Jimmy," she said.

Then like a spring opening a Jack-in-the-box, Jimmy jerked. I don't mean a small jerk like a sleeping dog makes. No, his whole body changed position in an instant. His workbook—the one about the Way of the Cross that we were supposed to have completed for Lent, but that some of us were still working on—flew into the air, and his arithmetic book smashed to the floor. The workbook hit the wall and fell to the linoleum. Sister Mary Ann first glanced at Jimmy, then at the workbook lying open on the floor, and then at the loose papers that fell out and the nearly totally used black crayon next to them. On the paper, drawn in a sharp black outline, was a large penis and a scrotum. It had the same detail and skill as the drawing we saw coming up the stairs nearly two years earlier.

Jimmy returned to his senses, or almost so. He was aware enough—conscious enough—to see his work on the floor. He leaped up to try to grab it before Sister Mary Ann could, but it was too late.

"You, you dirty filthy, filthy boy," she began as she picked up the paper.

We had never seen her pick a paper up from the floor before. When a nun dropped something, she waited for a boy to race up, pick it up, and hand it to her. I suspected that on some boring days, Sister Mary Ann dropped her chalk or pointer stick on purpose, just to check the obedience of the boys—to see them try to reach the item first, but without running or racing, and to hand it back to her in exchange for her grand, but guarded, "Thank you."

But not today. Today, she raced for the paper—and not one boy other than Jimmy ventured forth to retrieve the item.

"Just wait until your mother and Monsignor Ward see this."

She was holding it high, with its disgusting lines facing her. Jimmy tried to grab for it, but she pulled it away. A shocked look raced across her face—not alarm from the drawing as much as from Jimmy's attempt to grab it from her hands. Then he leaped again, but this time he grabbed the front edge of her veil. She started pushing him off, like one would do if a bird crapped on you, but his grip tightened—both hands tightened, although his left hand held nothing. Then his whole body began undulating; it appeared both comical and tragic. He was like an out of control puppy on a man's leg—but at the same time, he looked like the hard mechanical machine in the Detroit assembly lines that we saw in a movie two weeks earlier. Sister Mary Ann grabbed his shoulder and began to shake him and push him to free herself from this disgusting thing—this dirty boy that had landed on her. Her veil and coif peeled away from her body like the skin of a banana—revealing the woman underneath. For the first time we saw her short cropped brown hair, her ears, and a small brown spot on the side of her neck. The white crown band that hoisted the top of the veil into a square shaped tower was toppling, while the rounded white collar stayed in place, leaving the coif dangling around her neck. Yet, Jimmy would not or could not let go.

She screamed, "Let go! Let go!"

But Jimmy had faded into some other place. I could see it, but didn't know how to tell Sister Mary Ann. He can't. He can't let go. He's not here.

Then he fell to the floor, dragging her veil and crown band with him, as the pins that held it secure tore loose. Jimmy was shaking, tossing his arms, and peeing. His pants were becoming wet, but he didn't notice, and neither did Sister Mary Ann. She was like a wild beast, all fury, like God must have been when he rained down the hell fire onto Sodom and Gomorrah.

With exaggerated swings, she slapped him like a boxer out of control, screaming, "I tried to help you! I tried to help you! Your mother told me about your father, but I tried to help you!"

Jimmy was turning red. Stanley James's eyes fixated—not on the wild swings or stinging slaps, they were harmless. He was intensely watching Jimmy's ribs, which were exposed sometime during the fray when his shirt was torn open. His ribs were not moving—not moving in-and-out—in the rhythm needed to maintain life. His skin, always deadly white, turned a bright red, and around his mouth and fingernails it turned faint blue.

Stanley yelled as he spun from his desk, "Stop it! Stop it!" in a voice deeper than his years, and stronger than a boy of twelve should possess. Then with his head down, he charged like a furious bull, or like young men charge when colliding on the football field. His head smashed into Sister Mary Ann with a dull thud, knocking her into the hall.

By this time we heard Sister Rose yelling, "Get Mr. Pearson, quick as you can. Run!" then "Oh, God, Sister Vincent, call the police, get help!"

There were other sounds, too. George Ann was standing on one foot, then on the other, screaming indiscernible syllables while urine ran down her leg. Dave, hands flat on his desk, like a lot of the other kids, had tears streaming down his face. Roger's hands were shaking like a loon attempting a take off from a northern lake. And poor Johnny was simply staring straight ahead—having escaped awareness—and took the opportunity to eat a large booger that he pulled from his nose without fear of being disturbed.

Our world was ending. Our image of God—the unchangeable God—the terrifying God who gave us constancy and justice—had been attacked, and was proven to be just a woman under a black veil. Our brains, of course, knew this; but our souls were never informed. And now here, before our eyes, she was attacked. She stumbled and teetered, but had not yet fallen.

Stanley James stood, bent slightly forward, hand clenched in a fist, but pointing back to Jimmy. His face contorted, and tears flowed from his eyes. With a voice that mixed both anger and grief he bellowed, "Stop, Sister Mary Ann! Stop, he is hurt!"

She did not—or did not want to—hear him. She charged back into the room, grabbing her pointer stick. This was both her scepter and her wand. She used it to both point out wisdom, and to enforce the wisdom when needed. It was modern in design, just a simple birch rod one-half inch in diameter with a convenient ring at one end for hanging and a black rubber tip at the other to prevent the disturbing sound of scratching on the black board when it was being used for its intended purpose. It was always her weapon of choice, and everyone in the room—even the good kids—felt the power of its sting, a sting that could be delivered precisely on the knuckles or randomly on the shoulders. Now, with both hands firmly grabbing it, she swung backwards first, much like a baseball player ready to hit a home run, and then forcefully swung forward—hitting Stanley James on the head and shoulders. He bent down, like a man bowing, and raised his hands in front of him—trying to deflect the blows. Jimmy continued to flop on the floor. Now the smell of poop reached us, and a thin telltale spot showed under him. He shit, too. The blue shadows around his mouth and fingers spread to encompass more of his body. His chest was unmoving, but his body still flailed uncontrollably.

On the third swing, Stanley grabbed the stick, and in an instant too fast to be seen, cracked it over his knee. He now held both pieces of the powerful rod in his right hand. She grabbed for it and he swung the broken parts. She was now bent and screaming. One of the swings scraped her face. The broken end of the stick ripped into her soft virginal skin. Blood—yes nun blood—deep red and human, ran down her check.

The students in the other classrooms, abandoned by their teachers—who either came racing to the Ungraded Room or fled in other directions recruiting help—were hanging out of their doorways. Then above this cacophony of noise we heard the clear thump, thump, thump of a man's work boots running down the hall. It did not sound like a mortal running, but more like a dancer leaping, dramatizing the race of a giant. It was Mr. Pearson. He grabbed Stanley James by the collar and belt, and reeled him around like a hockey player swinging a stick. Bang! The swing ended with Stanley James' head hitting the edge of Sister Mary Ann's Steelcase desk. The corner connected just above Stanley James' eye causing blood—also human and also red—to spatter all over Sister Mary

Ann's desk, the newly mimeographed papers for this week's final lessons, and the long narrow black book where our sins and our punishments were recorded. In a continuous move from the edge of desk, Mr. Pearson swung Stanley James into a chair—landing his ass precisely on the seat.

Stanley desperately yelled, "He's dead! He's dead!" and looked at Jimmy, but wasn't able to manage the bodily control needed to point.

Sister Mary Ann, now halfway recovering, yelled, "Oh my God, you have killed him."

Mr. Pearson rushed to the body, tipped his head, and managed to clear the vomit from the child's mouth by rolling him over and prying his mouth open. The foul blockage flowed out, and a sharp movement sucked in painful air. Then, nothing. Then another breath, and then sporadic but repeated shallow breaths. The police and ambulance arrived. Monsignor Ward raced from the church— still wearing a white Amice, the first vestment put on in preparation for Mass, over his back and shoulders.

The adults switched automatically from panic mode to clean-up mode. Jimmy's mom arrived from her house, just three doors down from the school. She was calmer than might have been expected. Sister Vincent worked with Sister Mary Ann in the hall to repair her habit to full—but soiled—order. The men with the ambulance took Jimmy to Saint Mary's Hospital. Sister Mary Ann and Jimmy's mother accompanied him. Because there was only room for two adults in the ambulance, Sister Rose said she would be there shortly with the car—after she called Stanley's father, if she could get a hold of him. A doctor at the hospital looked after Sister Mary Ann, and another treated Jimmy.

The police took Stanley James. They said that they probably needed to stop by the County Hospital on the way—the gash in his head looked like it might need a few stitches. They would take him into custody over at the county jail. It was obvious that he was totally out of control. Mr. Pearson expressed some concerns about putting such a young boy in with the other men, but the officers assured him that the county jail had a cell that was separate from the others that was used for women and for juveniles awaiting a hearing.

It was too late for Mass now; so Monsignor returned to church, gave the few parishioners and the other children a blessing, and distributed communion. As Mrs. Beasley was now a fulltime teacher, there was only one tutor coming in this afternoon, Officer Beecher. He normally worked with Jimmy, so there was no need for him to come in unless they asked him to cover the Ungraded Room, so that Sister Mary Ann could take the rest of the day off to recover. But Sister Mary Ann assured everyone that she was quite capable of holding class that afternoon, and that it was best for continuity that she manage her class rather than someone that many of the children didn't know. Sister Vincent took George Ann to the office, called her mother, and arranged for a change of clothing to be brought to school.

The efficiency with which the adults worked was amazing to us. There was just one last task—The Explanation. Sister Rose made it clear to us that the adults would handle that just as efficiently as she was leaving. She said, "This could reflect badly on St. Mary's School. I hope that you will let the adults handle it. Do not speak about what happened—in this room, on the playground, or with others. I will send home a note for your parents at the end of the day. I can promise you that St. Mary's is safe, and that it is a good place for children."

Sister Mary Ann did return to school that afternoon. Her desk was cleaned during lunch, and the bloodstained handouts were reprinted. The trash was taken out, and the only sign left of the drama that occurred only an hour and fifteen minutes earlier was the small bandage on Sister Mary Ann's face. It hid three small stitches—stitches that one day would develop into a barely visible scar. There was, of course, another difference—the absence of Stanley James. It was like he was sucked into a hole in the universe, but the hole was filled so completely that no trace of him remained. His desk was moved out of the room, and his name was taken down from the wall. When I caught a glimpse of Sister Mary Ann's long little book, I saw that his name—which had topped nearly every page—was gone. It was carefully and completely erased.

The note that went home that day simply said, "A disturbed student from a mixed marriage, who the school tried to help, attacked a nun. However, he was quickly removed from the school. No Catholic students were hurt or involved, and the school is developing better testing procedures to prevent similarly troubled students from enrolling at the school."

Stanley James wasn't mentioned ever again at the school.

Stanley Begins his Journey

Trusting in the promise that whatever we ask the Father in Jesus' name He will do, I now approach You Father, with confidence in Our Lord's words and in Your infinite power and love for me and for [insert name], and with the intercession of the Blessed Virgin Mary, Mother of God, the Blessed Apostles Peter and Paul, Blessed Archangel Michael, the guardian angels of myself and [insert name], with all the saints and angels of heaven, and Holy in the power of His blessed Name, as I ask you Father to send forth Your Spirit to convict [insert name] and to allow him to see any and all wrongs that he has done and how they offend Your infinite goodness.

Hedge Prayer for Return of Wayward Person

The Sorrowful Mystery

The police first took Stanley James to the Douglas County Hospital; they had an arrangement with the administration on discount rates, and besides, taking a criminal to a Catholic hospital might violate some church-state regulation. The officers gave him a gauze pad to hold on his head in the car. They were polite enough, but joked, saying, "You beat a nun? Boy, you're gonna get the book thrown at you!" Stanley, unaware of legal terms, thought that a book tossing was the prescribed punishment, but was unaffected anyway. He had no sensation; his life was over, and he knew he would never return to the school, his home, or to his friends. He was on a new path.

As they sat waiting, Mindy came into the waiting room, wearing her volunteer apron over her white uniform. The same uniform doubled for waitressing, but she always changed into a clean one between jobs. She volunteered at both hospitals. She started at the Catholic hospital, but then a friend asked her if she could fill in once in a while at the county hospital—just when one of the volunteers called in sick. She said she would, but had only filled in a few times. So, she was still unfamiliar with the procedures here. She hurried over to Stanley James. She recognized him from church. She saw the police officers and assumed that a car or something had hit him.

"What happened?" she asked.

"Oh, we have a nun beater here. But don't worry, we have the little bastard under control," one of the officers said.

Stanley recognized Mindy, too. Everyone in church—no, by now everyone in town—knew her as the Trailer Park Saint, but never said it to her face.

"Oh, let me get you a new pad."

She quickly disappeared, and reappeared with a paper cup of water and a new clean gauze pad for Stanley James to press against his wound. He thanked her and she took the old pad in her hand. In those days no one worried about blood, or the possibility that it was contaminated. Only doctors wore gloves, and then only in surgery in order to protect the patients, not themselves. She asked the officers if she could get them anything, but they were fine. As she walked away, one of them whispered something to the other and she heard a low chuckle, but not the comment. As Mindy made her way to the trash to dispose of the gauze, she looked down at it, and was staring at it when Monsignor Ward walked in the door.

"Look Monsignor, I think I see the face of Christ in that boy's blood."

Without looking down, and keeping his eyes clearly fixed on hers, he took the gauze from her and dropped it into the trash. "There is no face of Christ on that gauze. Miracles don't happen in Alexandria, Minnesota, and they certainly don't happen like this. It is time to get a grip on reality, Mindy. A boy almost died today because of that kid. I have prayed and prayed for him, for his soul. Now this happens! How in God's name does this happen?"

"I don't know Monsignor, but I know God loves every one of us. He has a plan for that boy, too. Maybe he is trying to show us something," Mindy said softy.

"I hope so."

He walked away and waited for Stanley James to come out. He asked the police officers if he could have a word with the boy. They said, sure, and moved a few feet away.

"Stanley, while you're in jail, you can ask for me. I do prison calls on Tuesdays and Thursdays, but I can only visit if you request it. Do you understand?" Monsignor was talking fast, providing instructions not to a boy, but to a man, who was entering a dangerous place alone.

"Yes, Monsignor," Stanley James responded like a dazed solider.

"Ask for me and I will come. You're only 12; you can still turn your life around. This doesn't have to be your path. I will say Mass for you tomorrow," Monsignor continued, as if laying out a battle plan.

"Monsignor, I don't have any money for that," Stanley said in a whisper. Poverty was never something to be announced.

"You don't need any. It is my gift to you. Please, Stanley, ask Mary and Jesus to help you," he added quickly, knowing his time was limited.

One of the officers cleared his throat; it was a gentle signal that it was time to take Stanley over to the jail. Monsignor Ward watched as the officers took Stanley out the door. He then looked around uncomfortably, like a man who was looking for a misplaced hat, but not finding it or knowing what he was missing. He walked out, got into his black Cadillac, and drove over to the Catholic Hospital to visit with Jimmy and his parents.

When he got to Jimmy's room, Jimmy's mother gave Monsignor the full report. The doctors thought that he might have had an epileptic fit, a grand mal seizure. Epilepsy didn't run in the family, at least no one had ever talked about it. The doctors planned to begin running tests, but for now he was safe and out of danger. One of the doctors said that perhaps the attack on the nun caused a stressful situation that triggered the episode. There was some evidence that there was a relationship between stress and fits, but not much was really known. He called another doctor that he knew at the University of Minnesota, who gave him the name of a doctor at the Mayo Clinic in Rochester. That was one of the best hospitals in the country. He would write to him; perhaps he might arrange for Jimmy to see him. But for now Jimmy would stay in the hospital for at least a week or two.

That night, Mom got a call from Sister Rose. They were unable to reach Stanley's father, and asked if she might call to let him know that Stanley was permanently expelled from the school. No matter what the court decided, he would not get a certificate of sixth grade completion. They would be pleased to forward his records. Mom said she would call.

Mom wasn't able to reach Bill, so she called Sally Mayfield and asked to talk with Bill.

"He knows all about it. The police were already here," Sally said, her voice a little slurred.

"But I need to tell him about the school's decision," Mom said.

"What about it?" the uncaring voice replied.

"They said that he couldn't go back there. They won't give him his sixth grade certificate."

"Well, who the hell cares? We ain't letting him go back anyway. It's all your fault. If he was in regular public school, this never would have happened. Those nuns are all squirrely. They should all have their asses kicked in. I'm telling Bill to just go and tell them tomorrow that his boy did good. They all need that, you know. They all need to get slapped around a little; those nuns need that," Sally advised.

She was drunk, and Bill most likely had passed out by now. Mom decided to try again in the morning.

The next morning—May 28, 1963—Mom called the police station at eight o'clock. She learned from the clerk that Stanley's hearing was scheduled for that very day, in Judge Wicker's court, up on the second floor.

"The Judge is leaving tomorrow. With Memorial Day on Thursday, he thought he would take the rest of the week off."

The clerk didn't know what time the hearing would be held, but gave Mom the number of the Juvenile Court Clerk. She called and learned it was at ten. Sally was right when she said tomorrow, but did Bill know, and would he show up?

Mom had washed the altar boy surplices over the weekend, and planned to get them back on Monday. But with everything that happened she didn't, and now they really needed them. Bishop Gonzalez would be there at three o'clock to celebrate his Mass and to talk to the church about the mission in Peru. He was even going to be on KXRA radio and be interviewed by Channel Seven News. All the altar boys were part of it; she had to get the vestments there on time. But she also wanted to make sure someone was there for

Stanley. She called Bill. No answer. So she called back five minutes later; after ten rings, he answered.

"What is it?" asked a man's voice, a voice that wasn't interested in talking.

"Bill, this is Faith. Are you going to court today? Your boy's hearing is at ten. Do you need a ride or anything?" Mom spoke fast, almost in a panic. Time was short and she didn't know how long Bill would stay on the phone.

"That damn boy! What the hell was he doing? Everyone was coming in the bar asking me about him, laughing at him—no, laughing at me. Faith, what the hell did I do?" whined the voice.

"Bill, you need to be there. He needs you," she begged him.

"Sure, I'll be there. Where is it?" Bill asked, slightly more coherently.

"On the second floor of the courthouse—Juvenile Court, Judge Wicker."

"Judge Wicker? I voted for that asshole. Is he going to send my boy up?"

"I don't know. Please, get sober and go down there. Tell Judge Wicker that you will get help for Stanley. Tell him anything. Maybe he won't have to go."

"Damn right, I'll be there. Where is it again?" Bill asked, his confusion returning.

"Second floor of the courthouse, Judge Wicker."

"I voted for that bastard. Did you know I voted for that bastard? Now he is going to send my kid up. What the hell, I voted for that bastard!"

"Bill, you gotta be there, you know, for your boy. Please, get some coffee."

"Sure, Faith. Sure, I'll be there. I'll be there for my boy . . ."

"Bill, are you still there? Bill! Bill can you hear me!" There was no dial tone—just the sound of far off traffic.

She turned and said to me, "Help me load up the surplices; we need to get them over to the church. I can't go to court like this."

I loaded the surplices as she changed her clothes. She put on a simple dress, hat, and shoes. It was nice out for May, so she didn't need a coat, and we were out the door. We got to the church and I helped her carry the surplices up the stairs. We just hung them in any order. If there was time later, we would return to arrange them in order of size; if not, the boys would just have to find one that fit. The cassocks, the other half of an altar boy's wardrobe, weren't back from the dry cleaners. They were all wool and couldn't be washed in water. Mrs. Anderson's husband owned the big dry cleaners in town, and gave the church a discount for the cleaning. She was supposed to have them back by now. Oh, well, we couldn't worry about that now. We drove over to the courthouse. No sign of Bill's car, or Sally's car either.

"Wait in the car, I'll go in."

Mom went in the back door of the grand courthouse building—a building that sat across the street from the Junior High School where only yesterday we were racing and everyone was cheering. It was the school I would be attending next fall. Stanley James would have attended it, too. Maybe if this all worked out, we would be together again, Stanley, Dave, and me. Maybe we could dig some more of our underground fort, or just lay in the shade and smoke cigarettes and talk—talk about cool stuff. I loved to just listen to him. He had a way of explaining things—real simple, so that a boy could understand. He wasn't a bad boy.

I told Mom what really happened that day at school. I knew that Sister Rose said not to, but I thought it would only be a venial sin to tell. It wasn't gossip, and it wasn't a lie, so it couldn't be really bad—except not obeying a nun, especially the principal of the school—that was bad. That was probably a double venial sin—but that only gets you purgatory. Besides, I was still wearing my Brown Scapular of our Lady of Mt. Carmel, so that was protecting me from hell anyway.

I wished that Mom had finished high school; then she would be able to talk really smart to the judge. The day got a lot warmer, so I rolled down my window, just as Joey and some of the other boys from the regular class came by.

"Hey, what are you doing here?" they asked.

"Nothing, just waiting," I said, squirming in the hot car seat.

"Waiting for what?" Joey said, perceiving how unconformable I was.

"Nothing. Mom had to do something in the courthouse," I said, attempting to appear unconcerned about some routine event.

"Is she on trial?" Joey was circling, savoring every moment of my embarrassment.

"No, she had to do something," I tried one last time to escape the unavoidable conversation.

"I know, it's Stanley James. He's your cousin and your best friend; he's on trial isn't he?" Joey said with his sneering tone.

"Maybe, but I'm not sure that he's my best friend." I said, still attempting to avoid a direct assault.

"Yes, he is. Your best friend is a nun beater—an unstable nun beater. He was thrown out of school forever, and he is going to jail. Your best friend is a criminal—just like Ed Guine. Maybe he will be put in a cell with Ed Guine, and they can talk about killing and eating nuns," Joey said with a meanness in his voice that I had not heard for a while.

For a second I thought about yesterday, how we were all running together. But today the magic was gone. We were once again mere mortals, and were competing for position in some undefined hierarchy.

"He's not my best friend, and now that his mother is dead, I don't think he is even my cousin anymore."

As I said this, the back door of the courthouse opened and out walked a police officer with Stanley James. He was handcuffed and wore yellow coveralls. They just started walking over to the sheriff's car when he looked at me. I looked at him, but with the other boys there, I was afraid to wave or to acknowledge him. He couldn't wave. He tried to smile at me by tipping his head, but stopped. I think he saw the worried look on my face and wanted to save me from the shame—in front of the other boys, I mean. I think he knew that I didn't want them to know that he was still my best friend.

The boys left saying, "He's gone, man. He's gone to Jailsville."

A few minutes later Mom came out. She was shaking. She got in the car, took a deep breath and said. "Stanley is going to go to the St. Joseph Home for Incorrigible Boys for a while." Then tears. "Damn! He didn't come, that bastard! What did Eva ever see in him?" She reached into her purse and pulled out a Kleenex, wiped her eyes while looking into the rearview mirror.

We drove back to the church; the cassocks still weren't there. We drove to the Viking Dry Cleaners.

"Oh, Faith, I'm so glad you're here. I had to get my hair appointment changed, and we are so backed up with deliveries, we aren't going to be able to get the cassocks over to the church until tomorrow," Mrs. Anderson informed us.

"But we need them for services this afternoon," Mom said.

"Oh. Well, as long as you're here, maybe you could just take them. Save us a trip and all," she replied.

"Alright," Mom said.

"Sam will find them for you," she concluded.

A few minutes later, Sam came out. "They're not all done yet," he told us. "Could you come back later, in about an hour? We can't really give these priority. We are doing them at a discount, you know."

"I'll just take the ones that are ready now and try to stop back, but I'm not sure that I can," Mom said.

"Well, I don't see why not," Mrs. Anderson said, with a hint of indignation implying that Faith was inconsiderate, and unsympathetic to her plight.

We loaded the cassocks and headed back over to church. Monsignor Ward was there.

"Oh, Faith, you do so much. I thought they were going to deliver these," he said.

"They ran behind, and I thought we should get some of these over here at least," she said.

"How is Stanley doing?" he asked, in a compassionate voice.

"Well, they decided to send him to St. Joe's, to the reform school there," Mom said.

"Oh, no. Bill wasn't able to convince them to give him another chance?" Monsignor asked.

"He didn't even show up. I didn't know what to say. I said I was his aunt, but I didn't know what else to say. Stanley just stood there. He hardly said anything. I didn't know what to say. What should I have said?" Then the tears came back and this time they were unstoppable.

"Faith, you did what you could. I'm sure that just being there helped. I will call the priest at the school, Father Shaw. It's long distance, but I think I should talk to him before they get there. He is the nephew of an old friend. I will make sure that he knows that Stanley is a good boy, that he just needs help, a little background. A lot of boys go through this and come out just fine. We will need to pray for him," Monsignor reassured her.

That afternoon I carried the campanile for Bishop Gonzales. Mom got the rest of the cassocks to the church just in time, and we got through that day. The nuns sat in the front row as they announced who would be the first nuns to go to Peru to start the mission school. Sister Mary Ann, because of her work experience with children who need special help, was included in the pioneering team. She and two others from Saint Mary's School, along with three more from the Little Falls Convent, would begin Spanish classes on Thursday nights at St. Cloud State College, so that they would be fluent by the time they left in the summer of 1965. They would only be with us two more years. Over those two years the parish hoped to raise $10,000 for the mission school.

Miracle or Coincidence: May 29, 1963

Wednesday we were back in school. This should have been our last day because Thursday was Memorial Day. This was a time in history before Memorial Day was conveniently placed on Mondays to provide a three-day holiday. Then Memorial Day was a day for parades, and services at the cemeteries, and long speeches in hometowns that people actually attended. It also, as it does now, signaled the unofficial start of summer. No one could remember ever attending school after Memorial Day. But because of the extra day off on Tuesday for the Bishop's visit, we would need to attend school for one more day next Monday. They considered adding Friday, but so many families had already made plans for the long weekend that Monday was determined to be the best for everyone.

At school that Wednesday things were kind of normal again. The weather became remarkably pleasant, bright and clear. Only two days had passed since Stanley James was here, but it seemed like more than that. He seemed to have evaporated right in front of our eyes. Mom promised to get his address so I could write. That would be fun, a pen pal.

As I looked out the window—pretending to be paying attention—I saw Mindy pull up right in front of the rectory and jump out of her car. She was wearing her white uniform and her volunteer apron from the Catholic Hospital. She pounded on the door. Sister Mary Ann saw her, too. She rolled her eyes and her face took on a look of both disgust and annoyance. I knew we both were wondering what Mindy was doing and thinking—another miracle, perhaps? Miracles seemed to happen around her all the time now. Last week the Madonna of the Trailer Park cured two women who visited Mindy's trailer. One was healed of grief—she was afflicted for 10 years. The other—what was the other? Oh yeah, another arthritis cure. That made seven of those. None of these were reported in church or in the newspaper, but they were reported in the bars, restaurants and barbershops of the town. One barbershop was keeping a running count, and one of the bars claimed it would soon take bets on what the next miracle would be.

I could see her talking to Monsignor Ward. Then, to our surprise, they both came out together and hurried across the street to the school. We heard them come in the north door, then up the stairs and past our room to the office. Oh, Lord did they decide to let her volunteer here after all, thought Sister Mary Ann.

No, they were both in too much of a hurry for that. Within minutes, a girl from Sister Rose's class came to the door with a note. Sister Mary Ann read it, and then said to the girl, "Tell them I'll bring them myself."

She looked puzzled, but went to her drawer and slowly pulled out the five-manila envelopes—four that had been archived in her drawer for some time and the new one, the one that Jimmy was working on when the thing with Stanley happened. She announced that she might not be back for a while, but if she heard one peep out of anyone, there would be a price to pay. She was wrong. She returned in very short order—about the length of time it would take to hand five envelopes to Monsignor Ward and be dismissed.

We saw them leave through the front door. Mindy started walking over to her car, but Monsignor signaled her to get into his. They drove off together. Sister Mary Ann returned with an even more puzzled look than she had when she left—and now she no longer had the pictures, the pictures that she was still trying to decide what to do with. Was Mindy going to show them to Jimmy's mother and tell her that Sister knew that he drew them? What would that mean? How did she even know? And why was Monsignor helping her?

Later that day, Sister Rose came to the door. Her face was grave and exhausted, like my Aunt Eva looked when she learned repeatedly that her cancer treatments weren't working. It's the kind of look people sometimes take on after they turn 50—when they know that life will be a series of continuous blows to the gut, and that everything will not work out for the better. Sister Mary Ann went into the hall, looking puzzled but expecting answers. They talked in lower whispered tones than ever before. No smiles punctuated the conversation, and neither one glanced into the classroom at the student or students that they might be discussing. No clues at all—just distant stares down the hall, then a nod, then Sister Rose walked on to the next door.

By the next day, whispers filled the town as people gathered for the parades and celebrations. They overflowed into the nearby villages of Garfield, Nelsonville, and Osakis. But strangely, they did not grow any louder. Silent whispers—even in the bars and at the corners downtown. Everyone talked like a disease was in the town, as if afraid that outsiders might learn about it. Then, in three days, it trickled down to the playground. The girls knew it first, they listened to their mother's whispered phone conversations, but they did not understand what they had heard. The adults talked in a code not yet known to children of that time.

Clare was the spokesperson for the girls; she assembled all the pieces of information they had gathered, and by Monday morning as we gathered at the door, she was ready to share them with the boys— hoping to get a few more clues to fill in the still missing parts. What the girls heard was that Mindy stopped by to visit with Jimmy while she was volunteering at the Catholic Hospital. She only intended to get him a book or a toy from the play box in the sun room at the end of the corridor. Sometimes she used her own money to buy children candy bars from the little snack bar that the volunteers ran on the first floor. She did that just for the children—and only if they were allowed to have candy.

Jimmy asked her if it was true that she was a friend of Mother Mary, and if Mary still appeared to her? She told him that Mary did. I guess she really believed it. Then he asked her if she could tell if he was going to hell? She told him no, only God knew that. Then he told her that he did things that he couldn't tell—not even in confession—but that he tried to tell by drawing bad pictures, because even saying the things he did was a sin. He didn't want to go to hell, but he didn't want to go to jail, either. He was afraid that if he told anyone, he would be arrested, and the police would shoot him, and he would go straight to hell.

Mindy asked, "Who would arrest you?"

"Officer Beecher. He is a policeman, and he can arrest people and send them to jail or shoot them—whatever he wants."

"What would he arrest you for?" she asked.

"For doing the things in the pictures," he said.

"Where are these pictures?" she asked. He told her that Sister Mary Ann had them. She didn't ask what he had done, but was moved to ask him, "Who did you do these things with?"

"Officer Beecher."

"She told him that Mother Mary would always protect him, and that if he told Monsignor what he had done, Mary would protect him from Officer Beecher too. No matter what happened, he would one day be in heaven with her little girl, and with Mother Mary. He should just try to rest until Monsignor came to him."

"Mindy had not heard about the pictures, but she knew that Mother Mary was telling her to go, to go right away to Monsignor. She left the hospital without telling anyone, and went right to the priest's house. They went back to the hospital and Monsignor and Mindy showed Jimmy the pictures together. He explained who the tall man was—and that the other person, the scribbled boy, was him. He said that he had only drawn the ones in crayon and had not drawn the one in pencil, the one of the Sister and a priest. He didn't know who drew that one. He would never do that. He cried, but he did not have one of his seizures. Monsignor told him that he needed to be brave, but that he had not sinned. Officer Beecher had sinned. Monsignor asked Jimmy whether he knew if Officer Beecher had done the same thing with other boys. I don't know what he said about that."

"Did any of you see the pictures?" Clare asked.

I saw the first one, and heard about the others, but I didn't want to talk about it with a girl so I didn't say anything. Neither did anyone else. We just sort of felt funny, looked around, and thought about scouts, and camp. The boys didn't look each other in the eyes after that, and we felt kind of shriveled up inside. We didn't want to know.

Monsignor called Mr. Patterson, the county prosecutor, right away, but he was in court. Monsignor told his secretary that he had a matter of utmost importance to discuss, and made an appointment to meet in the prosecutor's office at 1:30 that afternoon. He also called his cousin, an attorney in St. Cloud—long distance collect, from a pay phone at the hospital—and he and Mindy drove to Sauk Center to meet him at the Center Café. All three of them came back to Alexandria and went directly to Mr. Patterson's office. There they laid out the evidence, and Monsignor told them that Officer Beecher was a volunteer at the school and active in the Boy Scout Troop. He was a camp counselor when the older boys went to Camp Willabee, camped with the boys, and counseled some of the boys in their Eagle Scout projects. Monsignor said he could get a list of names together, but asked that he be allowed to talk with the families first. He assured the prosecutor that he would tell the boys and their families that they had a responsibility to assist in the prosecution of this case. He then asked for assurances that if Officer Beecher were prosecuted, it would be kept out of the papers—for the sake of the boys, the town, and the school.

Next, Monsignor went over to the gift shop and met with Jimmy's dad. He couldn't leave the store because it was Sara's day off, so they talked in the back. Mr. Langley peeked out occasionally at the lone customer in the store, who left in the end without making a purchase.

Police Chief Larson went over to Jimmy's home and met with Mrs. Langley. She was shown the pictures and agreed to encourage Jimmy to cooperate. The police chief and the prosecutor went to Judge Monroe's office to get an arrest warrant for Officer Beecher, and a search warrant for the house Officer Beecher rented on 5th Street—just a block down from the church. Monsignor returned Mindy to her car, but before she left, they went into the church and prayed together. He returned to the school and told Sister Rose. She told the other nuns.

"But what did Officer Beecher do?" One of the girls from the regular room—who had not seen the pictures—wanted to know.

Clare, who seemed to know everything, could not say. "I don't know, they never say, but I think it was something really bad, something that you're not supposed to talk about."

While we didn't know the details of the crime, we knew that we should not ask the adults for an explanation. Robert had moved back to the projects, to the Cities, so that link to the mysterious and sophisticated sphere of worldly knowledge was gone. All we knew was that it had something to do with the pictures, wieners, Officer Beecher, boys, and that it was over.

Jimmy Langley never returned to the school. He went to the Mayo Clinic, and then his mom decided to move to Minneapolis—so he could be closer to doctors. His dad stayed in Alexandria—for the store. He stopped going to church, and then we heard that he married Sara. I guess Jimmy's parents got a divorce after she moved to the Cities.

The only newspaper account that I ever found—42 years later—was in the Weekly Echo's badly maintained archives. There was just part of the story. The first page was missing, "Continued from B-3-Columun 2, Chief Larson picked up two of his officers, Officer Hill and Officer Williams, and they arrived at Officer Beecher's home at 2:30 PM. Officer Beecher was wearing his uniform, all but the belt and the gun. They requested that he change, which he did. Later that night he confessed. After entering a guilty plea, he was sentenced to 19 years." Prison records I later located at the St. Cloud Reformatory revealed that he served 11 years, seven months and nine days before being paroled.

Just Too Much

The phone rang early on Saturday, June 1, 1963. It was Helen. She had been a co-worker of Eva's, and a good friend.

"Faith, did you hear about Bill?"

"No, what now?" Mom replied, with a voice that conveyed both weariness and disgust.

"He's dead." Helen replied quickly, in order to preempt Mom from saying anything that would cause her pain later.

"Oh, no! How? I just talked to him Thursday morning."

"He was working at the bar—drinking a lot, I guess—and then he just fell over."

"What do you mean? Was he hurt?"

"No, they think it was a heart attack. I'm surprised no one called you."

"Oh, God, poor Stanley! Have they told him?"

"I don't know anything, really. When I got to the hospital, the nurses told me. They knew that Eva and I were close. Everyone loved Eva at the hospital. She was such a good person. Bill was a good man, too. He changed so much after Eva died. He just didn't have anything to live for. It hit him so hard. He blamed himself—and that dry cleaners. He said he thought she got it on her hands because of the chemicals—but that can't be so. They have to be safe, you know, or the government wouldn't allow them. They test all that stuff. So, I know it wasn't that. But he blamed himself, and everyone loved her. He was worried about Stanley getting it, too. I think that's why he just let go—lost everything—so Stanley wouldn't be tied to it, tied to him. He just got it in his head that he was like poison, and that the people around him always suffered. Nothing turned out good for them. He went a little crazy after Eva died. My husband Hank tried to talk to him, you know, but you know how that goes. Didn't do no good. He just wouldn't know no different. Anyway, Faith, I don't know anything else. I guess his mother is still alive. She will most likely make the arrangements at Peterson's—that's where they take most of the Protestants. Give them a call, and they can let you know. Well, I just thought I should give you a call." Helen realized that she was babbling and brought the call to an end.

Mom raced out to the gas station to talk with Dad. I couldn't tell what they were saying, but he acted like he didn't care. He and Bill were never really close. It's not that they didn't like each other, it's just that they were never really close—and after Eva died, we hardly ever saw him, just that one Sunday, that one before . . . well, before that day.

Mom called Peterson's Funeral Home. "Oh, yes, he is here, but it is going to be a small service here, not in a church, just family. That's the way they want it," Mr. Peterson said in his cool official voice.

"Well, I'm family; I'm his sister-in-law," Mom informed him.

"No, I think they mean immediate family only," he firmly stated.

"Oh, I see," Mom said.

Having conveyed the proper message—a task that he was ashamed of—he shed the mechanical voice and resumed his natural tone. It was a warm tone, well-suited to his position, and one that despite nineteen years in the funeral business still remained true to the man.

"Faith, I'm very sorry. I know how close you were to Eva. I'm just doing what they have asked. I hope you understand. That's what we have to do, you know. We have to respect the family, and his mother is now the closest relative."

"What about his son, Stanley?" Mom asked.

"Well, Faith, I don't think they are going to bring him here. I asked that, too. I mean, everyone knows, but she said that he should not be disturbed from his treatment; it might be too much for him. We don't have any control over what they want. It's just going to be small—a small service. His mother seems very hurt, very hurt over how everything turned out. You know, she goes to our church and always tells people he should never have married Eva. I mean, I met Eva, and I always thought that she was a wonderful woman. But I'm just doing what she wants. I'm so sorry to have to tell you this."

He, too, was rambling. It's what people do when they are saying things that hurt—like if one puts enough meaningless words around the hurtful ones, it will soften them. People do it, even when they know that it doesn't really help.

"No, it's alright. I'm glad you told me on the phone; it would have been awful if I had just shown up without calling. I'll just send a card or something, maybe some flowers," she said.

"They are asking that all flowers be delivered to Douglas County Hospital as gifts to the sick. They don't want any delivered here. So, I wouldn't even bother. Just send a card. God knows, they don't need any money," he said bluntly.

"Thank you so much; I really appreciate your frankness. Thank you, bye now."

Mom put her hands on her face, then bit her first knuckle, and opened her little address book. There it was, Bill's mother's number. She had called her once or twice about something during Eva's illness—to find Bill or something—so it's not like they hadn't met. Should she call? Ask about Stanley? Maybe they just needed someone to pick him up. Maybe the embarrassment of driving up to the school would be too much for them.

She called. "Hello, Mrs. James. This is Faith, Eva's sister. We talked a few times."

"Oh, sure, of course, I remember you," the reply was polite, almost warm, but reserved.

"I know that you plan to have a family-only service for B . . . , William,"—she remembered just in time his mother's preference for William over Bill—"and I certainly understand. I am calling to give you my condolences and to offer to pick up Stanley for you. I'm sure you are all so very overwhelmed, his death being so sudden. I would be pleased to be able to help out by picking him up. I wouldn't come in or anything. I'll just wait in the car and then take him back right after."

"Thank you for your call, Faith, and your offer is appreciated, but Stanley won't be attending. We have talked it over and we really feel it is so much better if he stays where he is. He really needs his therapy and we are afraid that it might upset him too much."

"Have you talked to him? How is he doing?" Mom was desperate to continue the conversation while she thought of something else.

"We had our minister call this morning and explain everything to him. They have a chaplain up there, so if he needs anything, he has someone to talk to. We really think it is best this way," she continued firmly.

"Well, ah, you have my deepest condolences; he was a very good man," Mom said.

"Thank you, and yes, he was. Thank you for calling. Goodbye now," she ended.

"Goodbye."

That was it. Mom never sent a card. Why bother? She had other things to do.

We Pause for only a Moment

The summer was underway; Dave, Doug, and I were becoming a new group of best friends. I intended to write to Stanley every week, but just never got around to it. Mom sent a little card on the Fourth of July, and I wrote at the bottom, "Hope everything is OK." Summers are like that—not good writing times—better for goofing around. Then there was the gas station. I helped Dad fill the cars in the afternoon when things got busy. When we went up to Pete's Supermarket, the new store in the far south end of town, we sometimes drove past the old Quick Dry Cleaners. Of course, it wasn't a dry cleaners anymore. It was just boarded up. The old owner got it back because no one was making payments, and was just trying to sell the building now. As the summer days grew longer, we started thinking about Junior High School.

"You know they have dances there," Doug said.

"Yeah, but I ain't dancing," I said.

Then, on Sunday, August 4, 1963, the phone rang early in the morning. It was Warden Stern from the St. Joseph Home for Incorrigible Boys. He asked to talk with Mom. Her face dropped like a razor blade had sliced her soul.

Her voice was barley audible. I could only hear, "No, did you call . . . I'll have to find out . . . ." Then she placed the black receiver back on the heavy base and said, "Sit down here, I must tell you something. Stanley is dead. There was an accident. It wasn't anyone's fault. He fell from the bleachers. They had a game and Stanley hit the winning home run, and I guess they were just celebrating, and he fell. Things like that just happen. I'll be right back; I need to tell your Dad."

She left and went out to the gas station, and returned soon after. She picked up the phone; she had not cried yet, there were practical matters to take care of first. Grief is a luxury that the poor ration. We learn how and when to weave it into the practical matter of life; now wasn't yet the time.

Mom called Monsignor and told him what had happened. He said he would call Father Shaw at the home, right after the eight o'clock Mass. He would find out the details, and see what arrangements needed to be made.

Mom looked in her little book for Uncle Bill's mother. It was long distance, but that didn't matter, it was an important call.

"Mrs. James, this is Faith, Stanley's aunt."

His grandmother already knew that Stanley was dead. She was prepared for the call. She told Mom that she would send her two hundred dollars to help with the funeral costs, but that she would not be able to be involved, and would not attend. She was blunt, and colder than the sound of ice cracking on a January night in Minnesota. Such a sound is unassailable, so intimidating as not to be questioned.

Mom could only—would only—say, "Thank you."

Mom sat there stunned, mentally calculating the cost of the most meager of funerals, and trying to determine if such a financial feat was even achievable. Then the phone rang again. This time it was like an alarm, unexpected; but then, when is a call ever really expected?

It was Monsignor again. He called to tell her that Father Shaw told him that Stanley had not attended Mass, and had not taken communion. Since Catholic children reach the age of reason at seven, such a decision at the age of twelve had to be considered a rejection of the Church. Therefore, while he was heartbroken, and sure that Stanley didn't mean it, Monsignor could not overrule Father Shaw. No funeral could be held in the Church, and Stanley could not be buried in the Catholic cemetery. His words were not harsh, just factual. He didn't want Mom to plead or ask him to challenge

Father Shaw—that would be to no avail. It was like a mercy killing with a sharp knife.

Now, Mom was even more perplexed. The cost of a plot would be more if he couldn't be buried in the Catholic cemetery. And where would they have the funeral? Maybe they could just have something down at the funeral home—like for Bill—but how much was that? She called Mr. Peterson at the funeral home. She told him she wasn't certain yet what they were going to do, but asked about cost.

"Well, you will have to come in; I can't really discuss it over the phone. But we do have some very reasonable services. You might check also with St. Joe's. The State may have some assistance for a child—well, a child that is really a ward of the State." He was polite and wanted to be helpful. He knew that we didn't have the money for a funeral.

She called Warden Stern back. He said that he would be very pleased to discuss everything with her, but that she should take a little time to adjust. There was no need to hurry. They needed to complete a full investigation anyway, and nothing could be done until that was complete. It was routine, but in cases like this, the State wanted to be sure that nothing could have been done to prevent such an unfortunate accident. Mom said she wasn't sure what the cost would be, as she never had to arrange a funeral before. He told her he would work with her, that there was State money available for the burial, so she need not worry about anything. The State had taken on the role as parent, and provided for all the children's needs. Sadly, in this case, that also included final arrangements.

He suggested that she come to the home in the morning. By that time, she would have time to think things over, and he would have the answers she needed. He again extended his sympathics, and told her that even though Stanley had been there only a short time, all the boys and the staff liked him. They knew he was really a good boy with just a few bad breaks. His voice was personal and reassuring—and when he talked of Stanley, almost fatherly—but he still maintained the professional tone needed for his role as warden and comforter.

Now was the time for tears and for grief. Mom held me—she cried and held me and rocked me—but I grew numb, as men sometimes do. In my mind I saw him—the last time I saw him—looking at me. I was afraid to wave, to acknowledge him. I didn't deserve to grieve;

I deserved shame and the numbness that comes when blood is shut off from a part of you, until the appendage is dead.

The next day Mom left early so that she could make the hour drive and still arrive at the start of business. By noon she was home, changed out of her good clothes, and back into the routine of the everyday. Dad came in from the station for lunch. She nervously tried to convey the message, to tell him what had been decided.

"I met with Warden Stern and Officer Shaw. They were both very nice men. Officer Shaw—his brother is the priest that is related to Monsignor Ward—was there when Stanley died. He said that the game was very exciting, and that Stanley was the star. He hit the winning homerun. Then somehow Stanley fell from the bleachers and died. The doctor said that it was from internal injuries. They didn't recommend an autopsy. They just didn't want to have him so dismembered the way they do, well, when they do that. I agreed. What good would it do? Now, he did say that if we claimed next of kin, we could take the body; but then we would be responsible for the burial and all. Generally families have costs around eight hundred to a thousand dollars for that. Well, some are much higher—but I mean for a simple funeral. He said that if we didn't claim the body, then the State would provide a simple funeral there with his friends and it wouldn't cost anything. We could be there; but it's kind of a two-way deal—to be there we have to be kin, but if we are kin then we need to claim the body. He thinks it is really unfair but he couldn't do anything about it. He would, if he could. He was such a nice man—and very understanding. I think he knew that we didn't really have that kind of money.

"Now it's over. They are going to do the service there. No one would have come from here anyway; his grandmother wasn't coming—so none of Bill's family would be there. And we wouldn't have been able to have it in the Church. Monsignor feels very bad about that, but he can't do anything. So, just having it there with his friends makes a lot of sense." Then she looked at me and said, "I hope you understand."

I said, "Sure. Sounds like the right thing. I'm sure he had some really good friends there, and if we had it here, they couldn't come."

After lunch, Mom called Bill's mother for the last time. She explained that she would not need the two hundred dollars; the State was providing everything. She failed to mention that she would not be able to attend. Mrs. James insisted that she wanted to send the money—and instructed Faith to keep it, or give it to whatever charities she thought best—but the matter was closed.

After considerable thought and struggle, Mom divided the money: ten dollars to Monsignor Ward for Masses—just in case Stanley made contrition just before he died and made it into purgatory; twenty dollars to the Church; twenty dollars to the Sisters for the mission school in Peru; fifty dollars to St. Mary's School; and one hundred dollars to the St. Joseph Home for Incorrigible Boys. The Warden set up a special fund for the needs of children and staff that could not be funded from the State allocations—for birthday and Christmas gifts for the boys, sometimes to help staff members who are having a hard time, and so forth.

After making the donations, thank you letters arrived. The most touching was from Warden Stern. He told her in great detail how her gift would help the children—and told her that some of the parents continued to make Christmas donations to the fund even after their children left the home. We made a commitment to send something every Christmas, but that fall money was tight. So we decided we would do it at Easter, but again it was postponed. And the next year it was only a fleeting thought. Then, like Stanley James, it all faded into the past.

Finding My Old Friend

A recap of Homecoming activities prompted discussion about the pep fest and bringing back class cheers and THE BAND! Concerns were raised about the band not participating in the parade as well. A better halftime show was suggested for future homecoming games. Fergus Falls' great halftime show was brought up as an idea for a class-act show. Components of that show that were favorable were band and choir mini production, fireworks (small) and a lovely presentation of the royalty.

PAC (Parent Advisory Council) Minutes
November 2, 2005
Jefferson High School
Alexandria, Minnesota
Submitted by Becky Galligan

Classmates.com

"Those damn pop-ups! I heard about this on the radio, NPR or something, Classmates.Com."

I moved my cursor to the box and before I knew it, I fell prey to the lure of the advertising industry. I didn't really give a damn about finding out what great successes everyone had become, and why would they care about me? But, as I filled out the boxes, I kind of wondered about some, and then scrolled the list. Oh, wow, there was Larry Porter. I popped it open—picture and everything! I admit it was amusing, like finding a missing reel for an old B-movie that one started watching a long time ago—but then either fell asleep or found something more interesting to do, and never saw the end. There was Joey Turner; he was a teacher in Duluth. Mary McDaniel, now married, was a California girl. Gary Boyd, and Doug Anderson, too. I dropped a few e-mails, and to my surprise, got responses—just enjoyable conversation. Then the flurry of exchanges stopped and we returned to the hectic pace of our lives.

Then, months later, a short e-mail from Mary McDaniel, the pretty red haired girl from the second grade, arrived. Fred Burch, who took over the Burch Travel Agency from his father, was organizing a class reunion for June 25, 2005. They had planned to do a thirty-fifth, but it didn't work out, and our class was always different anyway. So, we would do a thirty-sixth reunion. There had only been one other. It was the twentieth. We were in our late thirties then, and doing all those late thirties things. Our lives were indistinguishable from our jobs and our promotions; we were totally inbred with positions and titles. A few of our number had begun to ripen into adults—and some were recovering from the wounds of life and the delicious, but taxing, sins of youth. Now, we were hitting our mid-fifties. Sixteen years ago, the event was held at the local Holiday Inn—a high-end stop for Alexandria. Some complained that the thirty-five dollar cost was way too high and didn't attend. This event was priced at twenty dollars, and would be held at the Forada Supper Club. I had no idea where that was. I looked at the note and thought that the effort to go to Minnesota was far more than I wanted to exert for a reunion that was sure to be disappointing.

The next day I got a phone call from my mother's best friend, Rose. Mom was taken to the hospital that morning with a heart attack. The usual flurry of phone calls followed. Should we come right away? A phone call with my mom that afternoon was reassuring. She was fine; she was getting out of the hospital that day. They ran some tests. It was a heart attack—but a very, very minor one.

"Please don't come now, but how about if you come this summer, when the weather is better?" she said.

My father had passed on years ago, and my mother came to see us twice a year, so there was not much reason to return to Minnesota—other than for those fast trips for weddings and funerals of distant relatives. But for now, everything was fine. My wife, Janet, and I decided that we would go to visit mom for her birthday. And since the reunion was taking place the same week, we would go to that, too. The reunion was planned for Saturday night. Mom's birthday was the next day. We decided to come in on Friday and stay until the next Thursday. My wife, an attorney, needed to be back for a hearing on Friday. This was a short trip—but with our workloads, it was longer than many of our trips had been over the years. Back on the Internet, I secured airline tickets, a rental car, and hotel.

We arrived Friday, and drove out Interstate 94 to the Alexandria exit. The town seemed to have moved. The two miles between the exit and the town, where farms had been when the freeway first opened, filled in with the typical freeway stuff—a rash of hotels, gas stations, and then the strip centers and what passed for shopping malls. My mom told me how the town had grown—how they first achieved the status of having a K-Mart—then a Wal-Mart. But the one hundred seventy-five fishing resorts present in my childhood were now reduced in number to a mere thirty.

I had told my wife about Alexandria's pride—the world's largest plastic statue of a Viking that stood proudly at the end of Broadway, and watched for invaders from Glenwood, the town that lay twenty miles to our south. The statue had stood there since 1965—after its less than triumphant appearance at the 1964-65 World's Fair in New York—the fair that promised "A future not of dreams, but of reality." That future has come, and the prediction has come true, also—for we no longer dream as we once did. We no longer believe that the future will be a dazzling world free of war, fear, hunger, and disease. We now only hope that we will be able to bear the reality.

The Minnesota Pavilion at the New York World's Fair was constructed well over budget, and while it featured a smorgasbord of over one hundred items, and information on a multitude of tourist areas in Minnesota, it was a disaster and threatened to close after only six months. Alexandria initially hoped to be included in the exhibits, but was shut out by the more powerful and more politically connected regions of the State. But now there was an extraordinary opportunity—the opportunity of the century. So, the good citizens developed a plan to save the state pavilion and promote the town. The town raised the funds to build a giant statue of a Viking and place it outside of the exhibit building. There was a speaker embedded in its shield—and while the mouth didn't move, the speaker invited visitors in to hear the story of Alexandria, the birthplace of America.

Alexandrians believe that they are living in the birthplace of America because in 1875, a farmer named Ohm discovered a rune stone on his property near Kensington and claimed that there were Viking writings on it. The stone is about 30 inches high, 15 inches wide, and about 6 inches thick, and the message on it reads: "Eight Swedes and Twenty-two Norwegians on an exploration journey from Vineland westward. We had our camp by 2 rocky islets, one day's journey north of this stone. We were out fishing one day. When we came home, we found ten men red with blood and dead. AVM save us from evil. We have ten men by the sea to look after our ships, fourteen days' journey from this island. Year 1362." The rune stone can still be seen in the local museum, and as can plainly be seen by the date, it arrived long before that Italian guy made it to some southern island. The town has been promoting the stone for years. It even made the cover of *Weird Minnesota: a Complete Guide to the Northland.*

The World's Fair plan also included renovating the exhibits inside the pavilion. The state agreed not to close the pavilion, if the town raised the cash. The statue was put in place just to the southwest of the Vatican Pavilion, which was doing quite well, both in numbers of visitors and by making a tidy profit. Its message of "The Church is Christ Living in the World," was perhaps less noticed than the presence of Michelangelo's, Pieta, traveling outside of Rome for the first time ever. This was when the sculpture was still innocent, unscarred by the damage that was inflicted by Richard Fredette on May 21, 1972 in Rome, when he rushed past the guards and delivered fifteen blows to the mother of God. I, of course, did not see the Pieta while it was in New York; I saw it years later in Rome after the attack, and the restoration by *Deoclecio Redig de Campos.* By then it resided behind bullet-proof glass, safe and unassailable.

I looked at the virginal face that the twenty-four-year-old Michelangelo had masterfully carved, and I grieved for her. Not for her sorrow, but for her inability to experience it. She was eternally the virgin-mother; her face was perfect, tranquil and ageless. In the 1,466 years between the death of her son and the carving of the statue, she still had not grieved. She remained ageless. She did not bear the scars of a significant life, no visible sign of any wisdom gained or treasured emotions stored in her heart. I looked at the cold marble. It did not permit any expression—certainly not the contorted expression of a grieving parent that I have seen on human faces when they behold their dead sons or daughters. I thought, "What was Mary's crime, that the church eternally imprisoned her in such an incomplete existence—why is she not permitted to age, to be transformed into a complete female deity?" And then I wondered, "Would the holy fathers ever let her free, ever let her grieve for her human son?" Perhaps Richard Fredette had only been trying to liberate her, not destroy her on May 21, 1972.

Anyway, the plan to save to save the State pavilion at the fair failed. The pieta won the interest of the World's Fair goers. The heroic Viking statue frantically called for visitors. Some came—but not enough—they closed the pavilion three weeks after it reopened. The town was crushed, and the statue, now named "Big Ole," returned humbly to town and lay behind the museum until a decision could be made. Finally, it was placed at the north end of Broadway. Surely, motorists from Interstate 94 would travel the three miles required to see the world's largest plastic statue of a Viking! And if that wasn't enough, at Christmas, they dressed it as Santa—then it was the World's Largest Plastic Statue of a Viking Dressed as Santa. Let's see any town around here match that one! So, it came to pass that Big Ole served as the town's new symbol of hope for a prosperous future. No one from the town read the 1964 World's Fair's announcement about a future not of dreams but of reality—so they still believed in dreams in those final years of optimism, before the Beatles and the reality of Viet Nam.

Traveling through the new sprawl, we transitioned into the older part of the town. It was desperately trying to hold on. The town's exceptionally wide streets were laid out like so many other American towns in the nineteenth century, in the belief that the town would become a major city. Now the design just made it look like an empty parking lot. Before the freeway was built, in the late 60's, the street was jammed with traffic and it served its purpose; people and cars crowded the small town and prices soared each summer during the three golden months of profit. But now, the few tourists left stopped at the Wal-Mart. The local stores were antique shops or flea markets. Traveler's Inn had remodeled in the typical fake brick and wallpaper borders of small town restaurants, and was still going strong—no longer a teen hangout, now a respectable restaurant. Olson's had closed.

As we got to the end of Broadway, an even greater shock hit me. Big Ole was gone! He was missing, no longer guarding the town. As we arrived at the intersection where he had always faithfully stood watch we saw him, peeking out from behind an old hotel, now ruling over nothing but a gravel parking lot. The town god, their last hope for glory, had been dismissed. We learned from my mom that he was moved for better traffic safety. "Someone might be distracted looking at him and crash or something," she told us. He seemed sad in his new location, and worshipers were few.

We turned left at the intersection and drove out to the old place. The gas station was now a restaurant, called Jan's, that specialized in breakfast and lunch. The milk powderizing plant and the Williams Brothers pipeline storage tanks had expanded. We drove past the Lakes Café where Mindy worked. My mom lived in an apartment on Willow Drive. We arrived at last. We talked of old times. I asked about various town characters, and if they were still around.

"Remember Old Ed? Lloyd the One-Armed Man? Mindy, the Trailer Park Saint?" I asked.

"Oh, you don't know," Mom replied eagerly, having found someone to share a local story with who hadn't heard it ten times over.

"Know what?" I said.

"About Mindy."

"No. I hope they didn't lock her up or something. She really did have a good heart."

"No, a group of nuns, cloistered nuns that live in Portugal, heard about her and asked her to join their convent. And they had the wall removed from the trailer and shipped over. It is in a chapel and she is a nun. She is a big hit over there. People come from all over to see her and have her pray for them. It has revived the convent; it is one of the only convents growing in Europe. They did a story on it, on Channel 34. She is more famous than Big Ole," Mom concluded.

"Just think, if the town had known, they could have had the Trailer Park Madonna in the Rune Stone Museum, and would probably get more tourists than that stone." She then commented that she hadn't been to the museum for twenty years.

The next day we found the Forada Supper Club. It was a yellow metal building without windows, just a large sign announcing that it was The Forada Supper Club. It was probably a good choice. No one would find it ostentatious. We decided that a trip to the local mall was needed. This was not a place for the suit I had packed. We found J.C Penny's, and decided that a knit T-shirt would work well. As we checked out, Janet's cell rang.

"Yes, I heard it buzz, but I haven't looked," she said into the phone as she pulled her Blackberry from her purse. Yes, she carried both a Blackberry and a cell phone. She stepped out into the mall. She talked with the phone in one hand and scrolled though the e-mails on her Blackberry with the other. As I joined her in the mall, she looked up and said, "Would you mind if we went back to the hotel for just a bit?"

I drove as she talked on the phone. We got back, and she connected her computer and joined a conference call already in progress. She turned, covered the phone, and said to me, "Honey, I'm sorry, I think this is going to take a while."

"I'll be back by 5:00; then we have to get ready to go." I again spent some time with mom, driving around the town as she proudly pointed out each new building. When we drove past where Bill and Eva's dry cleaners had been, the McDonald's that had replaced it was now also gone, and a Taco Village was in its place.

When I got back, Janet was still on the phone. I got ready and started stomping around—my signal for, "OK, it's time to get off the phone. The world can survive for a few hours."

She did—and raced to get ready. We arrived, and to my surprise, most of my classmates had matured into real people. Gone were the pretensions and the fears. Sure, there was the class doctor, who was always the cool guy in school, with a new young wife and announcing that he had two toddlers. But for the most part, there we were—survivors who were not worried about scars, or sagging skin, or our disappointments. We realized that life was a story, and that we were fortunate just to have a role. Maybe we were pulled even closer because another one of our classmates died just three days before the reunion. He did not survive. He committed suicide.

In looking around the room, I noticed a lot of guys from high school, but none of the boys from St. Mary's. The girls were there— but not the men. All of the girls at one time were going to become nuns—and a few did, but not for long. Even at the last reunion years ago, the remaining nun from our class had just "Kicked the Habit." She seemed bitter, hard, like she had been cheated. She commented that there wasn't really any fellowship at the convent, just petty jealousies and dysfunctional women. She wasn't there this time.

As the drink and the evening wore on, I found that a small cluster of us—the women from St. Mary's and I—formed a gathering of our own. We talked about the nuns, and laughed uproariously at stories that only this cult could understand.

"Gee, I remember," started one the women, "when Sister Mary Ann took you by the ear, twisted it, and dragged you down the hall. I went home crying, and made my mom promise to never let Sister Mary Ann take me in her class. I was so glad I wasn't one of . . ."

"One of the retards." I finished the sentence that she was too embarrassed to finish when she realized what she was about to say.

"I didn't . . ." she started to say.

"Oh, don't worry. You know, they never even tested any of us, they just decided," I assured her. "It was wild in there, but frickin' bizarre stuff happened. Some of us were retarded, but being there didn't help," I said.

"Remember when Sister Gene went berserkers and had to leave? I guess she had a nervous breakdown," Clare said.

"Well who wouldn't after someone drew that picture of her and Father Reed. They sure got him out of town fast. I heard she went to work for the Department of Mental Disabilities after she left the convent," added Susan.

"God, remember Monsignor Ward? We were all afraid of him, but we also liked him. He was kind of like God—powerful, but really kind underneath," Mary said.

"Remember the first day when he was calling everyone's name, and Stanley didn't answer, and then he stood up and said defiantly, 'It's Stanley James, not James Stanley.'" Susan said. We all remembered, and laughed. Then the chill of sadness submerged us. Not like a wave, but more like cold water had instantly risen from the floor drains as we connected the end of the story. "He was your cousin wasn't he?" she continued.

"Yes, my cousin, and my best friend." I said confidingly, remembering the last day that I saw him, when I didn't have the courage to recognize him.

"What happened? He went away; then later we heard that he was dead," Susan inquired.

"Yeah, he was sent to the St. Joseph Home for Incorrigible Boys, and he died there, just a few months later. He fell from the bleachers or something. He's buried there, but I've never been there," I added.

"My aunt worked there at one time. She said that it was pretty rough in the late fifties and early sixties, but that it really changed when the new warden came in '64. My mother said it was closing—moving, or something. It was in the paper," Clare said as the conversation moved to mellower, sadder tones.

"A lot of those places are. They're all moving to group homes and stuff," Susan concluded.

"Well, Stanley James was a great kid. I wish he was here. Let's drink a toast—he wouldn't want us to be sad. To Stanley James, not James Stanley," I proposed, thinking that this was the closure I needed—an easy closure with old comrades and moderately priced scotch.

The next morning was Sunday, and as I opened my eyes, the image of my wife came into view. She was not romantically lying beside me as we planned for our brief vacation—but was sitting at the small table, connected to the Internet, typing on her computer.

I got up to pee and she said, "Honey,"—"Honey" was always the way she started when she had news that she knew would disappoint me. "I have to go to Washington."

"No, not today. It's mom's birthday."

"No, in the morning," she assured me.

"How early?" I inquired.

"4:00 A.M." she said.

"Oh, shit," was my not very enthusiastic reply.

"I can get a car and drive down to Minneapolis to catch the plane. You can stay here," she tried to assure me.

"No, you won't be able to rent a car one-way from here. We'll drive down after the party and get a room near the airport, and I'll drive back here Monday. Our tickets are not refundable. Do you want to come back here later in the week, and then we can fly back to Ohio together?" I was trying to salvage at least a day of our so-called vacation.

"I don't think I will be able to do that. I'm really sorry, but I really need to go." She knew she was disappointing me but, sometimes that was what marriage was about—the worse part. I loved the fact that she worried that she was letting me down. If she wasn't concerned about my feelings, then I would worry.

"Ok," I said, and that was the end of it.

The party ended about five o'clock, and we hit the road, southeast down Interstate 94. As I passed the sign for St. Joseph, I remembered how difficult the journey was before this last leg of the freeway was completed. "We went though all these small towns, and St. Cloud—that was a nightmare." I said, then continued, "I think

I'll stop at the college on my way back to tomorrow—walk around the campus, maybe drive over the Tenth Street Bridge. I wonder if it is still there?" I thought about old college friends that I hadn't seen in years. My roommate, Mark Pearson, last I heard he was with USA Today. Man, we would talk for hours. I could tell him anything. Well, maybe not everything. I never told him about Stanley James. Maybe we only told boyhood stories where we were the heroes, or the victims. Maybe only with age do we recall the stories where we lacked character, were cowardly, and where we betrayed friendship with a simple glance.

"At the reunion, Susan mentioned your cousin. I didn't know you had a cousin who died," Janet said.

"Yeah, all the time I was in college I never did go over there—where he is buried. I just stopped thinking about him, after he was gone. He got in trouble. It wasn't really his fault. It was one of those things where I think he was just protecting another kid and things got out of hand. Anyway, he was only supposed to be there, at the home, for a short time—but then he died. It's a long story, and I'm not really sure about a lot of it." I replied without thinking too much about it.

The next morning we got up at 2:30 A.M. I took Janet to the airport and she got through security by 3:30. I went back to the hotel, lay on the bed until six, and then decided to check out. As I drove back, I thought less about college days, and more about Stanley James. He slowly began to take shape in my memory—the thoughts, the talks, and the pain. I felt the emptiness of never having wept for him, but still, I could not feel much. I remembered that day, the Class Olympics, but did I remember it right? It always seemed so unreal— the feelings, the things that happened. I thought about camp, too. Then I realized that both days had a common component; on both days I was connected, felt a oneness with the other boys. At camp that feeling was at the expense of a boy whose only crime was being fat, but at the Class Olympics, it was achieved by—by what? By caring for, by loving a boy whose only offense was being weak.

I had kept my medal, the ribbon from running the first race, the relay race that the blue team won. I ran across it every now and then, but each time I saw it, things seemed less real, more like a movie. I decided that I would skip the college tour and try to find the Home. Directions and an unsolicited confirmation that it was closing came from a gas station attendant, and I was on my way.

The Return

"Greater love hath no man than this, that a man lay down his life for his friends."

John 15:13

The Home

There were only a few cars in the parking lot, but the doors to the Home were open. I walked in; it looked like it was nearly empty. I found a young black woman in one of the offices. She had a clipboard, was writing down notes and putting small circular stickers with numbers on the various items that still remained.

"Hello," I said.

"The auction isn't until Friday and the review of items isn't until Wednesday. Sorry, I have a lot to do before then, so I can't help you."

The response was automatic; I must have been the hundredth bargain-hunter wanting to scoop the crowd.

"I'm not here about the auction. I want, no, I need to find out about a boy who was here in the early 60's. He's a relative. Is there any possibility that there are records or anything?" I asked, trying to be positive, so as not to be chased away.

"Well, if there are, they are downstairs, in room seven. Mr. Harris is down there cleaning it out. If they're not sealed he might be able to help you; but I think most of them have already been shredded," she said, pointing the way to the stairs.

I walked at a quick pace, as if a few minutes might matter after these forty-some years. I found the room, with records piled all around, and Mr. Harris standing next to a stack of three boxes. He was old—in his sixties—and slightly bent over, gray-haired, what there was left of it. His eyes were sad, and the lower lids sagged so much that you could see the inner red surface. He looked at me and waited for me to speak first.

"Excuse me. I don't know if you can help me. I . . . my cousin was here in the early 60's. Well, actually, he died here. We were very close, and I was just wondering if there might be any records," I said, more clumsily than my usual speech.

"You were close, and you waited over forty years to look him up," the man said to me with a tone of what's this bullshit in his voice.

"I guess, life just got a hold of me, and I forgot—forgot about him and things," I said, not even convincing myself.

"There isn't much left. We got rid of stuff, and now that we are moving, I've been assigned to clean this mess up. Makes sense, I filed most of it. I filed it for decades. What was the boy's name?" he finally asked.

"Stanley James," I pronounced clearly, with a sound that faintly echoed off the bare walls of the room.

He stopped. "I wondered if anyone would come for him, wondered all these years. I came across his file three days ago, but I couldn't shred it, just couldn't do it. He was the first file I brought down here." Then he just stopped like a computer sometimes does while processing information; and you can only wait, and hope it will start again. "I had just started. I was 23 years old, and I was the first black man ever hired by St. Joe's. They were very proud of that, how progressive they were and all. I went to a two-year program over at the Business College. Not the first there, though.

"I was given some files to bring down here, and the first one had the name Stanley James in the corner. Right away, I thought, is it Stanley James or James Stanley? I didn't want to make a mistake on the first day, not when I was the first, and all. I wasn't supposed to look in any of the envelopes, just file them, you understand. I looked again, but couldn't tell if the little speck was a comma or not. In business school we always learned to put the last name first, you know. Well, I opened the flap to see how the name was inside. Oh, God, how I wished I'd never opened that envelope," again he stopped and I waited, "just done my job, not looked inside. After that I could never again sleep at night, never get it out of my mind; kept thinking, I should tell someone. But who? They—the higher ups—they all knew. They put the stuff in the file. I thought I should go to the newspaper office; but then I was new, and I would be fired, and who would want to hire me then, and what good would it do? Even three days ago I thought, what should I do? But I have never done anything. Yes, I know where it is." He walked over and sitting on the corner of a tall box was an envelope with the penciled name of Stanley James in the corner. "Take it, but please don't open it here."

"I think he is buried on the grounds. Can you tell me where?" I asked

"You'll need a map. Here," he said, as he pulled out a paper from a stack of badly reproduced photocopies. "A lot of folks come looking for relatives and stuff."

The back of the sheet had all the names in very small print, and the front had a map showing the location of the graves. The rows were by letters and the graves were by numbers.

"Not all of the stakes with the numbers are still there. Find one that is close, and then count over five feet for each new number, and you will be close."

"Thank you," I said and walked out. I drove the short distance to the graveyard; past a small shed and the bleachers. The bleachers were only four feet high. I wondered if they were the same ones that were here then. How could anyone die falling just four feet? Well, it could happen; and back then they might have been higher. Maybe they lowered them so that no one else would get hurt. I stopped the car and started looking for his name on the paper. The list was arranged by last names, first. It wasn't there. So I looked for the last name of Stanley, and there it was, H-36. I walked out into the well-kept cemetery. I found row H, and then walked past 30, 32, 33, 34, to 36. I was at the site.

I knelt down and said, "Hey, I'm here." I thought that I might, maybe I should, say a Hail Mary or something, but it didn't seem right. We were no longer boys; instead I opened the envelope.

The first item was a routine itemization of Stanley James's last costs to society. The document coldly listed each item and carefully calculated the cost to the State. It read like a shopping list—yet from it, I desperately tried to assemble a sense of his funeral, clues to its humanity, to put myself there at the funeral, to be present for him. Next was the investigative report. It was a carbon copy on yellow paper—the kind that was once attached to a two-part form. The top copy was intended for some other office, and the bottom copies were filed. Next came a hand-written letter in blue fountain pen, written in cursive—the kind that was once universally recognizable, but that has begun fading with the rarity of ancient hieroglyphs. I had to focus and re-accustom myself to reading what once was the most familiar form of communication. But these few lines, these were the arrows that would pierce my soul, the last three were on thin sheets of paper that we used to call onion skin. These three flimsy things would boil my gut.

Application for State Reimbursement of Expenses
For Investigation of Death, Funeral and/or Internment Expenses
Related to Juvenile Wards of the State of Minnesota:

Name of Institution: St. Joseph Home for Incorrigible Boys

Date: Aug. 12, 1963

Name of Deceased Inmate: James, Stanley

Date of Death: Aug. 3, 1963

Cause of Death: Internal injuries from accidental fall

Cause of Death Verified by Death Certificate: Yes

Investigation Complete: Yes

Findings of Investigation: Accidental death (See Attached)

Further Action required: None

Internment Complete: Yes

Internment Location: On the Institution's Grounds H-36

Reimbursements for plot only applicable to internment in non-religious affiliated cemeteries, not to exceed $50 per plot. No reimbursement for internment on institutional or State-owned sites.

List each item separately, including extra staff time and purchases.

Additional time for salaried staff is not reimbursable, nor are expenses related to application for reimbursement. Overtime for guards and other hourly staff shall not exceed 1.5 times base hourly rate. Total reimbursements shall not exceed a maximum of $475.00 per ward of the State.

```
Overtime for Officer Shaw
        8 hours x 5.24 x 1.5 (Overtime Differential)   $    62.88
Overtime for Officer Brown
        8 hours x 4.35 x 1.5 (Overtime Differential)   $    52.20
Robert McCain Photography
        Photography (Materials and Fee)                $    18.88
Ed Clawson
        Grave Excavation                               $    30.00

Shaw's Department Store.
        Coffin                                         $   110.00
        Clothing: Shoes                                $     9.55
                  Suit                                 $    27.00
                  Shirt                                $     5.50
                  Tie                                  $      .75
                  Socks                                $      .30
Body Transportation                                    $    47.00
Body Preparation                                       $    50.00
Total Requested in Reimbursement                       $   450.61
```

Incident Report
Minnesota Department of Juvenile Delinquent Rehabilitation
Saint Joseph Home for Incorrigible Boys
Stearns County
1217 Hill Road
Saint Joseph, Minnesota

Incident: Death of Inmate: James, Stanley   Number J-2369-61-9

Guard(s) on Duty: Senior Guard, Shaw. Second Guard, Kevin Brown

Description of Incident:

(Use additional numbered blank pages if needed)

After the inmates were permitted a recreational baseball game, they returned to their barracks to prepare for showers. Sometime in route to the showers or after arriving at the showers, Inmate Mr. James escaped. Most likely means of escape was through a propped open door in the corridor that runs between the kitchen and the guard's locker room. The discovery was made during showers. One of the inmates, Mr. Judd Anderson, reported that Mr. James had left the group and was planning on returning before the end of showers. Admittedly in violation of policy, both guards left the shower facility in order to apprehend the escaped inmate. An honor inmate, Mr. Judd Anderson, was put in charge of the group, and no incidents occurred during this time. A preliminary search of the grounds was made, taking approximately an hour. When no sign of Mr. James was found, the guards returned to the shower facility and escorted the inmates back to the barracks. The guards believed that Mr. James would make an attempt to return, and therefore did not report the incident for several hours. When he failed to return, Officer Shaw made a report to one of the night guards, Officer John Rockman. A decision was made to alert the night guards, but to delay a search until daylight.

In the morning, the body of Mr. James was found near the bleachers where he had fallen. It appeared that he had stolen a baseball bat. The body was not clothed, as he escaped during movement to the shower facility. Dr. James Sanford was called; he examined the body and determined that death was caused by internal injuries. He was not able to positively determine the extent, or the precise cause of the injuries, but was certain that they were received that night in the fall.

While the guards do admit to a procedural violation, by leaving the inmates while they conducted the initial

Incident Report
Minnesota Department of Juvenile Delinquent Rehabilitation
Saint Joseph Home for Incorrigible Boys
Stearns County
1217 Hill Road
Saint Joseph, Minnesota

Date Aug 6, 1963
Page 2 of 12

search, they did so in order to quickly remedy the situation, and no boy was harmed by them doing so. Had they been able to act even faster, they may have been able to save the life of the errant inmate.

End of Report

I have read this Investigation Report, and accept the factual description of the incident set forth above:

Officer P. Shaw

Officer K. Brown

Incident Report

Minnesota Department of Juvenile Delinquent Rehabilitation
Saint Joseph Home for Incorrigible Boys
Stearns County
1217 Hill Road
Saint Joseph, Minnesota

Incident: Death of Inmate: James, Stanley   Number J-2369-61-9
Guard(s) on Duty: Senior Guard, Officer Shaw. Second Guard, Kevin Brown
Witness Interrogated: Mr. Judd Anderson, Honorary J-76696-59-7
Interrogated By: Officer Shaw. Second Guard, Kevin Brown

(Use additional numbered blank pages if needed)

Mr. Anderson stated that after the baseball game the inmates returned to the barracks. While preparing for showers, he overheard Inmates Bobby Lendermen and Stanley James discussing plans for an escape. Mr. Lenderman wanted to steal a bat for reasons unknown to Mr. Anderson. Mr. James volunteered to assist with his plan. He heard them say that Mr. James planned to escape during showers and then rejoin the group without detection. Mr. Anderson, under the inmate code of honor, felt obliged to inform Officer Shaw of the plan and did so at the first opportunity. Mr. James still escaped, and when he did, the guards immediately followed, leaving Mr. Anderson in charge. Mr. Anderson then supervised the inmates during showers without incident, and waited for the return of the guards before returning with the inmates to the barracks. Mr. James failed to return.

END OF REPORT

I, the undersigned, attest that this information is correct as recorded, and represents both the events described and my best recollection of them:

Judd Anderson

Mr. Judd Anderson, Honorary J-76696-59-7

Incident Report

Minnesota Department of Juvenile Delinquent Rehabilitation
Saint Joseph Home for Incorrigible Boys
Stearns County
1217 Hill Road
Saint Joseph, Minnesota

Incident: Death of Inmate: James, Stanley   Number J-2369-61 9
Guard(s) on Duty: Senior Guard, Officer Shaw. Second Guard, Kevin Brown
Witness Interrogated: Bobby Lendermen, J-768997- 61-9
Interrogated By: Officer Shaw. Second Guard, Kevin Brown

(Use additional numbered blank pages if needed)

Mr. Lenderman stated that after the baseball game the inmates
returned to the barracks. He admits responsibility for
encouraging the escape. He stated that he had inadvertently
failed to return a bat to the storage shed and that he
remembered this only after returning to the barracks. He feared
the loss of baseball privileges by the unit would result in
retaliation by the other inmates. He planned to escape in order
to return the bat to the storage facility. He was aware that
many of the inmates knew the combination to the storage
facility's lock and asked Mr. James for the information. In
doing so, he confided his plan. Rather than providing Mr.
Lenderman with the requested information, Mr. James volunteered
to escape and to return the bat, stating that he was a faster
runner. Mr. Lenderman's agreed upon role was to create a
diversion by falling on the way to the showers near the door so
that Mr. James could escape by the side corridor, next to the
kitchen and out the side door. The inmates knew that the door
was often propped open so that re-entry would be possible. Mr.
Lenderman did attempt to create a diversion by falling, however,
the guards immediately followed. He remained in the shower
facility until the guards returned.
END OF REPORT

I, the undersigned, attest that this information is correct as
recorded, and represents both the events described and my best
recollection of them:

Bobby Lenderman

Mr. Bobby Lenderman, J-768997-61-9

Incident Report
Minnesota Department of Juvenile Delinquent Rehabilitation
Saint Joseph Home for Incorrigible Boys
Stearns County
1217 Hill Road
Saint Joseph, Minnesota

Incident: Death of Inmate: James, Stanley   Number J-2369-61-9
Guard(s) on Duty: Senior Guard, Officer Shaw. Second Guard, Kevin Brown
Witness Interrogated: Thomas Johnson, J-768983-60-12
Interrogated By: Officer Shaw. Second Guard, Kevin Brown

(Use additional numbered blank pages if needed)

Mr. Johnson stated that after the baseball game the inmates returned to the barracks, prepared for showers and then proceeded to the shower facility. Mr. Lenderman fell by the door of the facility. Mr. Johnson stated that he did not see Mr. James escape, nor the guards leave, but was aware that Mr. Anderson was in charge until they returned. After completing his shower, he waited with the other inmates in the shower facility until the guards returned before returning to the barracks.
END OF REPORT

I, the undersigned, attest that this information is correct as recorded, and represents both the events described and my best recollection of them:

Tom Johnson
Mr. Thomas Johnson J-768983-60-12

Incident Report
Minnesota Department of Juvenile Delinquent Rehabilitation
Saint Joseph Home for Incorrigible Boys
Stearns County
1217 Hill Road
Saint Joseph, Minnesota

Incident: Death of Inmate: James, Stanley   Number J-2369-61-9

Guard(s) on Duty: Senior Guard, Officer Shaw. Second Guard, Kevin Brown

Witness Interrogated: Robert Olofsson, J-768983-60-9

Interrogated By: Officer Shaw. Second Guard, Kevin Brown

(Use additional numbered blank pages if needed)

Mr. Olofsson stated that after the baseball game the inmates
returned to the barracks, prepared for showers and then
proceeded to the shower facility. Mr. Lenderman fell by the
door of the facility. Mr. Olofsson stated that he did not see
Mr. James escape, nor the guards leave, but was aware that Mr.
Anderson was in charge until they returned. After completing
his shower, he waited with the other inmates in the shower
facility until the guards returned before returning to the
barracks.

END OF REPORT

I, the undersigned, attest that this information is correct as
recorded, and represents both the events described and my best
recollection of them:

Mr. Robert Olofsson J-768983-60-9

Rob Olofsson

Incident Report

Minnesota Department of Juvenile Delinquent Rehabilitation
Saint Joseph Home for Incorrigible Boys
Stearns County
1217 Hill Road
Saint Joseph, Minnesota

Incident: Death of Inmate: James, Stanley   Number J-2369-61-9
Guard(s) on Duty: Senior Guard, Officer Shaw. Second Guard, Kevin Brown
Witness Interrogated: Timothy Karlsson, J-769004-60-9
Interrogated By: Officer Shaw. Second Guard, Kevin Brown

(Use additional numbered blank pages if needed)

Mr. Karlsson stated that after the baseball game the inmates returned to the barracks, prepared for showers and then proceeded to the shower facility. Mr. Lenderman fell by the door of the facility. Mr. Karlsson stated that he did not see Mr. James escape, nor the guards leave, but was aware that Mr. Anderson was in charge until they returned. After completing his shower, he waited with the other inmates in the shower facility until the guards returned before returning to the barracks.

END OF REPORT

I, the undersigned, attest that this information is correct as recorded, and represents both the events described and my best recollection of them:

Tim Karlsson

Timothy Karlsson J-769004-60-9

Incident Report
Minnesota Department of Juvenile Delinquent Rehabilitation
Saint Joseph Home for Incorrigible Boys
Stearns County
1217 Hill Road
Saint Joseph, Minnesota

Incident: Death of Inmate: James, Stanley   Number J-2369-61-9

Guard(s) on Duty: Senior Guard, Officer Shaw. Second Guard, Kevin Brown

Witness Interrogated: Steven Olsson, J-768983-60-9

Interrogated By: Officer Shaw. Second Guard, Kevin Brown

(Use additional numbered blank pages if needed)

Mr. Olsson stated that after the baseball game the inmates
returned to the barracks, prepared for showers and then
proceeded to the shower facility. Mr. Lenderman fell by the
door of the facility. Mr. Olsson stated that he did not see Mr.
James escape, nor the guards leave, but was aware that Mr.
Anderson was in charge until they returned. After completing
his shower, he waited with the other inmates in the shower
facility until the guards returned before returning to the
barracks.

END OF REPORT

I, the undersigned, attest that this information is correct as
recorded, and represents both the events described and my best
recollection of them:

Mr. Steven Olsson J-768983-60-9

Steven Olsson

Incident Report
Minnesota Department of Juvenile Delinquent Rehabilitation
Saint Joseph Home for Incorrigible Boys
Stearns County
1217 Hill Road
Saint Joseph, Minnesota

Incident: Death of Inmate: James, Stanley   Number J-2369-61-9
Guard(s) on Duty: Senior Guard, Officer Shaw. Second Guard, Kevin Brown
Witness Interrogated: Roger Mattson, J-768971-61-9
Interrogated By: Officer Shaw. Second Guard, Kevin Brown
(Use additional numbered blank pages if needed)

Mr. Mattson stated that after the baseball game the inmates
returned to the barracks, prepared for showers and then
proceeded to the shower facility. Mr. Lenderman fell by the
door of the facility. Mr. Mattson stated that he did not see
Mr. James escape, nor the guards leave, but was aware that Mr.
Anderson was in charge until they returned. After completing
his shower, he waited with the other inmates in the shower
facility until the guards returned before returning to the
barracks.

END OF REPORT

I, the undersigned, attest that this information is correct as
recorded, and represents both the events described and my best
recollection of them:

Roger Mattson

Mr. Roger Mattson J-768971-61-9

Incident Report
Minnesota Department of Juvenile Delinquent Rehabilitation
Saint Joseph Home for Incorrigible Boys
Stearns County
1217 Hill Road
Saint Joseph, Minnesota

Incident: Death of Inmate: James, Stanley   Number J-2369-61-9
Guard(s) on Duty: Senior Guard, Officer Shaw. Second Guard, Kevin Brown
Witness Interrogated: - Mr. James Gustavsson, J-768993-60-9
Interrogated By: Officer Shaw. Second Guard, Kevin Brown

(Use additional numbered blank pages if needed)

Mr. Gustavsson stated that after the baseball game the inmates
returned to the barracks, prepared for showers and then
proceeded to the shower facility. Mr. Lenderman fell by the
door of the facility. Mr. Gustavsson stated that he did not see
Mr. James escape, nor the guards leave, but was aware that Mr.
Anderson was in charge until they returned. After completing
his shower, he waited with the other inmates in the shower
facility until the guards returned before returning to the
barracks.

END OF REPORT

I, the undersigned, attest that this information is correct as
recorded, and represents both the events described and my best
recollection of them:

James Gustavsson

Mr. James Gustavsson J-768993-60-9

Incident Report
Minnesota Department of Juvenile Delinquent Rehabilitation
Saint Joseph Home for Incorrigible Boys
Stearns County
1217 Hill Road
Saint Joseph, Minnesota

Incident: Death of Inmate: James, Stanley   Number J-2369-61-9
Guard(s) on Duty: Senior Guard, Officer Shaw. Second Guard, Kevin Brown
Witness Interrogated: Paul Jansson, J-768964-61-5
Interrogated By: Officer Shaw. Second Guard, Kevin Brown

(Use additional numbered blank pages if needed)

Mr. Jansson stated that after the baseball game the inmates
returned to the barracks, prepared for showers and then
proceeded to the shower facility. Mr. Lenderman fell by the
door of the facility. Mr. Jansson stated that he did not see
Mr. James escape, nor the guards leave, but was aware that Mr.
Anderson was in charge until they returned. After completing
his shower, he waited with the other inmates in the shower
facility until the guards returned before returning to the
barracks.

END OF REPORT

I, the undersigned, attest that this information is correct as
recorded, and represents both the events described and my best
recollection of them:

Mr. Paul Jansson J-768964-61-5

Incident Report

Minnesota Department of Juvenile Delinquent Rehabilitation
Saint Joseph Home for Incorrigible Boys
Stearns County
1217 Hill Road
Saint Joseph, Minnesota

<u>Findings of the Investigative Panel:</u>

While Officer Shaw and Officer Brown did violate policy, they
did so in an attempt to prevent harm to an inmate of the
institution. They did, however, take adequate precaution by
arranging for an Honorary Inmate to assume responsibly. Such a
role for an Honorary Inmate under the direct supervision of a
guard is permitted and encouraged; however, in this event, both
guards left the facility in order to apprehend an escaped
inmate.

While we feel that the guards should be commended for their fast
response to the escape, we cannot overlook the procedural
violation. Therefore, Officer Shaw, being the senior officer on
duty, will receive five days of suspension without pay. Officer
Brown will receive two days of suspension without pay.

Inmate Lenderman's role and culpability in the incident will be
determined by Officer Shaw, and will be dealt with on the block
level, as this panel does not have jurisdiction for inmate
discipline. The panel will nevertheless commend Mr. Anderson
for his admirable actions and recommend him for additional
privileges. His actions demonstrate that this institution is
providing rehabilitation to young men and meeting its mandate.

These are the Findings of the Investigative Panel:

Mr. Sam Stern,
Warden
August 12, 1963

Officer Al McDonald,
Chief Officer of the Guards,
August 12, 1963

Father Raymond Shaw,
Civilian Member
August 12, 1963

James Sanford, MD
812 ½ Eighth Avenue South
Saint Cloud, Minnesota

Telephone Number: 129-6414

August 8, 1963

Dear Warden Stern,

I consider it necessary to clarify the cause of death noted on the death certificate of Stanley James. While I did a cursory examination of the body where it was discovered, near the storage shed, on the morning of August 4, 1963, and remain convinced that the cause of death was internal injuries, as the Death Certificate correctly notes, I believe that a full autopsy is warranted.

From the injuries and the location of objects that I observed at the scene, I believe that Stanley James's injuries may have been caused by being sodomized with a blunt instrument, perhaps the bat found nearby. The amount of bleeding around the rectum was excessive, and the presence of feces was clearly evident. The upper portion of the bat was bloodied.

I am not a forensic pathologist, nor am I experienced in autopsies. I am under contract to the St. Joseph School for Incorrigible Boys as a general practitioner. Therefore, an autopsy would be both outside my area of expertise and the scope of my contract. I recommend Dr. Charles Johnson. He performs the autopsies for both the St. Cloud Hospital and Stearns County.

I only bring this matter to your attention in the event that you are not aware of it. As I am not experienced in these matters, my observations are not to be considered a professional opinion.

Yours truly,

James Sanford MD

Minnesota Department of Juvenile Delinquent Rehabilitation
Saint Joseph Home for Incorrigible Boys
Stearns County
1217 Hill Road
Saint Joseph, Minnesota

August 14, 1963

Dear Dr. Sanford,

I thank you for your letter of August 8, 1963. I can
assure you that the matter is being investigated fully.
I am, of course, not at liberty to discuss the details
of the investigation with you. You are correct, you
only serve this institution under a contract for
limited services.

I also believe, given that you have only recently
regained you license to practice medicine, that your
opinions might not be viewed with the level of the
credibility needed in an investigation in this matter.
I thank you for your services and your rapid response
to our call on the morning of the tragedy. We have
been very pleased with your work at the St. Joseph Home
for Incorrigible Boys, and hope that, even if your
private practice should ever again become viable, you
will remain on retainer with us and to serve our
limited needs.

Yours truly,

Sam Stern,
Warden, St. Joseph Home for Incorrigible Boys

Special Needs Fund
Saint Joseph Home for Incorrigible Boys
1217 Hill Road
Saint Joseph, Minnesota

Name: Officer P. Shaw

Request: As five days without pay would place a severe burden on my personal finances, making it impossible for me to meet my financial obligations, I request that the pay be reinstated. Conversely, I do not object to the finding of the panel in regard to the suspension.

Response to Request: In as much as the withholding of pay would create a financial burden, making it impossible for Officer Shaw to meet his financial obligations, his pay shall be reinstated with the exception of one-half day's pay or $25.00, whichever is less, which shall be withheld as a penalty for violation of policy while on duty.

Authorized:

Mr. Sam Stern, Warden.

August 12, 1963

Special Needs Fund
Saint Joseph Home for Incorrigible Boys
1217 Hill Road
Satin Joseph, Minnesota

Name: Officer K. Brown

Request: As two days without pay would place a severe burden on my personal finances, making to impossible for me to meet my financial obligations, I request that the pay be reinstated. Conversely, I do not object to the finding of the panel in regard to the suspension.

Response to Request: In as much as the withholding of pay would create a financial burden, making it impossible for Officer Brown to meet his financial obligations, his pay shall be reinstated with the exception of one-half day's pay or $20.00, whichever is less, which shall be withheld as a penalty for violation of policy while on duty.

Authorized:

Sam Stern

Mr. Sam Stern, Warden.

August 12, 1963

Then there was another white envelope. One of the metal clasps had broken off from too many bendings, and the other hung tenuously, holding the flap in place. It contained something firmer than the papers. Opening it, I found 8x10 glossy black and white photos. Their images looked ghostly compared to the colored photographs that we have become accustomed to.

Oh, God. The first photo was of the body of a naked boy, lying face down, with a baseball bat lying beside him. The photos were taken in sharp focus, the morning sun obviously present from the intense light and the long shadows. His body was facing west. Patterns of dark and light tones were sharply depicted on his body. The bright white of his clean skin set off the deep black where blood and dirt covered his buttocks and legs. Spatters of the dark shades extended over his back and arms. On his back, between his shoulders, was the imprint of a heel in the dark shades of mud made from blood and earth. Such a mark could only have been made by a booted foot placed on his back, just below his head. The bat was only white on the grip end. The hitting end was painted in the same dark hues that covered his buttocks. Oh, God. What? Why had they done this?

The next photo was a close up of the back of his feet. A deep mark with shallow cuts in an absolutely straight line was imprinted at the back of his ankles. Next was a photo of his arms—with a thumbprint and fingerprints in shades of black and gray. Next—a close-up of the heel print and the cut on his head. This was clearly photographed. The photographer had parted his hair and held it in place with tape while taking the shot. Then, the last—the last was the face of a dead boy. His mouth was partly open, his face dirty, and his eyes open. I could see in the bright gray tones the brilliant blue eyes of Stanley James. His eyes looked so knowing, so kind, so forgiving, even in death.

I could feel a sound rising like steam—painful, hot, and dangerous. It collected in my intestines—filling them with a bloated discomfort that ascended to my stomach, where, heated by my gut's furnace, it grew in fury until it boiled into my lungs, where it became frothy and foamy, like a wild tidal wave. Then at last it erupted from my throat and blasted into the sky.

It was the cry of rage, pity, and defeat, full of syllables and terrible tones that shook the poles. Earth's gravity leaped in scale and pulled everything into despair. It was the cry that knew the fury and cruelty of justice. Yet, at the bottom of that cry, in the thick residue among the sinews and muck of indifference, there was—like a shining silver drop of purest water—there was still love. It was the love of a crucified man-child who had not cared about justice, law, or commandments, and by whose kind heart man's redemption could be known. At last, I wept.

When the world reassembled itself, time again began ticking its relentless moments, and forms again became solid. I slowly realized that another human was standing, just standing behind me. Its presence was like a spirit that seemed to materialize out of the chaos of the sound.

"They never even washed him. They just buried him. The cook told me."

The voice had a man attached, it was Mr. Harris.

"It was the Tuesday after when they buried him. Ed, the cook—well, he was just the assistant cook then—he told me. They were feeding over three hundred a day then you know, so we had more help. Anyway, he saw her leave. He told me one day when I was standing by the grave. I was standing right here, right where you are standing. Ed, he was the cook, he came over to me and just started telling me everything. I guess he needed to tell someone before he retired. And he saw me standing here, just standing here looking, you know. I do that sometimes when I get to thinking.

"Anyway, he came over to me and said, he heard that there had been an accident on Sunday. Then he saw the car parked in front of the administration building, one that he didn't know, or anything. Then the boy's mother came out—a real classy lady, wearing a blue dress and a white hat, a little round one just like Jackie Kennedy wore, with shoes and a belt that matched—a real classy lady. He noticed her because she was so classy. Thought at first she might be someone real important, but then decided that important people never came that early, so it must be the boy's mother. Anyway, she was alone. Some of them are. A lot of the boys don't have dads, and some never did. Well, anyway, she just drove away. I guess she didn't care, or maybe he had been a real handful, but you know, no matter what the boy had done, no matter how bad, even if he had killed someone, they shouldn't have done that.

"The next day Officer Shaw came over and asked Ed if he wanted to make an extra $30.00, and of course, he did, that was two day's pay. They asked him to dig the grave, had a couple of the honor boys cover his kitchen duties, and gave them each a quarter. That was a lot for the boys then, you know.

"He knew it was for the boy, the one that had the accident. Officer Shaw then went into town and came back with the coffin. It was made of plywood. Ron Tillman, one of the teachers who taught carpentry over at the vocational school, had figured out a way to make a coffin out of plywood. Poor folks used to buy then for $30.00, $50.00 if they had a lining. They looked pretty good, too. But the one he came back with, it was just made with plywood sheathing, you know the kind they use, with no good side? There wasn't no lining either—just dirty, low-grade plywood like they put under siding made into a coffin. Well, anyway, he came over to the grave with it in the pickup and then asked Ed—Ed, you know, he was the cook—and asked him if he was done. Ed said he wanted to go a few more feet, but Officer Shaw said it looked all right to him and then asked Ed to help him put the boy in the coffin. Ed followed him over to the shed and he unlocked it. There the boy was. He was still all dirty, and the blood had all dried. He had been lying there since Sunday morning. After they took the pictures they just dragged him a few feet to put him in the shed. Now it was Tuesday at around 5:00 p.m.

"They didn't want to touch him. You know, you can get stuff from a dead body like that. So, they tied a rope around his knees and then they worked one down behind his head until they got it to the chest and then tied it, too. They lifted him into the box, just a plywood box without a lining or anything. They tossed the ropes in because they didn't want to get their fingers dirty untying them, and then Ed didn't think it seemed decent to bury him that way, so he took the dishtowel that he had been using to wipe the sweat from his head—it was a hot day you know—and covered up, well, you know, the parts that should be covered on a boy. Ed said that Officer Shaw laughed a little, and said, where that boy is going, he won't need to be covered. Then he picked up the ball bat and he put it in the coffin too. He said the boy had a great day, and hit a home run, and that he thought he should take the bat with him.

"They nailed the box shut, and then they lifted it onto the truck. Officer Shaw drove the few feet over to the grave and Ed walked. Officer Shaw did not invite Ed to ride, and it was just a few feet anyway. They lowered the coffin down with the rest of the rope, tossed that in, too, and then Ed covered the grave by himself. He got his $30.00, but he told me he never slept too good for a long time. He hadn't told anyone until he saw me standing there, right where you're standing. Just looking, just wondering, why that boy had to die."

"Mr. Harris, do you know where they are? Where the bastards that did this are?"

"Please, call me Jake. I feel like I know you, like I've felt you for a long time. They're gone. Gone to hell, I pray. Officer Shaw was a nice looking blond guy who never said much, but always seemed to be looking over his shoulder. He had this kind of practiced smile that some people kinda bought into. But if you could see, see beyond that, there was something evil, something dead about him. He and the warden were real close; I always thought that he knew something about Warden Stern. I didn't know what, but sometimes he would hint at being just a little disrespectful, just joking kinda, with his fake smile and all. Warden Stern—he would laugh, too, but I think chills were running up his back when he did. I don't really know, but there was something there.

"After Warden Stern died . . . . Oh yeah, Warden Stern was overweight—tall, but real fat. He always wore double-breasted suits, even though they weren't in style, to try to cover it. He thought it helped but it didn't. He was still fat, and bald, too. But he thought he was good looking. A fat, bald, fifty-nine-year-old that thought he was good looking. Don't figure, but then he just fell over dead one day. He was in his bathroom. He didn't use the same one we did. There are bathrooms here for inmates, guards, staff, visitors, and then one just for the warden. They say he had a heart attack—a big heart attack—and it just took him. That was at the beginning of October on a Friday afternoon. I remember it because the moon was full the night before. I was going up north to Lake Cowdry to do some night fishing. I was thinking about how the moon would grow darker each day, and how the days were also getting darker. And then when I heard about the Warden, I thought how everything had become dark for him; but he must already have been very dark, very dark inside, you know.

"Anyway, Officer Shaw was the last to see him. During the summer it was real hot, and the warden had a small air-conditioner in his window. He was the only one. If you needed to meet with him, the afternoon was the best time, because of the air-conditioner and all.

Even though it was October and he wasn't using the air conditioner, they still met on Friday afternoons. Officer Shaw was in charge of officer's grievances, so if anyone had a problem, they would talk to him and then he would talk to the Warden. It was one of those kind of meetings. There wasn't much to talk about that day, so it didn't take too long.

"That evening one of the guards saw the Warden's car in the parking lot. Sometimes he worked late, but not on a Friday. He went up and checked the office, and the door was still open, so he called the Warden's house. His wife said that he hadn't come home yet. He sometimes stopped off for a drink on the way, especially on Fridays, but this was getting really late. The guard, Officer Reinhart, knocked on his bathroom door, and then opened it. It wasn't even locked. I guess when it's just yours, you don't need to lock it. There he was, deader than dead with his pants down, just laying there all bunched up. He called some other guards in. They laughed about it later, kind of a sick inside joke. His body was beginning to get stiff with his legs all folded up under him and his pants down. They couldn't get his pants back up. He was just one fat ugly bundle of hairy flab. They even had a hell of a time getting him out the bathroom door and out of the office. It was a heart attack all right. They did an autopsy over at the hospital. He had high blood pressure and everything was all blocked up. But you could tell that by the way he breathed and all. Well, I tell you, not many were too sorry to see him go. He spent most of his time in that air-conditioned office anyway, you know.

"Oh, yeah, I was telling you about the guards. Well, Officer Shaw decided to leave when the new warden came in, that was Warden Watson. We called him Dr. Watson. He wasn't a medical doctor; he was one of those college doctors. I'm not sure what in, but had to do with something. He came December 16, a little more than a week before Christmas. The night before had been real dark, no moon, you know. I was thinking, 'Well, it might be dark tonight, but tomorrow night it will be a little brighter, and soon the days will be brighter too.' He was real different from Warden Stern. For one thing, he was younger—about 45—and he was an outdoors guy. He started working with the boys, was always out of the office, watching, actually talking to the boys, and asking them questions. Not accusing questions, just stuff, like, 'How's it going? I heard you weren't feeling good, are you better now?' He learned the boys' names and would call them by their names. He cared; he cared in a real good way. He started changing stuff real fast.

"So, some of the officers started complaining, but he didn't care. He was like a man made of metal—of gold, that's the most precious metal, you know. And that's what he was. Nothing could get to him; he knew what he wanted to do, and he just did it. The boys loved him. They really did. They would study hard, be good, just so that he would notice. So he would say, 'Good job,' and he always did. Even after the boys were out for years, Dr. Watson would get letters, or they would stop by. He talked to them, told them to join Big Brothers, get involved with kids. He really cared. When he retired in '83, thousands came. It was the biggest deal ever here, even the Governor came down. He moved down to Florida and is still going at—well, let's see, he must be in his late 80's by now.

"Well, at any rate, after he came, some of the guards didn't like the changes. They said he was letting things get too loose, and that someone could get hurt. Officer Shaw tried to organize the guards, and there was talk of a strike, but not many of the other guards wanted to go along with that. A lot of them liked Dr. Watson. Dr. Watson was trying to get them a raise, and they knew it. Warden Stern would never have done that. So Officer Shaw just left. He joined up with the Marines and that same month Officer Brown went, too. He went to Philadelphia, and joined the police force there. They were gone and things started getting better—better for the boys, and for us, too.

"I tried to forget about the file, but every now and then, it called me back. Like a ghost who didn't want to be forgotten, it would call me back. I would go to the file and open it, just to see if it was really like I remembered it. I should have just not looked, but I couldn't help it. I thought about giving it to Dr. Watson, but that would only make St. Joe's look bad. Bad press and they might try to close it, and now it was doing good and all. So, I didn't.

"Then I read in the St. Cloud Times that Officer Shaw had been killed in Vietnam. He was an MP, and was working in that prison there, the one that had all the bad stuff written about it later, the one with the cages where we tortured the Vietnamese, that one. Well, anyway, he was killed off-duty, by Viet Cong sympathizers in the city. There weren't a lot of details, but he was dead. And in hell, I'm sure of that one. If there is a hell, he is there—with his fake smile, blond hair and white teeth—all burning to ashes.

"Then, about a year later, there was a real short notice in the obituary that Officer Brown was killed in Philadelphia, in the line of duty. I went to the library, not the downtown one, the one over at the college. They have all the papers there from all the cities and I found an article about him. He had been accused of police brutality three times, but each time the investigation cleared him. The last time involved a Haitian boy who died, beaten with a nightstick. He died of internal injuries. After he was cleared, there was a protest, and twenty people got arrested, all black men. That was only a few months before he was killed. He was shot in the line of duty. His partner went into a building where an informer told him a dealer was selling dope. Then there were shots fired, and he called for help. Officer Brown ran in and got caught in the crossfire. A bullet fired by his partner ricocheted off of something, they think, and hit him right in the head, killed him instantly. The dealer got away, but the police chief made his capture a top priority. Officer Brown was given a bunch of medals and stuff, and a big funeral. There was a picture in the paper. Not the St. Cloud paper, in the Philadelphia paper, the one over at the college. Officer Brown had a new baby and a wife. It's sad about that part, a kid growing up without a dad. But maybe some kids are better off without one.

"Back in 1991, Labor Day week, I went to Washington D.C.," Jake continued. "I went that week so that I could get the extra day off. You know, I don't get that many days here. I just had to see it, see the memorial, the Vietnam one, and see all the names. I had a lot of good friends that died there, too. I knew I was going to see it, but I put it off until the last night. I went down Sunday night. The full moon was just coming up, hardly anyone was there. I started looking for his name, Patrick Shaw's name. It shouldn't be there, a name like that, it shouldn't be there. I walked past an old man—he must have been in his eighties—and his wife. At least I think it was his wife, they were together. She brought a rose, like a lot of them do. They even sell them at one of the stands, but that was closed, so she must have brought it. He was trying to get it into the little space between the slabs of stone, you know, like they do. Then I saw it. Just where the map said it was, there about five and a half feet from the ground, there it was. PATRICK F. SHAW. Carved there between two men who deserved to be there. I looked at it and I just got sick, angry kind of sick. I felt dizzy, like all my life collapsed into a single moment, the life that they had taken from me. All the anger, guilt, shame, everything. The pictures, the pictures of the boy, his eyes staring at me and making me never forget. They did this, they did it to him. They did it to me.

"I spat right on that name, on the black granite and the carefully carved letters. I spat. The old man next to me turned, his eyes were on fire. He wanted to kill me. His wife looked terrified; she grabbed his shirt to hold him back, tears were in her eyes. Not the same tears that she was shedding a few minutes ago, this time tears of fear. Fear that there was still enough fire in her husband to kill me. I couldn't explain. I didn't want to explain. They didn't deserve an explanation. My anger was so overwhelming at that point, I wanted to fight, too. I was angry at everyone—at him, at me, at the world. We just looked at each other, just stared across a universe nine feet wide and we hated all the hate that souls are capable of. Then, he just called me nigger. Nigger. Well, I guess that is the word. I walked away. By the time I got back to my hotel, I had forgiven him, and strangely, forgiven myself. His word, painful and cutting, hurt me, punished me. I always wondered how much being the first black man to work here had affected my decision not to do anything. That word was always at the bottom of my pain, festering, never permitting the wound to heal. Then he said it, and unknowingly pried it lose.

"The next day I came back here and didn't think about it again until I found the file three days ago. But even then, it was different. It felt like someone was coming for him, and that I needed to be here, for him. Not because of the pain. Because this time I wanted to; it's like giving him something. How could anyone do something like that to a boy of twelve? How could they have destroyed him?" Jake asked, bent slightly forward and looking up at me.

"They didn't destroy him. They delivered the blows, but they didn't defeat him. After they did it to him over by the bleachers, they must have left him for dead. But see, he was found by the shed. Even after they did that, he dragged himself, and the bat, to the shed. He was still struggling to accomplish his mission for Bobby—Bobby, the boy who left the bat out. He was trying to save Bobby. They killed his body, but they never damaged his soul. His soul is still bright, clean, and glowing. It never stopped loving. He defeated them.

"They had to kill him, because he was a boy who would have become a dangerous man—a man who could convince us to reject justice, power, and authority, and to choose forgiveness and charity. I know that in him, charity lived and danced. They couldn't have that. That would contradict the world in which we are comfortable—a world that seeks retribution, that we call justice; payment, that we call obligation; obedience, that we call culture; and power, that we call civilization. No, Jake, they couldn't have that. That's why he had to be crucified. He had to be purged from the earth—just like Jesus Christ—or any man whose soul whispers the truth."

Jake's head nodded, he understood. He said, "My soul is so tired, I've waited so long . . . I don't deserve it, but I know, even to me he has given a gift. What's going to happen?"

"I don't know how, but I'm going to bring him back to life—back from this miserable unknown grave. Not his poor beaten body, that's not important; but I'm going to bring his spirit back, his words back, and his story to life. That's all we really are anyway, just a story; and I'm going to tell his to the world."

Post Script

On April 12, 2006, there was a fourteen-minute uncontested court hearing in the St. Cloud Probate Court that resulted in me being named next of kin to Stanley James. Three days later, his body was exhumed from the burial plot at the St. Joseph Home for Incorrigible Boys.

I stood there alone, watching the three workmen. Ralph, an American in his fifties, and two Mexicans in their twenties who seemed not to have names, did the work. I hired Ralph, the owner of Internment Care, a small grave digging company, after talking to him about how the body could be moved. I was not disappointed by them, and highly recommend them to my readers, should they find themselves in need of such service.

They dug by hand—starting far away from the center of the grave—using wide, flat-ended shovels, rather than pointed spades. I knew from my earlier conversation with Ralph this was to protect the coffin. They reached the still intact—but delaminating—plywood box, and dug trenches on all sides, until it sat on an earthen pedestal. It was not buried very deep. This kept it out of the water table, and the heavy use of rat poison in the cemetery prevented any animals from burrowing into it. The fact that it was made of cheaper plywood sheathing intended for outdoor use, rather than finished plywood, made it more durable. Then the two Mexican men, at Ralph's direction, carefully worked a heavy canvas under the box. They wrapped the box with the canvas. Next, they worked five boards beneath the canvas. These they bolted to planks that were placed on each side. Four chains were attached to the planks, and the box was raised by a small crane and placed in the bed of an over-sized pick-up truck. Ralph asked if I needed some time alone, but I wanted to keep moving, so the truck bed's cap—that was removed to facilitate loading and was now sitting beside the truck—was replaced. The crane was placed in the flat bed of another, heavier duty truck. The two Mexican men got into that truck and Ralph drove the pickup. As we left the cemetery, I felt like we were the last flight out of some county that was collapsing under an invasion. I was getting Stanley James out, but leaving all these unknown, uncared for boys behind. I stopped thinking and simply followed the small caravan.

We arrived at a small cemetery, which for the sake of peace I will not name in this writing. The coffin was placed in a concrete coffin vault. The flat part had already been placed in the grave, and the cover would be lowered after the coffin was placed. It was like an upside-down shoebox. Ralph explained to me that this arrangement would prevent water from entering the grave, like holding a glass full of air upside-down under water. This gave me comfort. I don't know why, but I felt that I was somehow protecting him.

Janet was standing there. I didn't want her to come to the exhumation—but here, that was okay—not quite so hard. She went to Jo Ann's Fabrics earlier in the week and bought red silk cloth for a cover. To make it wide enough, two strips were sewn together. She lined it with white linen. I wanted red. Red is the color used for the mass of the martyrs. It was the color of the priest's robes and the altar boys' cassocks that Stanley James and I wore for the feast day of Saint Tarcisius—Saint Tarcisius, the patron saint of altar boys, who like Stanley had been murdered by guards while he was serving the needs of prisoners. As in the story of Saint Tarcisius, the guards never found the secret treasure that lay deep inside him. Red was also the color of his team, the team back on that day in 1963. The white side went next to the coffin. White is for the mass of the innocents—and while he had passed the age of seven, after which white is not used, his soul was as bright and innocent as a baby's. The two colors together were right, right for him.

A priest, from the Newman Center at the St. Cloud State University, agreed to come. I told Ralph that if the coffin was intact, I would not want to open it. So, it was simply lowered, and the priest said a few words that I didn't really hear—but I was glad that they were being said. I brought the gold ribbon that I won in the relay race that day. Stanley James had been the real victor then, as he was in life, so I placed it on his coffin, on top of the red cloth. The breeze was blowing, and I thought of the funeral for Mindy's baby so long ago.

The priest left, but we stayed to see the concrete cover lowered and the grave filled. I had ordered a stone, but it was not yet ready.

We returned two weeks later to see the stone in place. I didn't want it to have his birthdate or his death date. To me he was so pure a spirit that he must have existed for all time. He could not be dead, because his spirit continued to live—in every kind act, every moment of courage, and in every instance of goodness. So, the stone was simply carved with his name, Stanley James.

A Request

I think *Stanley James* is an important story—one that celebrates the triumph of love and the ability of the human spirit to transcend the cruelest of circumstance. I have decided that the profits from the sale of the book will be used to help those in need. Therefore I have established the Stanley James Foundation. The website for the foundation is *www.stanleyjames.org*. Information on the foundation's operations, profits from the sale of the book and their distribution will be posted at that site. I welcome your suggestions for worthy spending. If you agree that this is a story that should be told, please help me. This is the first novel that I've written, publishers found it impossible to fit neatly into a genre, consequently giving it little chance for success. But like Mindy, I, too, believe that miracles can happen and that everything happens for a reason. The success of this book is in your hands just as the feather was in the hands of the would-be hero in the old Russian fairytale at this book's opening. I hope you will choose to help. Here are some suggestions, I'm sure there are many more.

- Recommend it to friends whom you think would enjoy it. It is readily available through Amazon.com, Borders.com, and BarnesandNoble.com or directly from xlibris.com/bookstore. Smaller book stores may or may not stock it; if they are currently out of stock, national distributors include Ingram Distribution, Baker&Taylor, or directly from Xlibris.
- Consider giving it as a gift.
- If you blog, internet chat, or have a website, please post or mention it. The power of the internet is greater than any publisher's marketing operation. A single post, if picked up and repeated, could move *Stanley James* to the top of the market. You never know how the smallest of actions will change the world.

- Suggest it for a book club or discussion group to which you might belong.
- Request it from your public library. Some public libraries will acquire a book if as few as two patrons request it.
- If you feel it appropriate for a school's reading list, please suggest it being added.
- Ask book reviewers to read and write a review.
- If you know a television or radio host (or are one) consider asking the author to be a guest to promote the book. (Email Oprah Winfrey at *http://www.oprah.com*)
- Track the book's success, funds raised and distributed at the website *www.stanleyjames.org*.
- Be creative and help in any way you feel comfortable, and let us know what you've done. Together and only together will we fund a foundation that can bring hope and help to the world while telling a story of love and courage.

I can be reached at clydehenry@stanleyjames.org. I hope to hear from you, and I profoundly thank you for reading the story of *Stanley James*.

Printed in the United States
135329LV00003B/140/P